Death's Inquest

Death's Inquest
Arrival of the Four Horsemen
Copyright © 2022 By Marcelle Valentine

Contact information: marcellevalentine.com/

Published in the United States of America by Medusa Publishing.

Medusa Publishing is a registered trade name of Medusa Publishing, LLC.

Stand tall when others kneel

Death's Inquest

Arrival of the Four Horsemen Series

Marcelle Valentine

Medusa Publishing

Table of Contents

And then shall appear the sign of the Son of man in heaven: and then shall all the tribes of the earth mourn, and they shall see the Son of man coming in the clouds of heaven with power and great glory. And he shall send his angels with a great sound of a trumpet, and they shall gather together his elect from the four winds, from one end of heaven to the other. Matthew 24:30-31.

Prologue

Death Winter 2019

THE YOUNG SOUL BEFORE me is at the end of his mortal existence. Soon I shall deliver him to his next life, to the true glory that one can only know after they have shed the trappings of their realm, the realm of man.

He was a dutiful child and would have been a great man had the soulless black heart masquerading as a man not cut him down. A coward who hid in ambush as this young soul returned from seeing the female he mistakenly fell in love with. Like the craven who holds her heart, she will be found wanting when their judgment is finally upon them, for his is not the only life they have stolen; it is simply the saddest.

Like so many others whose life is circling the edge between his realm and the glory of their afterlife, he fights to cling to the only reality he knows. What impresses me most about the young man, who has only seen twenty summers, is he fights with the strength of ten soldiers. My brother would be pleased to witness the courage, tenacity, and fortitude he shows in his fight to live, yet he would also find him wanting to have ended up in the situation that led him to this; his final moments.

My brothers still slumber while they wait until the day our almighty benevolent creator calls us forth to deliver his final decree, the day humanity will meet its end. Maybe then I will at long last be permitted to rest. Until then, I stand.... I watch.... I wait.... And I deliver because that is my purpose, for I am the pale rider, known by some as Thanatos, but my most common moniker and the one I am certain you will understand is Death.

"Come forth, my child." The call of my creator is a beckon I cannot refuse; however, seeing the soul before me failing fast, I am honor-bound to deliver him to the next phase of his existence. So even as the summons is building within me like venom for not heeding my creator's call, I wait, I watch so that when he finally succumbs, I will be here to deliver.

As the pain builds to an excruciating degree, I allow my eyes to slip closed, concentrating on holding my creator's will at bay.

"Where am I?" The same question I hear from every soul who is passing through purgatory.

I open my eyes to focus on the young man's confused face. "A better place, one where you will find your lost loved ones waiting. A place where pain does not exist."

"Am I...." This is the second question they all ask.

"Yes, young soul, you have slipped from the realm of man."

"But my mom."

"Will greave you. She will have to learn how to live in a world where you do not exist any longer until the day she takes her last mortal breath, and then I will bring her to join you."

"*Come Death, for my patience grows thin.*"

Taking the young man's arm gently within my grasp, I escort him towards the gathering souls waiting to welcome him home. I stay until the boy falls into the embrace of his grandmother before I turn to heed my father's call.

*****

"I have summoned you because I have a task you must fulfill."

"I have a task already. Can one of my brothers not be awoken to oversee this new endeavor?"

"No, for when my lamb breaks the seals that will wake them, it will be too late for those I send you to judge."

"Judge?"

"You will live among my children and determine if they are worthy of redemption or if it is time."

"Time?"

"Yes, my Son. Time for me to call them home."

"I do not believe I am best suited for this, father."

"I disagree. Regardless, steel your heart and steady your soul, for this is not a request, faithful rider." And with his final decree delivered, I am thrust into the realm of man, the land of the living. My task is to judge these beings and determine if they are worthy of his divine forgiveness.

Chapter One: Faithful Decision

*The Bible says, in the beginning, God created
the heavens and the earth. That our world was
formed from the void. He wanted to separate
the light from the dark and saw the light as
good. Does this mean only evil blooms at night?
If this is true, how do you explain the souls like
me, the ones who thrive in darkness?*

Avalon Spring 2022

I FIND A QUIET peace in the darkness. It is the only time
I feel really alive since it is the only time I don't have to hide
who I am. A lost soul who has seen far more than my fair
share of brutality.

Tonight is the best kind of night, made darker by the
steady rainfall. I exhale, watching the continuous drops

trickle down the windowpanes; yes, this is the perfect night for someone like me.

If I had known how dramatically my life was about to change, I might have just climbed into bed to hide until the end.

Everything is perfect until shouts echoing off the sides of the building outside my apartment disturb my quiet peace. I peer down towards the road only to discover five men attacking one. This, in itself, is not unusual. Hell, it wouldn't be a normal Saturday night if there was not at least one assault within the five blocks surrounding where I live. What is most interesting about this time is that the man seems unwilling to protect himself as they repeatedly hit him, knocking him to the ground.

"Hell yeah, kick him again."

"John, finish him," another guy interjects.

"If you are in such a hurry, Isaiah, you can fucking do it." Oh shit, I know these guys. They are a bunch of ruthless thugs who terrorize the neighborhood. John glares at Isaiah, who puts his hands up and backs away from the sadistic prick.

"I see you're not so interested in shoving the fucking blade into him yourself. No? Then keep your fucking mouth closed, or you may find yourself lying next to him," John snarls.

The man they have been beating is currently lying unconscious and bloody. He has no idea of the danger coming his way. John kicks the man in the head several more times before he bends down in front of him to jerk his head off the wet pavement. I hear the click before I see the glint of steel from the knife he pulled from his waistband.

"What, nothing more to say now, asshole? No words of wisdom you want to give us."

I can't believe it, but the poor guy actually mumbles something, although it's too low for me to hear clearly from my vantage point.

"Still talking shit, I see. Well, maybe this will teach you the lesson you seem so fucking unwilling to learn." John slams the knife into his gut before ripping it out to plunge it into his chest.

I can't help the gasp that follows. Son of a bitch, did I really watch John kill another man in cold blood? And like the sound that carried from them to me, apparently, mine filters down to them as well. Throwing my hand over my mouth, I duck behind the wall; my only hope is that they didn't see me standing in the window because the room I'm in is concealed with darkness. The only sound I can hear is the pounding of my heart.

After what feels like an eternity, I take a chance to peek around the curtain down to the street below. John and the rest of his gang are still staring at the building I call home.

"Get this piece of shit off the street. No point in making it easy on Detective Asshole." John snaps. Pulling a pack of cigarettes from his back pocket, he lights one. The flame briefly illuminates his face, which chases away any doubt of who I just witnessed killing the man unfortunate enough to cross paths with these assholes. His eyes move back up towards the building, and I swear to God, I think he is looking directly at me.

"You all know who I am and what I'm capable of, so if you know what's good for you, I suggest you mind your business and keep your fucking mouths closed, or that asshole won't be the only body the police will be investigating." He shouts before flicking his cigarette toward one of the first-floor windows, but I cannot erase the feeling he is looking at me. I watch as his goons each grab an arm or a leg to cart the man into the deserted building across the street.

I remain pressed against the wall, my breathing ragged until I am sure they have left. With one last glimpse out the window, I call it a night. Crawling into bed, I concentrate on calming my heart, knowing I am tucked safely between my sheets.

The longer I lay here, the more the images of the beaten man plague my every thought. Here safe and warm in my bed, I feel guilty for not doing anything.

I know there is no way possible he could have survived the injuries he sustained, but what if? What if he is lying down there right now, praying someone will find him, praying someone will come to his aid?

"No, Avalon, keep your ass in bed. He's beyond help, and the only thing you will accomplish if you go over there is getting a knife in your back when John returns," I mumble to the empty room.

The ticking of the clock is a constant reminder of time winding down, of the life slipping away right across the street. I grab the blankets and yank them over my head, hoping to drown out the sound. When it does little to help, I bury my head under the pillow.

"That's better. Now, close your eyes, Ava. Close your eyes and go to sleep."

Tick-tick-tick, tick.... tick.... tick.... .... tick.... .... Tick.

"Oh, for fuck's sake! Okay, I get it." I scream as I throw my pillow at the clock, knocking it off the wall. The damn thing is finally quiet when it shatters on the floor, sending bits and pieces flying everywhere.

"I can take a look outside; as long as I don't see anyone milling around out there, I can check it out. The dude is probably dead already. If he is, I'll bring my happy ass right back up here, climb into my nice warm bed, and sleep until I have to go back to work." Walking over to the window, I stand there for several minutes, watching the road and the shadows.

"Shit-shit-shit. Just get it over with Avalon. Standing around isn't doing anything but assuring he dies."

Slipping on my shoes, I jog down the stairs. Once again, I take a second to survey the road before I exit the building. Cautiously, I creep across the street; each sound I hear has me damn near jumping out of my skin.

When I arrive at the entrance to the building they drug him into, I wish I could hear if anything was on the other side of the door, but I can't hear a damn thing over the thud of my racing heart. Carefully opening the door, I inch along the wall, wishing the entire time I had brought a flashlight with me.

The burst of lightning from the approaching storm outside illuminates the space barely enough for me to make out the shape of someone lying in the middle of the room. I am not sure if I am more hopeful I will find him alive or discover he has succumbed to the wounds dealt out by his attackers.

"That is a shitty thing to hope for." I chastise myself for letting such a horrible thought materialize.

When I arrive at his side, I place my shaky hand against the side of his neck. Holy hell, I think this guy might still be alive or is it purely my imagination? I lower my head toward his chest, trying to listen for a heartbeat. Hell, any signs of life would be great right about now. When a low groan rumbles from deep in his chest, it scares the hell out of me, and I end up on my ass.

After a couple of seconds, my legs stop shaking enough to let me stand back up.

He's alive. Now I just need to.... Shit, I don't know what I need to do. I guess I didn't think this through all the way. I let my eyes drop back down to the man who was injured more by the assault than I realized. I know I need to get him out of here and back to my place if I have any hope of saving this guy's life.

"If you can hear me, I have to move you. I'm sorry. I know it is going to hurt like hell, but those guys will definitely be back around to make sure you will not be able to identify them."

Grabbing under his arms, I slowly begin pulling him towards the door. Inch by inch, one painful second at a time, I make it a little more than halfway across the room when I realize I will never get him all the way up to my apartment, not like this anyway. Maybe I have something over at my apartment I can use to help me.

"Ava? Are you in here?" My neighbor's voice is unmistakable. This is the help I need is the thought echoing through my head as I rush around the corner to find her standing just inside the door.

"What the hell are you doing over here, Suki?" I ask, mindful not to raise my voice too loud.

"I was on my way home and saw you coming into this dilapidated shithole. What are you doing?" Good question. What the hell am I doing? Seeing her timely arrival as an opportunity, I decided that asking for her help rather than replying with one of my typical snarky comments would be most beneficial.

"Will you help me with something? We need to hurry."

Suki's mom was obsessed with a book series that came out in 2001. I remember her laughing when she told me the story.

Apparently, her mom either misspelled her name or elected to go with the Japanese version.

Suki follows me around the corner and almost pisses her pants when she realizes we are both over here to help the man lying motionless in front of us.

"I need to get him out of here and over to my apartment before John and his band of thugs come back to finish the poor guy off."

"John did this?"

"Yeah."

"Oh, hell to the no. What the hell are you thinking, Avalon? Those crazy assholes will kill us if they catch us in here."

"Suki, what if this was someone you knew? Wouldn't you hope somebody would have the guts to risk saving them?"

"I sure would, but I ain't about to risk my life for some guy I don't know." She tells me as she starts her trek towards the exit.

"Suk, I can't do this without you."

"Then don't."

"I can't just leave the poor guy here. Please, the only thing I need you to do is help me get him across the street; I'll take it from there."

"Once we're across the street, the dangerous part is over, A." A is the nickname she took to calling me right after I met her. To be honest, I like her name better anyway.

"Please. Suki, I'll do your damn laundry for a week."

"Not worth it."

"Two weeks then."

"Make it three."

"You have got to be shitting me."

"Take it or leave it."

"Alright, three weeks. Now, will you help me? Please?"

"You better be damn glad I like you."

"Love me." I correct with a smile.

"Right now, it's damn debatable."

Even with Suki's help, progress is slower than either of us is comfortable with. I also know dragging the guy across the road has to hurt like a bitch since he only has on a thin shirt. I don't think I take my first breath until we are safely back inside my apartment. Thank God the super fixed the stupid elevator because there is no damn way we could have gotten him up the stairs.

Our next challenge is getting him up on the freaking bed. Like before, we both grab an arm and pull until we have the top half of his body on the mattress. I stay with his upper half while Suki lifts one leg at a time until we have him mostly on it. Panting heavily, I drop to the floor next to Suki, who is as winded as me.

"You know, we could have saved ourselves a lot of hassle if we had just called the cops."

"With how long they take to respond around here, the poor guy would have bled out before we heard the first blip of a siren in the distance."

"So, what are you going to do with him now?"

"I don't have the slightest idea."

"Okay, since he's not in danger of John coming back to finish what he started, why don't you call the police?"

"Now, there's a great idea. I imagine the conversation would go something like this. *Hi, I would like to report a guy who has been near fatally stabbed. Yep, he's in my bed as we speak. How did he get in there, you ask? Oh well, that's easy; see, it's like this, my neighbor and I drug him over here from the abandoned building across the street before we wrestled him onto my bed.* Yeah,

I can definitely see how that call would work out in my favor, not to mention if John comes back and discovers the police here, he is not going to let it go."

"Okay, point made." She glances over her shoulder at the man who hasn't moved or made a sound since we got him situated on the bed. "Welp, toots, I'm outty. Good luck with the stiff."

She stands up to look down at the guy we risked our lives to save before she swipes a piece of hair from his face.

"I'll say one thing. At least he's easy on the eyes, and if you have to share space with a nearly dead man, a fine-ass-looking one like this is always the best candidate."

"I hadn't noticed." She glares at me through squinted eyes with her hands planted on her hips.

"What? In case you weren't paying attention, I was kind of busy." This grants me one of her patented eye rolls. Followed by her shaking head as she turns to leave.

"Alrighty, sugarplum, I'll call you mañana." She takes one more look at the guy passed out in my bed and clicks her tongue as she wiggles her brow before she turns to shuffle out of the apartment, leaving me alone with a guy I don't have the first fucking clue about.

Yeah, this was a brilliant idea.

Now that I think about it, he could be some damn ax murderer or something much worse. I mean, I don't have the slightest idea why John and his band of thugs attacked the guy in the first place. It doesn't matter at this point because he's here, and I don't think I have the strength to remove him.

A muffled moan coming from him has me shaking off any lingering doubts. The first thing I need to do is check his wounds to see exactly what I'm dealing with.

After grabbing all the medical supplies I have in the house, I return to assess the damage. Still afraid John may return at any time, I conclude the most prudent decision is to leave my lights off, but if I hope to evaluate how bad he is, I need something to illuminate my surroundings. As a result, I end up lighting several candles.

The flame is enough for me to see the injuries they inflicted on him, but it is low enough that you could never see it if you were standing on the street. I try to slide his shirt up to give me better access, but this guy is huge, and trying to lift him by myself is next to impossible. I should have had Suk help me before she left. Shoulda woulda coulda isn't going to help with this issue right now though, so I do the next best thing.

"I hope it isn't one of your favorite shirts," I quietly tell him as I cut the mangled cloth away from him. I don't know why I'm worried about it because it's not like the thing isn't already ruined by the blood and multiple holes where they stabbed him.

He has eight puncture wounds, confirming my original suspicions that they continued their assault and stabbed him a couple more times after he was inside the building. Most of them have stopped bleeding except for the chest wound. Luckily for this guy, it's nowhere near his heart, and I think it's far enough away to have missed his truly essential organs.

Even if he survives the actual knife wounds, he could still succumb to infection, so I need to clean them as much as possible.

I begin by cleaning around the worst of them with Betadine before using simple soap and water to clean the punctures themselves. After I bandaged the wounds as best I could, I turned my attention to tend to the more superficial injuries on his face from where they punched and kicked him.

He has numerous large, angry-looking bruises already visible. With my limited knowledge of medicine, I check his belly, which doesn't feel hard or distended. The last thing I do is clean some of the dirt and debris from his hands and arms.

"Well, that's about the extent of my medical skills. If you make it through tonight, I think you stand a good chance of pulling through this. God, I hope you pull through because I have no damn idea what I'll do if you die, so if you have any sympathy for the dumb girl who is trying to save you, please pull through this." I tell him as I slide the blankets over him. Lowering myself to the floor, I lean my head back on the bed while waiting to see what the next hours will bring.

Angry shouts snap me awake. Shaking my head to clear the grogginess, I bolt upright when I realize the voice belongs to none other than John, and suddenly, the night's events slam into the forefront of my mind.

Looking over my shoulder, I discover the guy is still unconscious, but I can just make out the rise and fall of his chest in the low lighting. No longer willing to risk the whole not being able to see the candlelight from the street thing, I blow out the last two burning flames. This movement causes the muscles in my back and legs to throb from falling asleep on the hard-ass floor.

Crawling over to the window, I peek around, and as suspected, I find John standing out there barking orders at his crew.

"Find him, goddamn it. He can't have gotten very far." I watch as quite a few of his men split off, each going in different directions. I also notice the car with the trunk lid open. They must have decided leaving a body, even here in this shitty-assed neighborhood, was not a good idea. And just like earlier, when he turns his attention to my building, I can't shake the feeling his attention is directed fully at me.

"I'm gonna check out that building. The rest of you scour the street." My heart falters upon hearing his plan to come over here. Slinking away from the window, I hear my unknown patient moan as he shifts.

"Mister, I really need you to be quiet right now."

Simultaneously, I hear several buzzers for apartments surrounding mine before his voice comes through the speaker, "Little pigs, little pigs, let me come in."

I know some dumb ass will inevitably press the damn button to unlock the door, and he will focus his attention on this side of the building. If they make it inside the apartment, I will need something to protect myself and the unconscious guy with. The only thing I can use as a weapon is the butcher knife, making my decision quite easy before I focus my attention back on the door.

Hoping to give myself a couple of extra seconds if he tries to get into my apartment, I shove a chair under the handle and bolt every lock on it. It's not much in the way of defense, but it will have to do. Sliding down the flimsy door, I keep my back against the only thing offering me any safety.

I briefly contemplate running, but I will never be safe even if I do because if they find this guy in here, they will never stop until they locate me. Besides, what kind of an asshole would I be if I left this guy utterly defenseless?

After a few minutes, I hear heavy footfall entering the hall. There are only three apartments overlooking the street where they stabbed this guy, and one of them is empty.

Trying to keep my breathing even, I clutch the knife against my chest, fully prepared to use it on the first asshole who tries to come in here.

The door handle over my head jiggles, and I can only pray now is not when the injured guy decides to come to or starts moaning again.

"Oh, hi, can I help you?" Shit Suki, what the hell are you doing?

"Who lives in this apartment?"

"My friend, but she's not at home."

"Where is she?"

"Intrusive much. If you really need to know, she left this afternoon to visit family." Family? What fucking family, Suk? The only people I have happens to be the crazy girl talking to the sadistic prick in the hallway.

"Are you sure about that?"

"Yeah, she called me about two hours ago to let me know she made it. Did she forget she had plans with you? She can kinda be a scatterbrain about this kind of stuff." Geez, thanks, Suk.

"What's her name?"

"Ava. But you would know that if she was expecting you." I quietly thank God when I hear his response.

"My mistake. I'm here to visit with someone else. Can you tell me who lives in that apartment over there?"

"That place belongs to Mr. and Mrs. Johnson; they're the sweetest old couple you would ever want to meet."

"Old?"

"Yeah, I think Mr. Johnson is like eighty-four, and Mrs. Johnson recently celebrated her eighty-first birthday. But I can't imagine you'd be here to visit them at this hour either since they go to bed at like 7:30." Suk, you really need to watch your step with this asshole.

"You wouldn't be lying to me now, would you?" Shit. I quietly stand because if he moves to hurt Suk, there is no way

I can continue hiding in my apartment. Not after she risked her life to save the guy over on my bed and me.

"Why would I do that?"

"To protect someone."

"And who is it you think I am trying to protect?" I can almost imagine her crossing her arms defiantly over her chest. Slowly, I remove the chair from under the handle and slide the chain lock out of place. My heart is pounding so hard right now it's entirely possible the asshole on the other side can hear it.

"Well, you have a pleasant evening then," John says. I listen to his footsteps fade down the hallway. I remain with my hand resting on the knob until I hear Suk whisper from directly outside my door.

"And this is why we don't get involved, A."

"I know. Now go inside your apartment and bar the damn door."

"Did handsome wake up yet?"

"No."

"If he does, don't do anything I wouldn't do."

"So nothing is off the table then?"

"Not with a fine piece of man meat like him." She chuckles lightly. A second later, I hear her door close. Looking through the peephole, I confirm the hallway is empty and she is safely back in her apartment.

Moving towards the window, I wait until John exits the building. His goons are already waiting for him. He's telling them something, but I can't hear what he's saying. Just before climbing into the car, he turns and lights a cigarette. Even in the low light, I can easily track his eyes as they roam over my building.

Marcelle Valentine

My heart nearly stops when he raises his hand like a gun and fires. I swear the worst part is he was looking right at me when he did it.

Chapter Two: Chance

$\mathcal{I}$ REMAINED BY THE window for several hours after they left, afraid they may return at any moment. But as the sun crests the night sky, I vacate my vantage point to check the bandages on my patient. I carefully uncover one of the smaller wounds on his upper abdomen, only to be left dumbfounded by what I find.

"What the hell?" I mumble when I discover the bloody wound that was there only a few hours ago now resembles little more than a scratch. Trying to rationalize what I am looking at, I conclude it may be possible in the low light I made a mistake and the wound was not as bad as I thought.

The problem is, I can't explain away the damage I know I should find here as I move to the next one. In fact, I find the same thing with every bandage I remove until I have to face the simple truth; his wounds are healing at an exceedingly fast rate.

As I try to clean the wound on his chest, his hand shoots up, grabbing mine.

"What are you doing?" He asks me breathlessly.

"Holy shit." My words escape me before I can stop them.

"What are you doing to me?" His inquiry this time is delivered with a little more force than he managed with his last question.

"Tending to your wounds."

"Don't."

"Don't?"

"This is what I said, is it not?"

"If I don't clean them, they'll get infected."

"No, they will not."

"While I admit I'm no doctor, I've seen enough injuries to know—"

"No!" He snaps as he tries to sit up. His abrupt action starts the blood seeping from the chest wound again. The pain from his movements twists his features and causes him to fall back onto my bed.

Grabbing more gauze, I press it to the gash he managed to rip back open. The instant my hand comes in contact with him, he knocks it away. I get that it probably hurts like hell, but he will have to suck it up so I can stop the bleeding again. He doesn't allow my hand anywhere near him this time before he knocks it away.

"Listen, asshole, I'm trying to help your dumb ass in case you haven't figured that out yet."

"I neither ask for your help nor do I want it."

"Is this how you thank everyone who helps you?"

"As I have already stated, I never—"

"Yeah-yeah, I know you never asked for it. Well, that's too damn bad because I already did, jackass," I snap as I climb off the bed, throwing the towel I was using to clean his wounds back in the soapy water.

"This is what you get for sticking your nose where it doesn't belong, Avalon," my mumbled response mirrors Suki's earlier sentiment as I get the asshole a glass of water, although I do not know why because he will probably knock this away too. "Next time, I'll just leave you out there to die at the hands of John and his band of misfits."

"Is this what you believe?"

"He did kinda stab you at least eight times that I can see." I thrust the glass out towards him, but the only thing I get in response is him rolling his eyes. "Did you seriously just roll your damn eyes at me?"

"I find your comments to be ridiculous." He winces as he tries to sit up once more. I am not ashamed to admit his reaction brought me just a little bit of pleasure. Serves him right for being such a jackass.

When he stands up, I notice him swaying. Before I can tell him to sit down, he falls, smacking his head on the nightstand in the process.

"Oh, for the love of God." Storming around to the other side of my bed, I find precisely what I thought I would find. He's out cold with the chest wound ripped back open and a huge knot on his head where he hit the table. I first try to shake him, but when he doesn't respond, I realize I will have to get this big lug back onto my bed.

This time, regrettably, I don't have the help of Suk to get him back up there. For a fleeting second, I consider leaving his ass right where he landed. I mean, after all, he's the dumbass who did it.

"You better wake up with a better attitude," I grumble as I push him up to get behind him, allowing me access to wrap my arms around his chest, careful to avoid the worst of his injuries. Once I get my feet back under me, I leverage the bed to arch myself up, bringing Mr. Warmth with me.

Lucky for me, the frame is solid enough that it doesn't slip away from me as I use it. Once I have him lifted high enough, I push back with my legs and slide us both onto the mattress. The problem is that he is lying on top of me, and his body is dead weight, making it nearly impossible to wiggle out from under him. Frustrated with my current circumstances, I blow several strands of hair out of my face.

After what felt like an eternity, when it was probably more like minutes, okay, probably closer to seconds, I somehow managed to wiggle out from under him. With most of my energy spent just getting the upper half of his body on the bed, I lay next to him, panting for numerous minutes, until I noticed the blood flowing down his side.

"Alright-alright, I'm getting up," I say to no one in particular since he is sure as shit not listening. Shoving his legs up on the bed, I struggle to straighten him on the mattress before I tend to the wounds again. Pulling the blanket over his torso, I brush the hair from his face. I hate to admit it since he seems like such a royal asshole, but Suki's right; he is kind of handsome in an "*I know I'm better than you*" sort of way.

Glancing up towards where the clock used to hang, I am reminded of my tantrum last night. I sigh, realizing it will have to be replaced. I'll have to fork out money I don't really have to spend, even to purchase a stupid five-dollar clock. I could always look at my cell phone to find out what time it is, but based on the light outside the window, I guess it's probably somewhere around 5:30 in the morning. Sitting in the chair next to the bed, I try to find a comfortable spot to close my eyes for a few minutes.

I wake up to the sensation of being placed on something soft. My thoughts are still muddled from being woken up, making me forget everything that happened last night and early this morning for a few seconds. Snuggling my head against my pillow, I can't help letting out a satisfied little sigh. I cannot recall why my back is so stiff, but I don't care because I'm comfortable for the first time all night. Which begs the question, why was I so uncomfortable? Then something else occurs to me.

The scent surrounding me is all wrong.

My eyes snap open and settle on the medical supplies I used on that guy. I realize I'm in my bed, and he's gone. Jumping out of it, I look around my apartment, which is pointless because he's nowhere in here. I need to find this guy, is the only thought repeating in my head. In my haste to get to the door, I inadvertently kick the bedframe, forcing me to hobble more than rush over to the door. The slew of curse words I mumble could rival any trucker.

I yank it open in time to see him disappear into the stairwell. Shit, I need to stop him. If John is watching the building and he strolls out the damn front door, it will only invite trouble for the residents who have to continue living here.

Ignoring my throbbing toe, I run down the hall after him and slam through the door he went through only seconds ago. I immediately start down the stairs, only to realize the sound of his footsteps is moving up, not down. Switching direction, I pick up my pace, racing up the stairs. The door to roof access echoes off the walls and makes me wonder what the hell this guy is up to. I smash through the door to find him standing on the edge of the roof, looking out over the city.

"What.... What are you doing?" I ask breathlessly.

"Waiting."

"Waiting for what?"

"Not what, who."

"Okay, I'll bite. So, who are you waiting for?" With him no longer debilitated, I realize how large this guy really is. I have to be honest; he's pretty damn intimidating, which makes sense why he didn't seem afraid of John when I mentioned him earlier. Yet John was able to incapacitate him enough to stab him eight —

What the fuck is going on? Every thought I have seems unimportant when he turns, and I see he is completely healed. How in God's name is he healed?

"You. I was waiting for you, Apple."

"My name's not Apple; it's Avalon," I mutter, still bewildered at how he is standing here without a blemish to be seen anywhere on his skin, including the laceration I felt last night could use some stitches.

"So it is."

"How?" I ask as I reach my hand out towards him. He steps away from me and closer to the edge.

Tilting his head all while his curious eyes assess me. I feel like a child being sized up by the person who holds the fate of their punishment in their enormous hands.

The entire time my gaze is moving over his torso, his muscled, toned, golden torso; I'm amazed when I discover not even a scratch. I've heard of miraculous recoveries, but to be honest, I never believed in them until now.

"Why did you come for me?" His question only semi-registers in my confused state.

"Huh?" There is no damn way possible the wound on his chest could be healed unless there is some witchy who-ha shit going on here.

"Why. Did. You. Come. For me?"

"It was the right thing to do," my absentminded response causes his brows to furrow.

"You risked much coming to get me. The ones who did this could have come back at any time."

"They came back," I mumble, massaging right above my brow line. Maybe this is all a hallucination. Did I fall and hit my head last night? Running my fingers through my hair, I don't feel any damage. I don't do drugs; I don't drink alcohol in excess, which leaves only one option.

"It has to be a brain tumor."

"Pardon me?" He asks while tilting his head.

"Brain tumor, I figured it out.... You're not really here because I'm not really here. This is all a hallucination brought on by a brain tumor."

"I can assure you that is not the case. You do not have a brain tumor, Apple."

"Then how the hell do you explain this?" I wave my hand, theatrically indicating his perfectly chiseled frame is.... well, perfect. Not a scrape, scratch, or blemish to be found, and definitely no life-altering knife wounds.

"I can also assure you hell had nothing to do with it. What did you mean by 'they came back?'"

"What I said. John and his goons came back last night."

"How did we escape them?"

"Simple. We were lucky. They didn't return until I had you safely tucked inside my apartment."

"Do you always take men you do not know to your dwelling?"

"Dwelling?" Who the hell uses the word dwelling nowadays?

"Home."

"I'm aware of what dwelling means. I was just shocked you chose to use it. You know, instead of apartment like most normal people would."

"Yes, well, it is what we call it where I'm from."

"And where are you from?"

He deliberately ignores my question to repeat the one I didn't answer, "Do you always save men you do not know?"

"If I can. Who are you?" He remains silent, unmoving, and the intensity of the gaze he has settled on me is making me uneasy.

"Okay, so I take it that's a no go on the name then. Well, how about I offer you a little advice instead?"

He tilts his head. I assume this means he's listening; if not, oh well, because someone needs to tell him. "You really shouldn't walk around in that loincloth, skirt, thingy you have on. There are a whole slew of assholes in this town, and if you walk around in that...." Come to think of it, where in the hell did it come from because he certainly wasn't wearing it last night? "John will be the least of your worries."

"Subligaculum."

"Come again?"

"As opposed to loincloth skirt thingy. It is called a Subligaculum."

"Isn't that just a fancy word for loincloth?" It could be the shadow cast across his face by the sun behind his back or my mind playing tricks on me, but I could swear he just smiled. No, definitely a figment of my imagination.

His eyes remain focused on mine until a light wind picks up and blows my hair forward across my face. I quickly push it aside. I don't know why, but something tells me I should always keep him within my sights.

I don't miss the slight wrinkle he does with his nose, like he smells something foul. I get I haven't taken a shower yet this morning, not to mention moving him last night was hard work, so I admit I worked up a bit of a sweat, but geez, gimme a break here; after all, if I stink, it's only because I helped his sorry ass. As I prepare to tell him this, his declaration cuts me off.

"You showed me a kindness, so I will return the favor. It would be in your best interest if you left this city, Apple. Take what is essential and leave this very day."

"Why do you keep calling me apple? My name is—"

"Avalon, yes, I know. Is this what you are most concerned about? What I call you?"

"Yes.... No.... I don't know. Is there something other than this crazy shit I should be worried about right now?"

"You are wasting precious seconds."

"What?" His warning is ominous. Is he planning on taking revenge against John and his crew? Is he afraid John will come looking for me? I want to ask him to elaborate until he gives me his final warning, which silences any further objections.

"I will give you one hour. After an hour, I will raze this city from existence. If you wish to live, you will be far beyond the confines of this place when I do."

Before his words fully register in my brain, he turns and steps off the building. My hands fly to my mouth as I run to the edge, certain I will discover his mangled, bloody body on the street below when I get there; instead, I find him standing on the road looking up at me. Then I watch as armor slowly materializes over his exposed chest and arms.

"What the hell?" This all has to be a nightmare. No way did I watch a man step off the building, live, and walk away unscathed. Maybe if I had the answer, I wouldn't have wasted so much of my precious time staring at the cracked and crumbled asphalt where he landed. I would have heeded his words and fled the city without delay, but how could I have known....

The man I thought I saved never actually needed my help because I had sheltered one of the fabled horsemen of the apocalypse. I just met Death, and it seems he is not in a forgiving mood.

Death

I cannot say why I felt inclined to give this mortal a chance at life. I know what I am preparing to do may very well set into motion the events which will ultimately end her mortal existence. Still, I felt obligated to someone who had risked their own safety when they could have so easily remained behind locked doors.

So I will give her a chance. If she does not listen to my advice, it is her mistake, not mine. Those who do not heed my warnings will pay dearly for their misstep.

My quest is to determine if these mortals are worthy, and I have found them wanting. In the few short years I have been trapped here, what I have discovered includes greed, sloth, gluttony, pride, envy, lust, and wrath. Each of the sins our father warned them about is alive and well within the beings of this plane. Seven deadly sins they have embraced when they should have shunned.

The mortal who attacked me last night exhibited all of these traits. I let my guard slip. It was a momentary lapse in judgment. One I shall never make again. The men who stabbed me did so because I tried to give them a chance to repent. I was pulled to them as they were attacking another, the call of a soul slipping away. I was so focused on my old ways I stood watch as I waited for his soul to pass. This is how they were able to gain the upper hand against me. The pain they inflicted was intense.

A gift my father bestowed on me when he set me on this task. He said to understand them, I need to know their pain, joy, and desires. I had to experience it myself; I had to know what it meant to be alive. I can assure you there has been no joy and certainly no desire unless you consider my constant longing to return to my previous life, but I have learned of their pain. More pain than I care to remember. I have existed since the dawn of time, and never have I known the pain I have experienced in the past couple of years.

I follow their path back to the bar where it all began last night. It is nothing more than a den of depravity. The rot emanating from this place rolls out in waves, destroying almost everything it touches. And like my other task, I wait, I watch, and I will deliver, just not anything they want.

Last night was the final time I will allow any of them to inflict the pain they so kindly showed me; this is not their divine right. It is mine. For I am Death, and their judgment begins now.

Avalon

What the actual fuck is going on? My heart is racing as I run back down to my apartment. I have no idea what I'm going to do, but I can tell you one thing.... I do not have any damn intention of waiting around to find out what his plan entails. Racing up to Suki's door, I pound on it until I hear her stumbling around inside.

I admit the fear John may yet come for me or the guy from the roof has changed his mind and decided that leaving me alive is a liability he's unwilling to take has me desperate to get away from this place. I shift my eyes from Suki's door down the hall. I don't see any menacing figures creeping toward me.

What I do focus on is Mr. and Ms. Johnson's door. I can't abandon them here. I need to get them out of here too, but first, I need to get Suki moving and a bag of my own packed, then I can wake up the Johnsons. And if need be, I'll drag them out of here kicking and screaming.

"There better be a goddamn fire, and it better be right outside my bloody damn door," she yells as she fumbles with the locks. I wonder if she even looked to see who the crazy person banging on her door this early in the morning was before she decided to open it.

"A? What the hell?" she asks, rubbing the sleep from her eyes.

"Suk, I need you to pack a bag and come with me."

"What?" she yawns while laying her head against the door.

"Suki, pack a damn bag," I tell her much more forcefully as I turn to run into my apartment. She must have registered the urgency in my tone, causing her to wake up and focus on what I am telling her. "Do it now."

"For how long?"

"A week, maybe two."

"A, I can't leave for two weeks. I'll lose my job, and so will you."

"I don't give a shit about a goddamn job." His warning echoes through my head. *One hour.* How long has it been since he told me to leave? I know I stood rooted in place on the roof for what felt like an eternity. Now I feel like I need to get my ass moving. Somewhere in the back of my mind, his ominous words ring true. He is giving me this one chance, and I am giving one to Suki. If she gets her ass moving, that is. As my door closes, one word drifts from the hall.

"John?" My heart stops. Did she say his name because she thinks John is why I want to leave, or did she say it because?

"Not by the hair of your chinny chin chin." I spin to see John standing there with Suki's throat in his hand. My mouth dries up like the Sahara while my hands refuse to stop trembling. Swallowing, I try to force any amount of saliva I can produce into my mouth as I battle to control my racing heart.

"Can — can I help you?"

"Funny you should ask. See, I was here last night, and your little friend here told me you weren't home."

Hesitantly I mutter, "I wasn't—"

He cuts me off, clicking his tongue as he raises his finger to wave it back and forth, "Let's not make an already bad situation worse. Where is he?"

"Where's who?" Hearing my response, he laughs, but there is zero amusement. The sound of it makes my skin crawl.

"See, now that would be an example of making it worse." Suki's hands, which until now have only been resting on the arm he has clamped around her neck, begin wildly clawing at it as he tightens his hold around her throat. Her struggle for that next precious breath becomes more apparent with every flex of his muscle.

"Who the hell are you talking about?" I scream as I take a step toward them. Faster than I can react, he shoves Suki in my direction. She crashes against me with enough force to knock us to the ground. The impact is jarring, causing my teeth to snap closed on my tongue. Coppery liquid fills my mouth, making me wish for the desert sensation over the taste of my blood.

John does not hesitate as he pounces on both of us. Twisting his fist in my hair as he begins repeatedly slamming my head against the ground. Pain explodes through my brain and down into my neck. The taste of blood becomes more prevalent as my teeth snap viciously on my wounded tongue.

Jumping to his feet, he rears back to deliver a brutal blow, but I move at the last second. Instead of kicking his intended target, this being my head, my shoulder takes the brunt of it. Something popped, and with little effort, he rendered my arm useless.

Before I can recover, he grabs Suki by the shirt and shakes her mercilessly. I try to sit up, hoping to help her so he cannot hurt her any further, only to have him stop me with a boot heel to my chest. The force freezes my diaphragm, halting any attempt I make at sucking in my next breath. Rolling, I push up on my hands and knees as I take one gasping gulp of air after another, desperate to alleviate the sensation of not being able to breathe.

I am vaguely aware of Suki screaming somewhere behind me, but there is another sound filling the space around us as well. Straining my ears, I question if it is the beating of my heart or the ticking of the clock, signifying the rapid rate at which my time is running out. Like sands through an hourglass, each speck brings me closer to meeting my maker, either by this asshole or the one who jumped off my roof.

I have to make a decision here. I either can stay here panting on the floor, waiting for my end to come by one of these two assholes, or I can stand and fight. Since I have never been one to wait around for the infamous and elusive knight in shining armor, my decision is easy. Why? Because I knew this fabled being does not exist. There is only one person in the world who can save me from this mess, and the person just so happens to be me.

As painful as it is, I force myself to my feet and begrudgingly slam my shoulder against the wall to pop it back into place before I grab the closest thing to me that can be used as a weapon before sneaking up behind John.

Swinging with every ounce of strength I can muster, the sound of the hit is every bit as satisfying as I had hoped. The first hit from the statue stuns him; the second sends him stumbling, but the third puts him on his ass. Not one to waste an opportunity, I grab Suki and sprint for the door. Leaving

43

everything behind, I drag her down the hallway into the stairwell.

Even with the repeated hits delivered to his head, he won't be down long. If this thought alone was not enough to get me moving, the bangs and shouts from above us pushed me to move faster as we descended two steps at a time. We rush towards the ground floor and what I pray is our salvation.

I know I'm a coward for not at least making an attempt to rescue Mr. and Ms. Johnson, but if I did, the only thing it would accomplish is killing them and still ending up dead at the hands of this bastard chasing us. We are halfway down the stairwell when the door above us flies open.

"I'm going to split your fucking skull open, bitch," his booming threat echoes off the walls surrounding us. As much of a head start as I believed we had, the sound of his rapidly approaching footsteps confirms it is quickly dwindling.

Shoving Suki through the door that will take us outside, I'm within a hundred yards of my car. Still, we did not move fast enough because John was suddenly behind me with my hair tangled in his grip, "I am going to slit your fucking throat and leave you to bleed out right next to the bitch over there and the asshole you so heroically tried to save."

"Run, Suki," I scream. She spins, seeing we are out of time, and I can see in her eyes she is torn between doing what I am begging her to do or helping me. He presses the edge of honed steel to my neck, which finally has her acting. Unfortunately, it's not what I was hoping for because she is running straight at us.

As much as I do not want to let go of the hand holding the knife that will claim my life soon. I throw my arms up, hoping to halt her before she can get too close. Believing she may have come to her senses when she abruptly stops. I continue to think this right up to the time her eyes go wide, and she mutters.

"What the fuck?" Her gaze is no longer focused on us; something behind where we stand has gained her full attention. John spins, allowing me to finally see what put the look of terror on her face.

The man I saved is standing behind us, still wearing the armor that magically appeared as he stood looking up at me from the street, but now it is covered in blood. This alone would be enough to have anyone quaking in their shoes, but the wings expanded out and away from his body are the most terrifying thing I have ever witnessed, and I've seen some pretty fucked up things in my life.

"What the fuck. What are you?" John screams as he levels the blade at the new arrival.

"Release the woman."

"Fuck you."

"Release. Her!" He demands again as he stalks in our direction. Hands-down, seeing him like this is the scariest yet most magnificent thing I have ever experienced.

Horrifyingly beautiful; talk about a damn oxymoron.

I can feel the asshole behind me tense as he prepares to do what he hopes will stop the thing prowling toward us; John presses the knife back to my throat, digging it painfully into my flesh.

"Stop right there, or I'll slit this bitch's throat." His threat is laughable. Why he would think my life would matter to the man closing in on us is beyond me. "I'm not fucking around here, man. Stop, or her blood will be on your hands."

One second, he was at least twenty feet away from us; the next, he had John's arm clenched within his massive hand.

John's screams of pain fill the air around us as the bones in his limb shatter.

"I told you one hour." The man's eyes, which have not left mine since he realized who John held, skim over my face.

"I was detained by this asshole," I hope my fear is not leeching out in my response. I prefer this man not realize how scared I am right now.

"So I see. Fortunately for you, you still have five minutes. I suggest you use those precious seconds to run."

He doesn't have to tell me twice as I hear what sounds like an explosion somewhere in the city. Whirling, I rush back to where Suki stands wide-eyed, mouth gaped open. I grab her arm on my way by as I dash to my car. The keys briefly fumble in my shaking hands as I chance one more glance over my shoulder. The man I saved still has John on his knees in front of him. John's arm hangs at an odd angle, and his guttural screams are unnerving, yet the man's eyes are still directed at me. The reality I am out of time is not only repeating in my head; it's screaming.

Jumping into the car, I say a silent prayer of thanks when it starts on the first try. Not wanting to be here when whatever hell he is prepared to release comes to pass, I throw it into drive, slam my foot down on the gas pedal, and peel away from the curb.

Suki's head whips back in the direction we came from as another explosion rips through the air. My eyes briefly flick to the rearview mirror, just in time to watch as the winged being snaps John's neck.

After our frantic escape, I would like to say that my life was able to return to normal and that nothing else bad happened because of this interaction. Regrettably, I cannot give you this peace of mind since this was the start of a new life, not only for me but for all of humanity. Because this was the trigger point that began Armageddon.... The end of days was near, and a whole new way of life had emerged.

Chapter Three: New World

THE DAY MY CITY fell was the day everything changed. All electronic devices ceased to work. Planes fell from the sky; cars stalled, never to turn over again; trains screeched to a halt. Gone was the internet, social media, phone calls, television, radio. News of what happened was all received by word of mouth, and we all know how trustworthy this can be. It all disappeared the second I crossed over the city limits.

He upheld his word and gave me a chance to run for my life. The instant my car died, I knew there was no point trying to fix it. Seeing all the other vehicles stalled around me, especially with their confused-faced occupants, didn't leave much room for denial. While they continually turned the key, hoping the starter would catch, sparking the now antiquated relic back to life, Suki and I ran.

We ran for our lives. We ran until our lungs burned, the pain in our sides damn near debilitating, our clothes soaked through with sweat, and our legs refusing to take one more step gave out, sending a sprawling to the grass still damp from the morning dew. After lying on the ground staring at the blue sky for an exceedingly long time, I got up and pulled my crying friend to her feet. I remember telling her we had two options: we could remain there and wait for whatever the hell was coming our way to arrive, or we could get our asses moving and try to stay one step ahead of it. That was just over a year ago.

"Hey, A, I don't think we checked that one, did we?"

Martial law has been enacted; however, there are too few honest people left to patrol everything, and the ones who are, tend to live within small communities, leaving the rest of the world to the deviants.

Suki and I briefly stayed with a group of survivors, but the self-proclaimed leader showed his true character when he began forcing all the single women into his little harem. Suk and I had no desire to join; the problem was he didn't care what we wanted. It seems options were not a part of his plans or vocabulary. And the other men who were his appointed forces were no better. When we told him we would leave, he refused. Things quickly escalated from there since he had no intention of allowing us to abandon them. Let's just say our separation was not amicable, nor was it without bloodshed.

The one thing all humans, regardless of whether they are decent or deviant, steer clear of is the being who started this all. There has been much speculation regarding who or what he is, although I have my own suspicions. Until a few months ago, no one knew for sure.... Well, let me rephrase that no one alive and outside his horde knew for sure.

Yes, you heard me right; the being who crumbled a city in less than an hour takes the humans he finds to serve within his horde. There are rumors he keeps some people to strengthen and build his army. Some are taken because of a particular skill they possess; some are cooks, builders, babysitters, servants, hell, maybe even a concubine or two, I don't know. I can tell you one thing I do know: I have no plans to find out what roles are available in his world. The one thing everyone proclaims is his reign is singular; he and he alone rules the ones around him.

To my knowledge, there are only two souls who have come face to face with him and walked away.... Suki and me.

Looking up at the sun hanging low in the western sky tells me it's time we start looking for a place to hunker down for the night. It's not safe for two women to travel the roads at night; between the assholes and the wildlife, I can't say for sure which one is the worst kind of predator. I am taking bets it is the ones who walk on two legs, not four. At least with the four-legged ones, I know precisely where I stand and what I represent; dinner. The two-legged ones normally have much more nefarious plans in mind for the women they find.

"Let's hold up here for the night. We can get an early start in the morning."

"You know we're getting awful close to Charleston."

"I know. We'll make sure we stay well to the south and west of it." Any city, regardless of how big or small it is, poses a risk to us, but the bigger ones are the worst, which is why we avoid them at all costs.

During our travels, we went from Ohio through Pennsylvania and New York on our way to Canada, but when we were told they closed their borders and were turning any refugees away, we circled back down, deciding if our northern neighbors didn't want us, maybe our southern ones would. We made it as far as North Carolina when we were told they also closed their borders. It's ironic if you think about it; so many Americans clamored for a damn wall to be built only to have it used against us when we were the ones running for our lives.

So now we are going back to where it all began. We figure by now he's moved further south with his hordes, or at least this was our hope. If we have to be out here on our own, it would be easier to be somewhere we are familiar with. Better the devil you know than the ones you don't. Right? God, I hope I'm right.

That night, Suki and I listened as an unexpected family got caught out in the open. I wanted to rush out to save them, but Suk stopped me, demanding I use discretion. Had I gone out there, we would have never survived the night. The next morning, the only item left behind was a teddy bear. My heart squeezes, knowing there was a child with them. People often view children as a hindrance in this new world, although there is no reason they should feel this way. I mean, hell, it's not like they are running from a damn zombie apocalypse.

After two more weeks, we cross the Ohio River, and I breathe a sigh of relief as I think about being home. Our progress is slower than either of us is comfortable with because there are bands of roving assholes on the first ten miles into Ohio. Seeing the Cambridge exit caused the first actual fight between Suki and me since she had family living there. She wanted to check it out while I was desperate to continue toward our chosen goal.

Marcelle Valentine

Ultimately, I relented, and we went to Cambridge because Suk was unyielding, even going so far as to tell me she would go by herself if I didn't agree. I guess I don't understand the pull of having a loved one since my family never truly gave a shit about me. If I thought I could get away with telling people I was an alien, and not the ones who move from one country to another but the little green ones who travel light years to get here in their little saucer spaceship, I would.

If my previous life and now my current life have taught me anything, it's this... trust no one. Regardless of who you believe they may be or how much you want to think they love you. At the end of the day, people will always look out for themselves first.

*****

We ended up staying in Cambridge much longer than I was comfortable with. If you talk to any escapee, they will tell you the first rule is never to put down roots. The second you believe you are in the clear is when life has a way of creeping up on you.

I got up early this morning to scavenge. I want to be ready to hit the road if Suki doesn't find whatever she hopes to locate here; if she does, I guess I'll wish her well and continue by myself. I have no desire to live in this city. It makes me uneasy every time I cross paths with anyone. I guess I'm a glass-half-full kind of girl. Yeah, I know this is no way to live, but it has kept me alive this far.

Today is a good day. I found five cans of vegetables and another thermal water bottle; these are better than gold in today's world. Cold drinks are a distant memory, but you never stop missing them; with any hope, these containers will help provide us with some.

I returned to the place we were staying, only to discover five men holding Suki hostage. I drop everything I'm carrying as I slowly begin backing toward the blade I have hidden in the corner.

"Stop." I don't heed his words; instead, I continue moving toward the only thing that may yet save our lives.

"I said stop right now." His tone is low and dangerous but with a hint of fear. Is he afraid of what will happen if I refuse to surrender or what will happen if I do?

He does the one thing he can to make me comply; he brings the knife he was merely holding at his side up to her neck. The blade bites painfully into her flesh as a soft cry escapes her. I raise my hands, conceding defeat, only to feel something heavy smash against the back of my head. As I Crumple to the ground, the one thought repeating through my head is *the devil just caught up with me.*

When I come to, Suki and I are both bound, held within a cage carried on a horse-drawn cart, because yes, this is our new reality. All that knowledge, all the advances humankind had made, only to end up right back where we started. It's a bitter pill to swallow at times.

The jostling of the cart has my head thumping from whatever they used against me. Surveying our surroundings, I find we are no longer in the city; only God knows why these men took us or where they are leading us.

I try to speak, but the words catch in my throat; it seems my vocal cords are too rigid to produce sounds. Clearing my throat, I make another attempt to get the question out. "Where are you taking us?"

"To him." This is the only answer we received. They will answer us no further.

I guess declaring Suki a hostage may have been the wrong word since they never planned on releasing her or me. No, the town Suk was so hell-bent on staying in betrayed us.

They have chosen us as a sacrifice for him. Who knew the man.... being.... whatever he is I met all those months ago, the one who gave me a chance to live would want human sacrifices offered to him. But then again, if the rumors are true, he is taking mortals to serve within his horde. So who the hell knows? Maybe he will accept this bargain. I can only hope he isn't looking for virgins because I can assure you this is not the case for my friend or me.

For two days we travel. They did not release Suki or me from the cage they held us in throughout the entire trip. I sincerely hope you will never understand the degradation we face having to use the restroom where we are forced to sleep.

The entire time we travel, I repeatedly try to tell our abductor he is not who they believe he is. The being I took care of does not want women in the way they may think. Like the men who serve him, women are simply a means to an end. It should come as no surprise these idiots refused to listen. They believed him to be like any mortal man. So they continue with their stupid trek to take us to him, regardless of how many times I try to convince them of their folly. They plan to offer us up like lambs for the slaughter, for him to use us in any way he saw fit.

Idiots, the lot of them.

They should have listened to me the entire time they were dragging us to this fate; had these dumbasses done so, these good and honorable men, as they repeatedly declared during our travels, may not be facing the uncertainty they are now.

*****

When we get within walking distance of the being who has crumbled every city that has opposed him, Suki and I are pulled from the cart and stripped before they throw freezing-cold water on us. I had to bat away the hands of these good and honorable men attempting to wash me on more than one occasion. Amazingly, the only parts of my body they felt needed to be cleaned were my breast and vagina. I guess the rest of the areas, you know, the ones which were left lying in piss and shit for days, are squeaky fucking clean, but these breasts, well, it seems they needed a generous rubbing, oops slip of the tongue, I meant scrubbing.

Of all the men present, only two do not touch us. When the leader of this ragtag little group felt we were presentable, he threw what passed as clean clothes with these morons at us. Then proceeds to bind our hands to lead us into the heart of Death's world.

The instant we enter his camp, we are surrounded by his army. Swords, daggers, bows, and spears are all trained on our every movement. With the number of weapons aimed at us, you would think we are the ones who hold all the power here. The sheer number of projectiles ensures nothing could be farther from the truth.

Twenty yards into his camp, our progress comes to a screeching halt when the men and women refuse to part; I turn to watch the swarm encircle us until there is nowhere left for us to run. As I said, these good and honorable morons did not know what they willingly ambled into.

"Idiots," I laugh as they all stand back to back, their minuscule weapons raised.

"Shut up, bitch," the one I had to block the most during our bath hissed.

The crowd in front of our group parts just enough to allow entrance for a tall, ordinary-looking man flanked by two smaller men to enter. When he finally stands before my captors, the ringleader steps forward. I know he is trying to put on a brave front, but I'm willing to bet he is shitting his pants.

"We want to see your lord," he is trying to make demands, but it comes out sounding much closer to a plea.

"He is not a lord. He is Thanatos."

"Then take us to this, *Thanatos*." He probably shouldn't have spit his name out like that if he doesn't want the mob to attack us. I admit I'm shocked by the whole interaction. Everything I've heard is they are his prisoners, but if this is the case, why does it feel like they are protecting him?

"As you wish," the man sent to greet our group laughs as he leads us through the other individuals surrounding us. I wonder who this guy is because the instant he agreed to take us to the rider, the rest lowered their weapons, allowing us to pass without further harassment.

When we arrive at the center of his camp, we are greeted by an enormous man sitting in the ugliest chair I've ever seen. All the men who brought us here step forward before they all take a knee. When the hell did we get transported back to the seventeenth century?

My eyes skim over the structure which holds the one these halfwits are bowing to, studying the other men who flank him. I look from left to right until my gaze settles on a hooded man leaning haphazardly against the beam holding up the ornate tent behind the throne.

"We are told your name is Thanatos." The man sitting on the throne grunts but does not lift his eyes from the plate of food he is consuming.

"We have brought you an offering. In exchange, we ask you to leave our town and the residents who live there alone so we may exist in peace."

The one they called Thanatos brings his eyes up to meet theirs. One second he was stuffing his face; the next, he was throwing the plate on the ground at their feet. Licking fingers that closely resemble stuffed sausage, he stands. Thundering down from his perched vantage point. He marches directly up to the leader of the group who took Suki and me.

"And what would I need with two half-starved females?"

"Whatever you want, they would belong to you. A gift from our community."

He pushes past our captors. When he arrives in front of us, he tilts his head from side to side as this mammoth man appraises the gift they are offering, all the while licking the grease left by his meal from those plump sausages. When he jerks Suki's head up, I've had more than enough of this shit.

"Don't do that, asshole." I snap. The hooded man shifts slightly but does not approach. The one standing before us slides his tongue over his teeth before snatching me by the hair.

"I will enjoy breaking you. I accept your offer, but.... I think it is not enough."

"We have nothing left to offer you."

"Then I claim you as well. Take the smaller one to the mess tent; the wild one can be delivered to mine." Suki's eyes widen as the assholes who started this all struggle to break the hold of the converging soldiers.

"Don't you need to ask the one who reigns over this horde first?" I ask with as much indifference as I can muster.

"I reign over this horde," he snarls.

"Shut up, girl," the leader of the men who took us scowls in my direction. I know he is hoping to gain favor with the asshole glaring at me, but he is honestly as stupid as the rest of them.

"No, you don't." I calmly respond.

"You are testing my patience."

"Maybe the leader of this group would have better tolerance then."

"You stupid girl, can you not tell one of the horsemen when he stands before you?" the one who took a particular interest in my boobs hisses.

"I can; too bad you dumbasses can't."

Sausage fingers grabs my face to yank it in his direction. "I will break you."

"Better men have tried."

"After you are nothing more than a shell of the insolent woman who dares to defy me, I will kill you."

"No, I don't think you will."

"A, what are you doing?" Suki whispers.

"Don't worry, Suk, that's not Thanatos."

Snarls and shouts circle around me, from the ones who brought me here to the beings who live within this camp, all screaming at my insolence.

"If I'm not Thanatos, then who is, girl?" He laughs as he raises his massive arms away from his side. I don't know if this was supposed to indicate no one else in this camp could possibly be the great and mighty Thanatos. The problem is this man, like his action, does nothing to dissuade me from what I know is true.

Leveling my eyes at the hooded being, I confidently declare, "He is."

Chapter Four: The Devil You Know

Avalon Late Spring 2023

AFTER REVEALING WHO THE true horseman was, they whisked me away to a tent where sausage fingers had me chained to one of the numerous posts holding it up. Looking around at all the shit in here, I have to wonder how much of a pain in the ass it must be when they tear this thing down and move all this shit every time they travel to the next city he plans to sack or raze or whatever the hell he is doing.

The rustling tent flap announces my newest captors have arrived. It matters little to me because I refuse to acknowledge them any more than the last ones. I will not give any of them, including the horseman, the satisfaction. Instead, I continue to look at the abundance of shit most people no longer possess.

I listen as more than one set of footsteps approach me. I merely don't give a shit which of the assholes who serve him is lumbering their ass in my direction; none of them have merited my attention. One object, in particular, has captured my interest though. It's a painting, and while it is nothing special, just some random meadow with the sun setting in the background, I'm captivated by it. The colors are bright and vivid. I am left wondering if the peace this picture is trying to convey is something we, and by we, I mean humanity, will ever experience again.

The one who pretended to be Thanatos grabs my face and yanks it in his direction. This is when I see the man I saved all those months ago float across my field of vision.

"Acknowledge your betters, bitch."

"Show me my betters, and I may acknowledge them. Until then, you can piss off." He raises his hand to smack me until the booming voice of Thanatos stops him.

"I can oversee it from here, Nevil."

"Are you certain—" I suppose they should know this from the start; I am not one of those girls willing to wait around as others decide my fate, and I tend to speak before I think, especially when I'm angry. And right now, I am pulse-pounding pissed. Which is why I interrupt with something I know will piss him off, if not the rest of the men surrounding me.

"Seriously, your fuckin name is Nevil?" A low growl rumbles from deep in his chest. Who the hell does this guy think he is? Some supernatural king? Pretty sure that doesn't exist, and if someone like that did, I'm willing to bet they wouldn't look like sausage fingers over here. "Your mom must have seriously disliked you. Were you a difficult birth?"

Nevil eliminates the remaining space between us. Apparently, I must have hit the right button this time. Thanatos intercepts him when he is preparing to grab me by my throat, which by the way, what the hell is the deal with all macho assholes going straight for the throat when they want to put the ones they deem to be weaker, specifically women, in their place?

"That will be all for tonight, Nevil." When the idiot continues to stand here panting like a rabid dog, Thanatos advises much more forcibly, "You are dismissed. Right Now."

I smile at Nevil as he turns to walk away. The malicious intent burning bright in his eyes confirms I accomplished my goal of pissing him off. Yep, I can count him among the ones who hate me. My reason for doing this is simple: people don't think straight when they're pissed. My gut feeling about this guy is he's a sadistic prick but one who is not used to being challenged. Making him mad may cause him to do something stupid enough that I won't have to worry about him in the future.

After Nevil, what a name for an idiot like this guy, leaves and takes the others who entered with them, Thanatos sits at a table in front of me. Well, this encounter is drastically different from our last one. Would it be so hard to offer me a chair rather than leave me chained to this pole? It's the least he could do since I so generously gave him my bed during our last interaction. Neither of us speaks until the whole situation becomes awkward. Not knowing what else to do, I clear my throat.

"Why do you provoke a man twice your size?"

"Because he's an asshole, and in my experience, the only way to deal with an asshole is by letting them know from the very beginning that they are, *in fact*, an asshole."

"And this has worked out for you?"

"In the past, yes."

"But not now?"

"Well, now sausage fingers knows exactly where he stands with me, but since I am currently chained to a post in the tent for one of the horsemen of the fucking apocalypse, I'm gonna have to go with no. Not so well recently."

Thanatos abruptly leaves his chair, stepping directly in front of me, his eyes following the lines of my face, shoulders, arms, and hips before settling on my breast for a brief second. Okay, maybe he *is* like all the other guys. I reflexively jerk away from the contact when he reaches out to me. This does not stop him as he pushes a strand of my wayward hair out of my face.

"Who are you?"

"You don't remember?"

"Should I? I assume from your response that you believe we have met before."

"No recollection at all of who I might be?" He levels his gaze at me but refuses to respond any further. I guess we are two very different souls since I would never forget someone who put their ass on the line to save me, him not so much. Now I understand why I'm still chained to this pole.

"I asked you a question."

"Yeah, so you did."

"My questions generally require answers."

"I'm sure they do."

"Your sardonic response is not the answer I seek, so we will try this once more. Who are you?"

"I'm nobody. I was born a nobody. Before you decided to destroy our world, I was a nobody. It seems I remain nobody, and I will die as one."

"I didn't ask you to tell me how you felt about yourself. I asked you who you are."

"And I answered."

"Are you always so obstinate?"

"Only when I'm held against my will."

"Are you deliberately refusing to tell me your name?"

"Nope—" the rest of my tirade dies on my lips as he moves closer to me. The hard lines of his body pressed dangerously close to mine. His presence is consuming, almost as if his mere existence commands the air around us. It is not until I bump into the pole holding me prisoner that I realize I have been unconsciously backing away from him.

He bends down until we are at eye level, and within his, I see a storm of emotions swirling within a sea of blue. Some innate part of me wants to reach out to run my fingers under these soulful eyes. Lifting my bound hands, I intend to do exactly that. Much like when I jerked away from him, he flinched away from my touch. He studies my face for another second before he straightens, going over to his bed.

The instant he blew the lights out, I knew he intended for me to remain here. Sinking to the floor, I wonder why he does not return me to wherever the others are sleeping. Curling up, hoping to find a comfortable spot on the hard ground, let's face it, it's a floor where there isn't much comfort to be found; I settle in for what I imagine will be an exceedingly long night.

Knowing my situation could be a whole lot worse, I quietly say, "You can call me A."

I have no way of knowing if he heard me or not since he did not respond. One thing I know for sure is for the first time since this all began, tonight, I do not have to be afraid of the things that come with the dark because the king of them is sleeping five feet from where I am lying.

And I don't reckon he likes to be disturbed.

Death

When my sentries advised of the approaching mortals, I knew they were coming for one of two reasons. They either intended to offer their services to me, or they intended to provide the services of another. It still amazes me how quickly our father's chosen beings will turn on one another when given the opportunity. There has been more than one occasion when the stronger will offer the weaker, hoping to escape my judgment. Husbands offering me their wives, mothers handing over their offspring, brothers giving up their sisters, friends betraying friends. The only ones who never try to hand off what they hold dear seem to be the children of this world but is that because they truly value and love them more than their own safety or simply because they do not fully grasp who and what I represent? If only they knew, none can escape the inevitable. I also care little for any who mistreat their brethren, and while I admit to having some of the very beings I despise within my ranks, I only do so to allow them to handle the miscreants I suspect are now approaching.

"Thanatos, we have a small group heading our way."

"I am aware."

"Should we stop them?" The one whose opinion I value most asks.

"No permit them access. I should like to see why they have traveled all this way and what they have come to offer. If you please, would you be so kind as to greet our new arrivals personally?" The man before me is not inherently wicked. He is a good, fair and honest man. He cares for the people who have joined my growing army by choice or force; it makes no difference to my first. "Oh and Xander...."

"Yes, sir?"

"Have someone fetch Nevil."

He smiles, knowing what I intend. Even though he has expressed his opinion of Nevil and his band of thugs on more than one occasion. He also recognizes the value of having such a being within our ranks. "Straight away, sir."

Taking flight, I soar well above them where my presence will not easily be detected. I watch as the men pull two human females from a cart before stripping them of their clothing. They intend to offer these women to me, believing it will appease me. I have no use for such trivialities since I do not desire the same things as the men within my horde; I have no needs regarding the matter of flesh.

What I see from their offering are two additional mouths to feed, although the one does not seem willing to allow their baser desire as she persistently smacks and pushes away their invading hands. I watch intently until the leader of this little band tosses the women what I assume is clothing before they bind their hands and lead them toward my encampment.

I arrive long before they crest the first hill, giving me ample opportunity to issue my directives. Nevil, who is always ready to play the part of me, strides up to the throne and immediately begins barking orders for his meal to be served. It is a fairly good representation of precisely who he would be if not for my presence keeping him in line.

Pulling the hood of the tunic I wear up over my head to conceal my identity in case these mortals have any indication of what I look like, we await their arrival. I could take the seat the others have deemed a throne, allow them to make their offering, and accept or decline the gift they wish to grant, but I have discovered I find out more when all eyes are not watching me. Besides, I do not belong on a throne. Only one is worthy of such a seat, and this is not me, nor is it the man who fancies himself a leader.

In the distance, I listen as Xander speaks with the new arrivals before granting them their request for an audience. Keeping my head down, I watch them pull the bound women before Nevil, who ignores them in favor of his meal. Watching their every movement, I feel the second the girl's eyes settle on me. She knows Nevil is not who he claims to be. I have to wonder if she will say anything to the others. So as is my way, I wait. I watch. And as is the human way, I am not left wondering for long. This is why she is now held within my private quarters.

"Are you sure, Thanatos?"

"You worry too damn much, Xander," Nevil tries to smile, but the ones around us do not miss his irritation, and neither do I.

"She didn't even hesitate. It was almost like.... Like—"

"The great and infamous death fucked up," Nevil interjects, causing everyone around us to fall silent while they all turn to focus on me, wondering how I will respond to his comment.

"It would behoove you, asshole, to remember who leads whom," Xander growls. If Xander feels the need to protect me, I will not interfere; however, there is no need to correct Nevil. His opinion means nothing to me; he is only here because I have deemed it so.

Entering my tent, I am fascinated by the interaction between them. His barbaric attempts to rein her in are met with an unbridled determination to show him she is not one to be controlled.

Shortly after dismissing him, I prepared for the onslaught of questions or pleas; it is normally always one or the other. She seems generally offended when I advise her I do not know her, as evident by the furrowed brow, dilated nostril, and pinched lip scowl she is giving me. Wanting an unobstructed view of her face, one filled with warring emotions, I push aside a strand of her unruly hair.

Her face softens as she meets my gaze, and for the first time since my arrival, I am astounded when this human does the unthinkable; she reaches out for me rather than recoiling. Returning to the pile of blankets that serves as my bed, I blow out the last light illuminating the tent's interior. She stands there for several seconds before the jingling of the chains holding her informs me she has slid to the ground.

A slight smile crosses my face when I hear her quietly advise, "You can call me A."

Chapter Five: Horde Life

Avalon Late Spring 2023

AFTER THE FIRST NIGHT, I am shown to my new quarters, a tattered tent I share with ten other women, and thus begins my new existence as a prisoner within Death's horde. Since I refuse to acknowledge who I am or what I did for Death? Thanatos.... Whatever you want to call him, he chooses to ignore me like the plague. Since his brother is responsible for the said epidemic, I'm sure you can imagine how often I see him. And before you ask, yes, I tried to escape once.

Why only once, you ask? Simple. Because after Nevil realized I would not leave Suki behind, he made sure Suk and I were never left alone again. He also beat the shit out of me. It took me the better part of two weeks before I completely healed from that confrontation. I guess he was still holding some animosity from our initial interaction. I can't imagine why.

"Hey, get your ass back to work," Steven yells. Steve-o is almost as nasty as Nevil, which isn't surprising since he happens to be his number one. Who knew a number two could have a number one? What I mean by this is — in my short stint with the horde, I have already figured out that Xander reports directly to Death, Thanatos, whatever (Yeah, I know I need to pick a name and stick with it, but that's a problem for another day.) and sausage fingers reports to Xander. Steve-o reports directly to his buddy Nevil; hence, the reason I said Nevil is ranked second, while Steven is Nevil's first. I don't make the power structure around here; I just try my best to avoid them.

"I am working. What I'm doing is typically called working," I grumble as I pick up another stack of dishes to take to the ones who are assigned to dish duty. Assuring we have clean plates to eat from before our next meal is a top priority around here. I hate this life almost as much as I hated the last one. I wish Suk would have listened to me when I begged her to keep moving, but there is no point in wishing because we did stop, and now we are nothing more than prisoners.

Two of the five men who brought us here didn't make it. They didn't like their roles within this group. They made examples of the leader and the only other guy who didn't touch Suki and me during our travels and then shipped them back to Cambridge to ensure no one else attempted what they had. Of course, the asshole who groped us the most thrives under Nevil's tutelage.

Spinning, I run directly into said asshole. Bob wastes no time grabbing my boob. The unwanted and intrusive contact caused me to drop the plates I was taking to the group of women chatting down at the water's edge, resulting in most of them smashing when they hit the ground.

"You need to be more careful, wench."

"And you really need to keep your fucking hands to yourself, prick." Bob takes offense to my response. He responds by taking the already nonexistent space between us and somehow manages to reduce it even further.

He's quite a few inches taller than I am. The only way I can continue to meet his gaze is for me to look up at him. I know the dipshit only did it to intimidate me. Little does Little Bobby know I've dealt with much bigger assholes and way scarier monsters than he could ever hope to be. This doesn't stop him from trying to be the top dog.

Advancing towards me aggressively, I can see Steven grinning from the corner of my eye. Okay, so definitely no help there. He leaves me no choice but to take a step back for every one he takes toward me; otherwise, I have little doubt he wouldn't have his hand viciously crammed between my legs.

His arm shoots out, hitting me in the center of my chest. The impact sends me reeling. Before I regain my balance, I slam painfully into a solid brick wall that seems to have appeared out of thin air. The problem is there are no brick walls in this field; even worse, I am painfully aware of who the body belongs to. Lifting my eyes slower than I should, I come face to face with the most feared being roaming this planet.... None other than Death himself.

"Lord," Bob exclaims as he lowers himself to one knee, pawing at me frantically to do the same. Mistake number one because this man who still has his arms wrapped around me does not like it when anyone refers to him as...

"I am no lord." Something I could have told the asshole if he wasn't such a pompous prick. Regardless, even if he did like this kind of admiration... I do not bow to anyone, including the man who continues to hold me against him. His eyes trained on mine, refusing to look at the dipshit still on one knee.

After a couple of tense seconds, he finally relaxes his grip enough for me to put a minuscule amount of space between us. Something flicks across his face as his pupils dilate and his eyes change from the color of the late-day sky to pristine crystals, but as quick as I see it.... It's gone.

"Bow before your betters, you insolent fool," Bob hisses.

"And you bend the knee much too quick. There is only one being worthy of such admiration."

"I can't imagine there is anyone more worthy than you," Bob's words come out in a rush. I know he is trying to garner favor with Death, but what he said is not how you do it. Death's hands tighten on my arms, and his lips vanish as he pulls his mouth into a thin, tight line. This is the first time since I ran into him that he looks away from me only so he can glare at the clueless idiot still down on one knee.

Deciding to step in before the dumbass could piss him off any further, especially since he seemed unwilling to release me. I quietly say, "His father is.... Your father is worthy."

Death brings his focus back to me, his eyes assessing the validity of my statement. My issue is I can't tell if he is trying to figure out if I was talking out of my ass, hoping to gain favor, flat-out lying, or meant what I said. I sure hope he doesn't look too hard, especially since.... his father.... our God, has never done shit for me.

The longer he holds my gaze, my eyes take on a mind of their own, betraying me as they drop to his lips. The lips pulled into a tight line only moments ago have relaxed, and now they seem to have garnered my full attention. What the hell is wrong with me?

He slides his hand down my arms before slowly releasing his grip. My skin wakes up, springing to life in the wake of his touch. I have no idea what the hell is going on; it's like every cell in my body would prefer to betray me by responding to my captor.

Damn it all to hell. No, just no. Categorically. Positively, NO.

When he finally released his grasp on me, I stumbled back, tumbling over a still-kneeling buffoon.

Death's hand streaks out to halt the inevitable but breaks just short of stopping me. As a result, I go ass over elbows across Bob. Heat flares to life, coloring my face in what has to be the deepest shade of red that has ever crossed these cheeks as my mounting embarrassment slowly creeps along them. At least the only three who saw it were Death, Bob, and Xander, who walked up just in time to witness the least graceful fall ever because Steven slipped away at some point. He may be the only smart one out of us.

"Watch where you're stepping, you dumb bit—" before he can finish, Death silences him when he steps toward us. Xander attempts to quell the situation with a hand on Death's shoulder, but he drops it almost as quick as Death's head slowly swings in Xander's direction.

"Bob, get your ass back to work, and you girl—"

"The girl has a name," I snap at Xander. I admit to being shocked when he seemed to be patiently waiting for me to finish, which is the opposite of what I figured his reaction to my interruption would be. As I open my mouth to tell him, Death mumbles something over his shoulder, turns on his heels, and stalks off in the direction of his tent.

All three of us watch him leave, although I'll admit we each do it for different reasons. One of us seems in awe, one enthralled and one biding their time. The sound of Xander clearing his throat snaps my attention back to him.

"Your name?"

"Huh?" I mutter, still trying to wrap my head around this entire interaction.

"You know, as opposed to girl."

"Oh.... Yeah. It's Avalon."

"Okay, Avalon, you need to finish whatever task you have been assigned. It is our last night here; tomorrow, we will tear down the camp. It is time to move on."

"To where?"

"I'm not the one who makes that call," he tells me as he tilts his head in the direction Death went a second ago. His genuine smile takes me off guard. If I had to venture a guess before all this, he was probably an elementary school teacher, pediatrician, or counselor; actually, I can easily see him in any position where patience is key.

"See you around, Avalon." He turns to head in the same direction as our illustrious leader, but before he can get too far away, I seize the opportunity to ask him the same question I have been asking for days. The one no one else wants to answer.

"Hey, would you happen to know where my friend is?"

"Depends on who your friend is."

"The girl who was brought in with me," his quizzical expression confirms I will need to provide some additional context for him to help me.

"Short girl, strawberry-blonde hair, a bit sassy." When he shrugs his shoulders, I figure it's pointless. His position within the horde probably has him seeing almost every person they.... Ummm, for lack of a better word, acquired at some point in time, and if Suk didn't open her mouth, she is so small she's easy to miss. This is part of the reason she has such an over-the-top personality.

"Maybe ask Nevil," he tells me as he wanders away. I can assure you that will not happen. I would rather talk to Bob, which should tell you a lot since I can't stand him or his damn roaming hands.

"Her name is Suki. If you see her, will you tell her I was asking about her?" I yell after him.

He waves over his shoulder to acknowledge my request. Still, with Bob's snarled response, I have little doubt I will not be discovering her whereabouts anytime soon.

"Keep dreaming, bitch. Nevil is all too aware she is the only reason you are being so." he hesitates to let his eyes drop from my face to my breast as his tongue slides over his thin lips. "Agreeable."

I hope this asshole isn't insinuating what I think he is because, first off, hell no. Furthermore, absolutely fucking not. I stand my ground, not wanting him to know how uncomfortable I am with his lingering gaze. A twisted smile spreads across his face as he brings his eyes back up to mine.

"What do you say, Avalon?" the way he says my name makes my skin crawl. "wanna show me how agreeable you can be?"

"Not even if hell was to freeze over." I snarl. Bob, who doesn't take too kindly to my refusal, lashes out grabbing my arm to yank me directly into his chest while he takes a menacing step toward me. As if on cue, several other men come around the corner.

Catching us in the middle of our standoff, two of them stop, "Is everything alright over there?" I know they meant the question for me, but they look directly at Bob.

"Yep, just finishing up over here," Bob replies with a little wave. Meanwhile, he tightens his grip on my arm. I have little doubt I will find an asshole-sized handprint there tomorrow.

"You're Avalon, right?"

"I am."

"Well, we could use an extra pair of hands to tear some of these tents down. Are you available to help us, Ava?" Ripping my arm out of Bob's grip, I hear him swear lightly under his breath.

"Don't think about it, bitch."

"Eff you, asshole," I hiss right back.

"Sure can. Bob here can finish this up all by himself." Without looking back, I approach the two men, who continue to eye Bob suspiciously.

"Hey, I need her help here."

"Then Dave can stay here and help you while Avalon comes with us." I think his name is Ryan, but I will definitely have to find out so I can thank both of them for their timely intervention.

Working with this group is much easier than dodging Bob's constant incoming hands. Who knew there were so many ways a man, or woman for that matter, could come up with to grope someone and make it look innocent? We are making excellent progress in tearing down the tents when the booming yell of Nevil interrupts us. Looking up, I find Nevil, Steven, and the asshole Bob all standing there.

"Who is the dumb fucker who pulled Avalon off the duty I assigned her?" Ryan (because yes, I confirmed his name is Ryan) glances at me. Before he can step forward, I jump in front of them.

"I left the stupid job. What of it?"

He snickers before his eyes move over to Steven. "Is this the asshole who thought he could run things?"

Bob sidesteps Steven and leaves him standing directly next to Nevil. You would think the way this asshole follows him like a lost puppy hoping to garner the minuscule amount of attention he is willing to grant Bob, that Nevil, not Death, was the one truly in charge around here. Seeing the glee in his eyes, I know this is almost like his big moment, his initiation into the sadistic prick club. I can't say I didn't see it coming, nor can I say I'm surprised since assholes tend to seek out others of their kind.

"Yeah, that's him."

"Let's go, big guy."

"Why the hell are you making this into such a big deal? What difference does it make where I work? It's not like there wasn't someone who took my place," I seethe while stepping in front of Ryan.

"When I assign duties, you do what I tell you, not what some pudgy fucker says."

"Maybe if that asshole knew how to keep his fucking hands to himself, I wouldn't have left the goddamn duty you assigned me," I yell, hoping maybe this might dissuade Nevil from whatever he has planned for Ryan and, more than likely, Dave too. But who am I kidding? He is just as bad as Bob, if not worse. Nevil does not hesitate to walk directly in front of me so he can lean down. With his face in line with mine, he quietly delivers his response.

"I don't care if Bob rips your pants down and fucks you in the middle of camp with every man watching. You will learn your place, *Avalon*...." The way he says my name like I'm the asshole here and not them is infuriating, but it's not until he finishes his thought that I do something I will probably regret. "Hell, if I had to guess, you'd love every second of it too."

Line fucking crossed!

Without thinking, I ball my fist up and slam it directly into his face as hard as possible. I'm fairly confident I broke my goddamn hand, but it was worth every bit of pain to see this smug bastard stumble away from me. Ryan reaches out and pulls me behind him before Nevil can retaliate.

"You were completely out of line," Ryan snaps through gritted teeth. At first, I thought he was talking to me. Perhaps hoping to save his own skin. But when I look up at him, I find his attention focused fully on Nevil and his band of thugs.

"Grab the big guy and the bitch," Nevil roars. As much as I had hoped the other men around us would have stepped in to stop this, they didn't. The sad part is that I am not even surprised by it. I mean, hell, people are nothing if not predictable. I learned early on that most individuals are either cowards or bastards. Very few people will stick their necks out for someone else, even when that someone is their own child.

Steven grabs Ryan leaving me held within the wandering hands of, Asshole. Yeah, I may have decided to change his name from Bob to asshole. What about it? My name seems to fit him much better than the one his mom gave him, but in all fairness, I'm sure this woman, whoever she is, didn't realize what a colossal asshole her baby would turn into.

Nevil leads, with Steven and Bob following directly behind. The closer we get to the edge of the camp, the more my heart rate increases. If it hammers any harder, it may crack my sternum.

We walk about two hundred yards into the thicker part of the woods when we finally see where they are leading us. Chained to a post with lash marks covering his back, we discover an unconscious Dave dangling by his wrist. The entire scene is disturbing. It doesn't take long to realize what their plan entails, and when I hesitate, it forces Nevil to grab my other arm. I assume he did this to prevent me from bolting after he gives his band of assholes his next directive.

"Take him down. Pudgy here has volunteered to take his place."

"Does Xander know you're doing this shit?" I bark.

"As much as you and that useless fucker believe he is running things around here, let me assure you, he isn't. I don't answer to him or anyone else." Nevil hisses the last part, so only I can hear his declaration. Twisting, I look up at him, shocked he would believe something so ludicrous.

Once Ryan is secure to the post, Nevil nods, giving the other two permission to proceed. I close my eyes, knowing what they have planned, and I have no desire to witness Ryan suffer the same fate as Dave. Yet Nevil has other ideas.

"You will watch what happens to your savior, or I will continue to have him beat until he has no skin left on his back." When they begin whipping him, regardless of how much I want to avert my eyes, I don't look away for fear his whipping will be significantly worse. I'm the reason he's here to begin with. I owe it to Ryan to ensure he does not suffer more than necessary. For this reason, I will not waiver, will not look away, and will never show these assholes how much this affects me. Squaring my shoulders and steeling my emotions, I look on as they whip him mercilessly for being a decent human being. Each snap of the whip they use causes me to jump. With each guttural scream he releases, I can't help but blame myself for the predicament Ryan currently finds himself in.

When they decide they have punished him enough, Nevil turns his gaze to me. "Your turn."

I struggle against his grip as he drags me over and chains me to the post. Bob doesn't waste the opportunity to reach around, so he can fondle my breast once he has me secured.

"After Nevil has his pound of flesh, I plan on collecting mine, just in a much different way," Asshole whispers before he runs his tongue along my jawline. Yanking my face away, he steps back so my first punishment can begin.

As I prepare for the sting from the first lash, I can't help letting the breath I have been holding escape in a whoosh when I hear Xander yell, "What the hell is going on here?"

"Discipline," Nevil responds coldly.

"Discipline for what offense?" I turn my head enough to see Xander stepping out of the tree line and into the damn circle they set up to punish anyone who defies them.

"Disobedience."

"And who did they disobey?" He asks as he takes several more steps toward us.

"Me."

"And who gave you permission to enact said punishment?"

"If you are alluding to yourself, then you're sadly fucking mistaken because I don't answer to you." Nevil snarls as he takes his first step in Xander's direction.

"But you will answer to Thanatos." Before Nevil can respond, various guardsmen from Death's army step out.

Seeing the forces they now face and knowing the soldiers will only listen to the horseman's first, Nevil, Steven, and Bob all make the first wise decision today when they keep their mouths shut. Still, I do not miss the sheer hatred Nevil harbors for Xander flaring to life within those beady eyes of his.

"Release her and take those two to a medic. You three will go with these men until Thanatos is ready to see you." Right before he walks away, Nevil does the only thing he can to ensure I will keep my mouth shut.

"If you say anything, I'll slit your little friend Suki's fucking throat after I let Bob have his way with her."

Well shit.

Chapter Six: Dream

Avalon late spring 2023

THREE HOURS LATER, THE entire camp is called to the, for lack of a better explanation, makeshift throne room, field, area, whatever the hell you want to call it. Nevil, Steven, and Bob all stand off to one side. Of the three, only Bob looks ready to shit himself. Nevil is too evil to care, and Steve-o is just too stupid. Death storms up on the raised platform which holds his throne, the one he refuses to sit on, opting to stand with his arms crossed over his massive chest, a look of annoyance covering his face.

"Nevil, we have gathered here, so you may explain why you took it upon yourself to punish two men who reside within this camp."

"As a lesson."

"A lesson for what affront?" Xander asks. I cannot help but wonder if Xander is the one who is going to question everything, then why did we have to wait for Death's arrival? Especially since he appears bored, annoyed, and ready to be anywhere other than here.

"They deliberately disobeyed me when they opted to switch out workers I had assigned to specific jobs." I begin to speak up until I see Bob slide his finger across his neck. You have got to be shitting me. What are we six years old, having a tiff out on the playground of some now deserted schoolyard? But it has the desired effect since I have now fallen silent.

"When I give an order, I expect it to be carried out, as I'm certain you would as well, Xander." Sausage fingers Nevil continues.

"I don't recall chaining you to a post and whipping you until your back more closely resembled ground meat than human flesh." Xander's response causes a low gasp from countless of the women present for this while the men all mutter to one another in hushed tones too low to carry beyond their intended recipient.

"You have your way of dealing with the horde, and I have mine."

"I'm not as confident your way will have many of these souls remaining with us for long."

"And talking us all to fucking death is better?"

"Better than having the fleshed ripped from your back? Yes, infinitely better, as I assume most people around us would agree." After more than a few tense moments, I notice Death's gaze assessing Xander much more than Nevil. Without knowing what this means, I make the only logical choice to end this standoff. Here's hoping I won't regret this later.

"It's actually all my fault." Death's focus settles on me. "If anyone should have been punished for what happened today, it should have been me. Dave and Ryan only agreed with what I wanted." Death quirks one eyebrow up as he tilts his head.

"I'm sorry. I didn't think it would disrupt anything since someone else had taken my place. Had I known, I would have done things differently." I would have shoved a knife in the asshole's gut instead. I know I may be asking for trouble with my confession, but I am also smart enough to know I might use this to my benefit. "The problem is ass—I mean, Bob and I don't get along so well. It's probably not the best decision to put us together as partners."

Xander appears to be shocked by my confession. Nevil appears vindicated. Bob is furious, and Death looks.... Intrigued. That can't be right, can it?

"It—it still does not give Nevil permission to beat anyone," Xander stutters while he tries to tear his gaze from me.

"And you do not make up the rules here," I am aware of the argument brewing around me, but I find it increasingly more difficult to remove my attention from the being watching me just as intently.

I don't care how nonchalant I pretend I am; his unyielding gaze has me shifting uncomfortably from such intense scrutiny. I hate to admit this, but his commanding presence is as much a turn-on as it is intimidating. I wonder what he would do if I marched up there and kissed him. Where the fuck did that shit come from, Avalon? I have one word for myself. Dumb.

Death's sudden booming response makes me jump, finally pulling me out of my head. Not to mention all the thoughts swirling within me regarding seeing him without that shirt on, you know, the one stretched tight over his well-defined physique.

"But I do. All matters of discipline moving forward are to be decided by me. Do I make myself clear about this?"

"Yes. Sir," Nevil confirms, although not without some effort if the ticking in his jaw is any clue to how he feels regarding this new directive. Relief washes through me, knowing his days of torturing the people of this horde are at an end. While this decree did not come in time to save Ryan and Dave, it may help the others in this camp from suffering the same fate.

"Is this the only thing we needed to meet about?" Death asks Xander, who merely nods. He surprises me when he doesn't immediately storm from the stage. Instead, he opts to lean over to his first, whispering something into Xander's ear before both of their eyes flick up to where I'm standing. I have to admit it's uncomfortable anytime I am the center of attention. But, it's a whole 'nother level when it is one of the horsemen of the apocalypse focusing on me. Bounding off the platform, he begins in the direction of his tent but suddenly stops to deliver his final directive to Nevil, "Oh, and she is no longer to be assigned to work with Bob."

I turn to make my hasty retreat before the three assholes can corner me, but it is Xander who shatters all thoughts of quietly slipping away and back to my tent.

"You girl." When I continue walking, choosing to ignore him. He yells again.

"Avalon." Let's see, can I feign ignorance? Claim I didn't hear him? Shit, doing that will probably get me tied to the post outside of camp again with no one to save my sorry ass this time. Taking a deep breath, I slowly turn to face the man lumbering through the retreating crowd.

He doesn't utter another word until he has forced his way past the people still gathered. When he is standing directly in front of me, he delivers his demand in a flat, emotionless tone. "Let's go."

Shit, is he in trouble with Death because of what I did? If so, I'll have to figure out how to fix this fast because the last thing I want is to get Xander in trouble. But all of this is for me to figure out another day because right now I want to know....

"Where to?" I ask, completely baffled by where or why he would want me to go anywhere.

"To Death's tent." Oh, hell no.

"Why?" the shock of where he wants to take me leeches out in my response.

"That's for him to know." He gently takes my arm to lead me back through the people returning to their tents. The look of sorrow covering most of their faces as we pass them confirms they all believe I am in as much trouble here as I do. My only thought is....

"And for me to find out the hard way. Fuck my life."

Death

She confounds me once again because she defies all my beliefs in humankind. To help another when she could so easily have remained silent. She truly is an enigma. A puzzle I feel I must piece together. Is it possible I have found the one soul worthy of our forgiveness? The one person who may yet prove my initial thoughts about humanity has been wrong.

Learning Nevil has a whipping post outside of camp infuriates me, and the instant I discover where he hid it, I destroy the damnable thing. I am unsure why he feels he has the right to decide the fate of any soul traveling with my horde; let me assure you, he does not. Nor will I allow him to continue doling out this kind of punishment. I am losing the ability to overlook his offenses.

Seeing the state of the posts and the blood covering the trampled earth, I comprehend this has been going on for much longer than Xander realized. I believe I finally understand what happened to all the men and women who suddenly went missing.

Fury races through me as I return to camp. They will not like what befalls them if they have the misfortune of seeing me this night. I know Nevil is not a kind man, nor has he ever been. I sensed it early on, but I figured if I could convert him, humanity must certainly be worthy of my father's divine forgiveness. Still, I quickly recognize this is an exercise in futility; it will probably never happen. Maybe this is merely my hope so that I may at long last return home, return to my rightful existence.

Storming into my tent, I come face to face with the one being who could calm my racing emotions. Avalon, my little apple and the only being who has ever shown me a modicum of kindness. She drops the antique hand mirror I found along my travels. I cannot say why I continue to collect such baubles. Yet, there is something innately beautiful about the craftsmanship, not to mention the soul who possessed it cared for it greatly because it looks the same today as I imagine it did the day the artist created it.

"I'm sorry," she mumbles as she picks it back up to return it to the precise position I had it in. She takes several steps back until she has centered herself in my tent, away from all the treasures I have collected during my travels. I admit I found a certain.... Contentment when I realized she survived after I destroyed her city. I cannot say why I allow her to believe I do not remember her because I have often thought of her during the time I have been separated from her.

"We are alone."

She shifts; her discomfort is apparent as her eyes dart around the empty tent. I have noticed how her gaze often lingers on me. I imagine this form I have taken appeals to her. Yet not tonight. This night, her eyes avoid even glancing in my direction.

As much as I enjoy seeing her frazzled, I admit I do not like her discomfort. Something deep within me wants to protect this being which is a new emotion for me. I detest the surge of emotions my father has deemed I need to endure, yet this one is the least unpleasant one I have experienced thus far.

"Ahhh, so we are." Not knowing what else to do, she begins fidgeting as she tucks a wayward strand of hair behind her ear.

"This would be the time to explain why you took responsibility out there tonight." Her eyes dart around the space again. I can only assume she is looking for Nevil or one of his crew. "As I have already told you, we are alone. There will be no interruptions."

This does not quell any apprehension she may have, yet she squares her shoulders as she tells me in a cool, unemotional tone, "Because it was my fault. I take full responsibility for the entire situation. Dave and Ryan are not to blame, nor should you punish them any further."

"I have no intentions of doing any such thing." Still, she refuses to elaborate; in fact, her pursed lips indicate her refusal to say anything else.

After we have stood silent for several minutes, in a flat, emotionless tone, she asks, "Am I free to go?"

"This would have nothing to do with the other female who arrived with you, would it?"

"Am. I. Free. To. Go?" When I nod, she turns to leave, but right before exiting, she softly says, "Thank you."

Hmmm, I wonder what I did for her to say this.

Avalon

I waste no time hustling back to my tent, only to find all the other occupants I shared it with gone. Now I am afraid. What if Nevil did this so I would have no witnesses? He could sneak in here with his two henchmen and do almost anything he wants, and there is very little I could do to stop him. Shit, maybe I should sleep elsewhere. Hell, perhaps the better option would be for me not to sleep at all.

Slowly exiting the tent I have shared with several other women since my arrival, I search my surroundings only to find most of them peering at me from behind semi-closed tent flaps. Marching straight up to the one holding the only person I have any faith will tell me what the hell is going on. I fling the tent flap back only to discover they have all slunk away from me. Searching their frightened eyes, I find the one person I pray will be truthful.

"Marisol, what the hell is going on? Why did everyone leave our tent?"

She lets out a deep sigh before stepping forward, "Some left because they were afraid Nevil would come looking for you in the middle of the night. They do not want to land in his crosshairs; in truth, none of us do. Others left because they believe you are nothing but trouble. I left when Xander asked me to."

"Why would he ask you to leave?"

"I don't know, Avalon. I can only tell you he did."

"Yeah, it's probably safer this way. Thank you for telling me." I drop my head; everything is perfectly clear. All the measures they have gone through were done to ensure that I will have to face whatever fate they have planned for me alone. Something I am not entirely unaccustomed to.

Slowly turning to make my way back to my tent, I know there is no point in trying to hide. They will surely find me, and whatever they have planned will only be that much worse when they do. I have to admit I am disheartened that Xander is involved in it. Since our arrival, I have believed him to be a decent man. I guess another life lesson for the dumb girl who doesn't seem to recognize who she should trust.

As I prepare to exit the tent, I hesitate only long enough to say, "No matter what you hear, don't come to help me. Stay in here. Hopefully, if you do, it will keep you safe."

I hear a slight sniff before Marisol quietly says, "I'm sorry, Avalon."

"Nothing for you to be sorry about. I did this to myself." And with this, I let the tent flap slip away as I search the open areas surrounding us. The only sounds I hear are the chirping of crickets, the hooting from a faraway owl, and the rustling of leaves each time the wind blows. Figuring it matters little if I linger out here or wait in the tent, I opt to enter the place I call home.

Not sure where to look or the best place to sit, I stand in the center and begin slowly turning in circles. I damn near jump out of my skin when I hear the tent flap rip open, only to be instantly relieved when I realize who just entered.

"A?"

"Suk?" Seeing her standing there, I rush over and pull her in for a hug. "Where the hell have you been?"

"Oh, you know me making friends and raising Cain."

"You may not want to say that too loud if you do not want to face our leader," Xander declares as he enters the tent. Pulling Suki behind me, I place myself between him and her.

"Ah, A, you realize he's the only reason I'm here, right?"

"You brought Suki here?"

"I did."

"Why?"

"Does it matter?"

"Yeah, I don't like owing anyone."

"No repayment needed. After everything you have been through today, we figured you might enjoy some alone time with your companion."

"We?" He does not respond, only giving me a lopsided smile as his answer. He dips his head before turning to leave, but I stop him by asking, "Why did you have Marisol leave?"

"As I said, I thought you might enjoy some.... Alone time."

"You know we are not a couple, don't you?"

"I call bullshit; you would totally do me," Suki declares with a grin.

"Nope, still totally into men, Suk."

"But I have seen you around several of the men in camp. You always seem... uninterested," Xander cautiously explains. His tilted head and quizzical expression almost make me laugh out loud.

"I said I like men, not little boys, and certainly not assholes like Nevil and his band of thugs. The rest have no interest in me."

"I think you may be mistaken. Regardless, please enjoy your evening."

"Oh, we are so gonna talk about you after you leave, handsome." Suk blows him a kiss, and Xander's response is to grin while dropping his head as he rubs the back of his neck.

"Well, I'll leave you to it then."

"Sweet dreams, handsome. Try not to think about us here tonight... all alone... all night. With nearly a stitch of clothing on."

"Suk," I hiss, trying to hide the laugh threatening to escape me.

I'm pretty sure this is the first time I have seen him this flustered. Clearing his throat, he confesses, "I will do my best."

"Or on second thought...." Suki starts but leaves the rest of her thought hanging for him to decode the rest. Although I can't imagine he will have a tough time deciphering her not-so-cryptic, hidden meaning.

We spend the next several hours talking about everything that has happened. While Suki isn't overjoyed to be held captive, she has come to accept being within Death's horde offers a certain security neither of us has had since this all began; I wish I felt the same. After piecing everything together, I now know why I haven't seen her in the last week. Nevil has made it his mission to keep us as far away from one another as possible. Simply one of his not-so-ingenious ways to keep me in line.

When we're both exhausted, Suki selects the best spot, opting to take the roll Marisol has been sleeping in, and falls asleep as soon as her head hits the pillow. I, on the other hand, am having a little more difficulty. Our experiences within this camp have been vastly different, and I find it exceedingly challenging to shake off the foreboding feelings from earlier.

Tonight may be one of the hottest nights we have seen thus far. Until now, I have been wearing yoga pants, but I opt to slide them off and sleep in my boy shorts. Which is a long way around saying my underwear. Having found a comfortable spot, I am beginning to drift off to sleep when I hear the tent flap rustle. Leaping up, the person I discover standing there is definitely not who I thought I would find.

"Death?"

"I came to see if you enjoyed your surprise?" he asks me in a whisper so he does not wake a snoring Suki.

"You did this?"

"Yes."

"Why?"

"I wanted to give you something." He tells me as he ambles towards me.

"I don't understand why you would do this."

"I find you most.... Intriguing." His eyes move down from mine, settling on my lips before sliding down to my.... Oh. My. God. I completely forgot I had taken my pants off.

"I'm so sorry." I blurt as I scramble to pull the damn things on. The problem is they keep wrapping around themselves,

93

almost like something secretly doesn't want me to put them back on. "Shit. I'm sorry. I wasn't expecting company."

Death's hand on mine halts my feeble attempt to pull the pants further than over my foot. Standing upright, I do not miss his gaze as it travels over the planes of my near-naked frame. I can barely distinguish the look of lust filling his soulful eyes. If what I believe I see in them is true, then I imagine he has to will himself not to touch me, as much as I repeatedly remind myself not to reach out to run my fingers over his well-defined chest and abs.

What the hell is the matter with me?

Before I can react, he is damn near against me as he runs his knuckles down the side of my face and along my jaw until they dip under my chin. Lifting it, he angles my face up to his as he slowly leans forward.

When he is mere inches from me, he abruptly stops. Mere centimeters would more accurately describe the space from me to him. I only need to pucker my lips to eliminate the distance between his mouth and mine. In fact, he is so close when I run my tongue over my lips, it brushes against his, and the low groan he releases sends heat rushing straight to my core, filling me with a needy desire I have never experienced before.

I am not sure if he is waiting for me to close the remaining space between us or if, like me, he is debating if this is a good idea. His arms loop around me, pulling me flush against him. If I am not mistaken, I would have to say what I feel pressed against my lower stomach is the hard arousal of an erection. Huh, who knew one of the horsemen of the apocalypse could get an erection? Let alone have the massive one I have pressed against me.

As if they have a mind of their own, my hands roam over the hard lines of his chest until I drape them around his neck, allowing my fingers to explore the silky hair barely long enough for me to grab.

Pulling lightly, I encourage him to close the remaining distance, and lord help me, but he does. This sensation of his body against mine is beyond anything I have ever wanted. I am damn near ready to come undone in his arms from the need and desire building within me. His lips brush against mine once, twice, before crashing to mine fully.

He deliberately backs us towards the bed roll I had been lying on when he entered. Hell, at this point, he could take me against the side of the damn tent; I wouldn't care as long as he doesn't stop what he is doing. I also could not care less who hears us or sees us. The entire camp can listen as long as he takes care of this burning need filling me.

Lowering us to my makeshift bed, he settles between my thighs, and I cannot help lifting my hips to grind against his ever-increasing erection. The low growl rumbling through his chest vibrates over mine, making my already hard nipples respond instantly.

Moving his head over to my neck, he kisses and sucks in all the right places while my hands dip down to remove the shirt, separating my touch from his bare skin. A heady groan escapes me when his hand drops down to pull my leg apart, granting him better access to grind against the spot I am aching for him to touch, fill, kiss; any of these options would be fine with me.

His lips return to my mouth, sucking my lower lip into his before he delivers a quick nip. My hips jolt up from both the pain and pleasure he is providing.

Marcelle Valentine

Running his tongue over my bitten lip, he confesses in a whisper, "You will be my undoing, Apple."

My eyes snap open only to realize I am alone. Heat pooling low, and dampness coats the insides of my thighs as the last memory of his lips on mine floats away. But it's his words that have me damn near moaning out my frustration.

Jesus Christ, did I really just have a wet dream? One in which Death played the starring role? Lord help me; I may never be able to look him in the eyes again.

Chapter Seven: On the Move

A SHOVE TO THE back gets me moving again.

"Announce him."

"Announce who?"

"Are you a fucking idiot? Death," Sausage Fingers snaps at me from his position on top of the horse.

We have been traveling for roughly a month if my count of how many night cycles have passed is correct. During that time, we did not set up camp; instead, we slept under the stars or on nights the weather did not permit in an abandoned building along the way.

Throughout our travels, I have only seen him a handful of times, and most of those encounters were him looking at us from a distance. I understand this thought is ridiculous;

actually, it's completely fuckin ludicrous, but it almost feels like he is avoiding me.

Crazy right?

I know it's batshit insane since I have no idea how he would have found out about it. I don't care that he's not mortal there is no damn way he could be aware of my dream about him because I didn't tell a single soul. Not even Suk, because she would have blabbed this shit to anyone willing to listen. There is no one else I would trust to divulge this information to, and even the thought of disclosing the truth to her about my toe-curling, almost sex dream where Thanatos took on the starring role would be.... Well, it would be weird. Especially since he is, in all rights, still our jailer.

Oh, and for reference, I have taken to calling him Thanatos during my internal monologs because referring to him as Death just doesn't feel right.

Although none of these things matters because even seeing him across the way has heat pooling low as all thoughts shift to how wonderful he felt against me. Being hot and bothered each time I catch a glimpse of him does nothing to help me make friends in his horde since I end up practically biting everyone's damn head off for merely speaking to me each time he's near.

Hell, I thought Suki would never talk to me again after I snapped at her when she tried to hand me a plate the other day when he came sauntering through camp with Xander. Okay, maybe it was more walking and less sauntering, but it's so damn hard to keep my mind from jumping straight to every smutty book I have read each time I see him. Which makes me slightly more than a little cranky most of the time.

Until a week ago, Nevil kept his distance from me. I don't think I need to tell you how much I appreciate this, but with

Thanatos's continual absence, he has grown bolder. So it should come as no surprise when he returns to his old ways of being a miserable prick and demanding how the horde should treat him.

This brings us back to him staring down at me from his perched vantage point. Apparently, he is sick of waiting for me to do as he instructed when he shoves me towards the city. If you haven't figured this out, patience isn't his strong suit.

Standing outside the massive makeshift walls they constructed, hoping to keep the troublemakers living in this world out, I cannot help but feel sorry for them. I suspect they never dreamed it would be the horseman's horde to stumble upon their quiet existence.

"Who the hell am I announcing him to?"

"The goddamn city we are preparing to raze."

"Well, that's super nice of him to introduce himself before he destroys their world." He does not find the humor in my comment, and he demonstrates it by backhanding me. The blow he delivers is enough to make my head snap to the side. My jaw instantly feels like I ran face-first into a brick wall. Hoping to relieve some pain, I rub my jaw as I move it back and forth.

Nevil, who is anything but a patient man, snaps, "Announce him."

Bringing my arms up, I direct them towards Thanatos, who seems completely oblivious to my conversation with this asshat. Gnashing my teeth together, I snarl, "City.... Death." After this, I point at the city, "Death.... City. Try to play nice."

"Don't be fucking cute; proceed him into the city, announce him, and lose the goddamn attitude." He spins his horse, preparing to ride back towards the rest of the riders before he stops to glare down at me. He gives his next warning in a dangerously low tone, confirming I have pushed my luck today as far as he will allow.

"If you choose to continue with the fucking attitude, I will enjoy knocking it out of you." To prove his point, he kicks me, knocking me to the ground. With my hands shackled in front of me, I cannot stop the forward momentum in time as I fly forward, slamming my head against the hard surface. White lights flash before my eyes as the sudden jolt rattles my brain. Shit, that fucking hurt like hell.

It's my own fault my hands have been constrained for the last three days. The shackles were only slapped on me when Nevil and Steven caught me trying to escape with Suki again. When they nabbed us, I took full responsibility for everything, basically telling them I forced her to leave. I believe they assume either I have a thing for Suki or we were in a relationship before our abductors delivered us to their front door.

One would think if they truly thought I was gay, they would lose interest in me; it is quite the opposite. It appears that Bob and now Steven have deemed it their mission in life to convert me. Although this would only work if they were transforming me into an asshole. Evidently, these assholes don't understand that a person's sexual preference isn't a choice.

The horde begins to move again, forcing me to scramble back up to my feet to avoid being trampled under the others who are walking but, more importantly, the clopping of the horse's hooves. Nevil rides right behind me as we trek into the city.

When we arrive, another boot to the shoulder shoves me forward. I was prepared for his attack this time, so I only stumbled a little instead of the full-on face plant he was hoping for. Apparently, he decided torturing me was more important than riding in with the rest of the assholes on horseback.

Glaring at him over my shoulder, it is not hard to figure out where he stands on the whole Avalon being a smartass thing; his expression showcases the depth of this man's loathing for me. I almost want to laugh thinking about how little ol' me can make such a colossal asshole scowl like he is. How the hell someone can hate another living being when they don't even know them is beyond me, yet there he sits up on his steed, a steed he only has because Thanatos has granted it to him, hating me with enough gusto; I can practically feel it flowing through him.

When I don't say anything, he brings his heavy booted foot back up; realizing he plans to kick me again or possibly worse, I step forward. He may be able to make me do this stupid shit, but he can't make me do it without my typical snarky attitude.

Clearing my throat, I shout, "Hear ye! Hear ye! Lowly mortal swine revel in his glory and bow before the great and powerful O—"

Another boot to my back knocks me down, cutting the words off before I can finish them. This time I get my hands up enough to stop my head before it smacks the ground, but I cannot protect my tongue, which is caught painfully between my teeth as they snap shut. Yep, I was totally getting ready to call him Oz. What of it?

Announcing Death is as stupid as introducing rain to a cloud. The cloud is all too aware the storm is coming, just as these poor souls are aware of Death's approaching horde. Besides, if you don't like the smartass comments, don't ask a smartass to do shit they disagree with.

Jumping down from his horse, Nevil lumbers towards me. Before fully regaining my footing, he grabs my shoulder, whipping me around as he prepares to fulfill his promise and knock the attitude out of me.

"Enough," Thanatos snaps as he rides through the horde.

"I was only trying to teach—"

"I have eyes."

"She needs to learn her place."

"And when did this mortal's *place* within my legion become your decision?"

This mortal?

This mortal!

Damn, if that doesn't just about sum up his feelings for me. I have to stop living in a fantasy. Xander, not Death (yep, we're back to Death now), is the one who brought Suki to see me that last night we were in camp. I always knew I was being silly, but a stupid girl with Stockholm syndrome never crossed my mind. Why would it? Somehow, I convinced myself he knew about the dream.

"Hell, maybe he was the one who put the damn thing in my head to begin with." Saying that out loud only serves to prove how dumb I have been. I let myself believe a falsehood only so.... What? I wouldn't feel so utterly alone? Jesus Christ Avalon, grab a damn clue.

I almost miss the look he gives me before riding ahead, and this, beyond anything else, helps solidify he never wanted anything to do with me because it was one of sheer disdain. Xander rides by, and like Death, I do not miss the look he is giving me, although his is much kinder since it is filled with question. I imagine he is trying to figure out why I looked at Death like he kicked my puppy. You and me both, Xander; you and me both.

Death

The raw fury I felt when I witnessed him kicking her was a new emotion for me. If I did not know any better, I would say it bordered on wrath. One of the sins I am judging the mortals for, yet I was on the verge of ripping the booted foot kicking her from his leg. I suspect my fascination with her is partly because of the dream I invaded the last night we were in camp.

I had instructed Xander to reward her for standing by her belief as she desperately tried to save the two souls who had no doubt protected her from the heinous coward who hides behind Nevil. He believes he can continue harassing her without repercussion; he is mistaken. But this is a problem for another day.

After Xander returned, he advised he delivered the other young female who had arrived with Avalon to her tent. He confessed he initially believed that they were romantically involved. Upon hearing this, a tightness spread across my chest.

I am aware if I were mortal, this could be a precursor to cardiovascular disease; however, any human conditions were eliminated when I selected my vessel.

As much as I have no desire to admit the sensation was directly related to his confession, the instant he advised he was mistaken, disclosing their relationship was nothing more than friends. The band around my chest released, and the pain subsided. I could have asked him to explain this phenomenon, but I no longer required it when I sensed his relief too. I have witnessed him around Apple's friend; he cares more for her than the others within my horde.

Shortly after Xander retired for the evening, I found myself wandering by the tent she had been sleeping in. I expected to hear the sounds of laughter or conversation; in place of this, I listened to the sounds one makes while sleeping. Cautious not to wake them, I quietly slipped inside her tent.

They were both sleeping, yet Avalon's rest seemed troubled. Her breathing was ragged, her pulse rapid, soft groans escaped her, and her skin was flushed. The longer I watched her, the more I wanted to know what could elicit such emotions; as a result, I did something I had never done before. I invaded her dream. I can assure you I was ill-prepared for what I discovered.

She was dreaming about me, not the dream I had long imagined humans would have about any of my brethren or me, but one that left a war raging within me. Part of me wanted to stay within her dream. Part of me knew this was wrong, and I was invading her privacy, but another part, a much larger part, wanted to carry her back to my tent and explore these emotions and her delectable sounds further.

Knowing this was not my father's intent, I remained within the dream. In fact, I stepped fully into it until it was my arms around her, my hands exploring, and my lips pressed against hers. The sounds of pleasure I elicited when I moved my touch, body, or mouth to a new location on her was one I reveled in much more than I should have.

I wanted nothing more than to remain with her that night, to end the need I felt coursing within her. Yet as I lay on top of her, feeling emotions and things I had never experienced, I realized I was very close to crossing a line, diving headlong into yet another sin. Lust. And had I crossed that line, I was unsure if I would be capable of completing the task my father assigned me.

My quiet confession to her before I withdrew from her dream that she would be my undoing is as true now as it was the night I told her.

Knowing I needed to distance myself from her until I could control my constant desire to feel her soft skin beneath my touch, I refused to allow them to set camp. I remained at a distance, observing my army without the temptation she evoked, and this worked until I witnessed Nevil's violence. I may not intend to speak with Avalon; however, I will not stand by and permit such abuses to be inflicted upon her.

I now believe that if I hope to fulfill my duty, I may need to release both Avalon and her friend from my growing legion, but more importantly, and the one I struggle with the most.... my protection.

Chapter Eight: Sacked

I HATE THAT WE came here and wrecked their peaceful existence or as close as you can get nowadays. Since the first day of our arrival, I have not seen Death or his cronies. They gave their orders and then disappeared. According to sausage fingers, we are to scour the city, collect everything of value, and flush out any citizens who did not submit when we arrived.

Yeah, I'll get right on that.

Bob, who has taken it upon himself to play the part of the supervisor, assigned me the last building on Main Street to sweep through and remove any valuables. Not in the mood to argue about it, I merely roll my eyes before strolling up to the building.

It once functioned as a bookstore; now, it's hard to tell what I'll find inside. When the residents of this town constructed the walls they had hoped would keep scavengers and thieves at bay, they only secured the area around the so-called downtown area. They converted some buildings into living spaces. In contrast, they transformed others into a store, a pantry with a meal cafeteria, and a makeshift medical center, but the largest structure houses the blacksmith, armorer, woodworkers, and jail. Had we never stumbled across this place, this tiny community could have thrived for years to come.

Not all the residents are happy with Death's invasion. We found that out the hard way when several of the residents led an attack against us the first night. Unfortunately, they were quickly put down, although we lost some people when they caught them unprepared. Luckily, Suki and I opted to stay outside the walls in tents, so we walked away unscathed. Hence, I opt for discretion as I cautiously open the door.

The interior of the building is dark, with row after row of shelves all crammed with books. I used to love reading, but now it's hard to find the time, let alone a book. I could happily live here, just me, some tea, and these books.

Running my fingers over the spines, I randomly pull one out. According to the back, this is a Paranormal Romance about a girl on the run (sounds familiar) from a demon who wants to kill her (yep, hitting close to home, although my demon is less underworld supernatural and more evil asshole) who meets a gorgeous man who is anything but normal. Shit, is this about my damn life?

Flipping through the book, I land on a particularly spicy page. Welp that sold it. Slipping it into my bookbag, I fully intend to read this later when my assigned jobs are done. Hey, don't judge. A girl needs her smut too. Especially when the only action I've had lately is a dream that left me hot, bothered, and finishing myself off while thoughts of another gorgeous not-so-human man starred in my dirty little fantasy.

If we decide to move on, I'll have to ask the residents if I can take some of these books with me. Yes, I said ask because I am not a thief.

After clearing the entire first floor, I open the door I believe will take me up to the second floor only to discover it goes down into a basement. Calling this a basement might be a stretch since the dank, musty darkness I am staring at is closer to an old root cellar than a true basement.

A shiver passes through me when I think about going down there. I hate spiders. Really, I hate any wiggling creepy crawly, but spiders are the worst, and without a doubt, I know that's what I'm going to find down there. I briefly contemplate skipping it. Hell, we haven't found anything during one of these damn sweeps so far, and I can't imagine they are hiding any valuables down there. Yet.... If I don't and fucking Nevil finds out, he will make my life a living hell. Ultimately, I would rather spend a month in a cellar with a bunch of spiders than one hour with Nevil and his band of assholes.

Running my hand over the wall, I breathe a sigh of relief when it skims over the light switch. I flip it on, hoping to chase away some of the little buggers before I go down there; sadly, nothing happens. I smack my forehead realizing what I did. There hasn't been electricity for a long time now. No electricity means no lights, dumbass. Wishing I had brought a lantern, I slowly descend into what I can only describe as my personal hell.

I again contemplate calling this area "checked" when I run my hand over what can only be a damn spider web. Great, now I'm going to be thinking about freakin' spiders climbing around in my damn hair the rest of the godforsaken night. Great. Just fan—fuckin—tastic.

When I pushed open the only door I found down here, I should have paid closer attention to what was in front of me instead of what I ran my hand through as I stumble into the room because had there been something other than what I found I could be in big trouble. When I turn to inspect the space, I damn near run straight into four women.

Three of them look to be my age, while the fourth is probably closer to her late forties, although I have never been all that great at guessing ages. I definitely could never work as a carnie. It's not the women who surprise me. It's the kids. Around fifteen children under the age of ten are staring back at me with pure terror filling their eyes.

"What.... How...." Shit, I don't know what to ask them.

"Please don't hurt them. They're only children."

Gasping, I stammer, "Wha—What—I would never hurt anyone."

"But aren't you with the horseman?"

"Not by choice. How long have you been hiding down here?"

"A few—" one of the younger women begins to answer until the older one grabs her arm, shaking her head.

"I promise I have no intention of hurting any of you." The women look from each other to the children and back to me. I understand their hesitancy; I would do the same if I were in their place.

"Have you had anything to eat? I don't have much on me, but you can have all of it." I tell them as I hold up some mini boxes of raisins and a granola bar, but it's not until I remove three candy bars from my pack that the kids perk up. Not wanting to startle anyone, I stretch my arm out for them to take the items without getting any closer to them.

"Thank you." A redhead says as she accepts the offerings before dividing the candy bars among the kids.

"Well, what do we have here?" Spinning, I am horrified at who I already know I will find standing behind me.

"Bob, what the hell are you doing down here?"

"I could ask you the same thing because from where I'm standing, it looks like you're trying to help hide these prisoners."

"They're people, not prisoners."

"Potato, potahto."

"Are you fucking kidding me? You will leave them alone." Damn it, I wish I would have never found this damn room. If I hadn't, I would have been upstairs when Bob and the other men assigned to work with us came in.

Clicking his tongue, he gives me a clipped response, infuriating me even further in the process, "No."

"No?"

"That's what I said. Chop, chop, time to go."

"Where the hell are you taking them?"

"Well, I got no use for the brats or the old bag, so you can leave them down here to starve or slit their throats. I couldn't care less which but those three," Bob runs his tongue over his teeth as he fixes his gaze on one of the young woman's breasts. His hand drops to the front of his pants as he begins rubbing himself. Did this asshole forget he's not alone?

Stepping between them to cut off his line of sight, he grins before hissing, "Yeah, your tits are way fucking nicer, but hers will do in a pinch."

"You're sick."

"Get rid of the brats; the rest can be rounded up for inspection except red over there. Take that one directly to my place."

"You can't do that," I yell as I move to reposition myself to keep them away from the kids.

"I just did."

"I demand we take them to death. All of them."

"You think the pale rider wants to deal with this shit? That's why he has guys like me."

"He didn't recruit you, asshole. You happened to be there when Nevil was considering your town's offer. A bargain your group offered, which this group accepted, and last I checked, it was only for Suki and me. You're merely the trash who tagged along. Funny how you're the last one of that group still alive. Now, I demand we take them to Death." Stalking toward me, he grabs my throat before shoving me against the wall.

"I don't give a shit what you fucking demand, bitch." His eyes drop back down to my breast while his free hand rams between my thighs as he roughly begins rubbing me. "Of course, you're always welcome to try to convince me. I'm sure you can figure out something we might want. Isn't that right, men?" Trying to break his hold, he tightens his grip as he licks the side of my face. His hand is barely loose enough for me to squeak out my response.

"Or I can tell Death you have been stealing from the horde and helping yourself to individuals who could be used within his service."

"What the fuck are you talking about? I never stole shit from Death."

"Really? Then how did you end up with three of the bows we took from the town's armory in your room?"

"Ahhhh, so the little snake has been slithering where she does not belong. Or were you wishing to find me there alone, maybe hoping I might fuck you stupid?"

"Only one of us gets to hold that award, and it sure as shit isn't me, asshole." He tightens his grip, cutting off the last of my oxygen.

"I think we should let Thanatos decide." Some young guy who joined us less than a week ago says, trying to distract Bob from crushing my throat.

"You don't get to call him Thanatos, asshole," Bob snarls.

"My mistake. Nevertheless, I agree with Avalon. This is his call, not ours." And certainly not yours, I think to myself.

"Fine, get them out of my fucking sight."

"Come on," the new guy says as he slowly herds them out of the cellar, starting with the woman Bob demanded to be delivered to his bedroom.

"She stays with me," he growls. For the first time since he pushed me against the wall, the hand he had between my legs snatches out to stop her from leaving.

Seeing an opportunity, I slam my head forward, drop my shoulder, and twist out from under his grasp. I instantly begin sucking in the precious air he blocked from me, but when Bob moves to where we are huddled, I know I cannot simply stand here and let him take this poor girl out of here.

"She goes with the rest of them." I snap, but it doesn't bite as much as I would like because my throat feels like I swallowed fire. Pushing her towards the new guy, he hurries them all out of the room. Leaving me alone with Bob and a guy I have only ever seen around camp.

Rage fills his eyes as he growls, "This is not over, bitch. Not by a fucking long shot." So, what else is new? Assholes like him always have issues with something I did or didn't do, so he can take a fucking number.

Later that night, the kids, the women, and I are paraded out to be judged by the one running this shit show; the big guy himself, also known as Death, finally makes an appearance. Of course, he has to show up now after being M.I.A. for better than a week. I mean, why wouldn't he since I stuck my ass squarely in the damn fire again.

Bob jumps up and immediately begins telling his version of the events, which is a steaming pile of horseshit.

Thankfully, the new guy admits his recollection differs slightly from Bob's. The new guy needs to be careful; if the glare he is getting from Nevil and his crew is any indication, I would say they don't care for him speaking up.

"Put the women to work. I have no use for them," Death says as he nods at the children. Holy shit, is he seriously going to let Bob kill these kids? Hell no, there is no damn way I am going to let that shit happen.

"You can't be serious? They're kids."

"Hence the reason I said I have no use for them. They offer nothing, nor will they earn their keep."

"I offer myself."

"In case you missed this, I already have you."

"I'll serve you."

"You currently serve the horde. As for me, I have no need for your assistance."

"Then take my life."

"Allow me to offer you some advice. You should not be so quick to offer your soul when dealing with my kind. Besides, I will reap your soul soon enough."

"What the hell do you want then, sex?" His eyes flash. I would have missed it if I had not been looking at him when they did. Schooling his features after the subtle shift from a strained appearance to cool indifference leads me to believe he has no desire to screw me.

"Okay, if not me, would you prefer the company of another man? I'm sure I can find someone." He glares as a low growl rumbles through him.

"Your flesh holds no temptation for me." Damn, this confirms my dream was my stupid desire, not his.

"No? How about drugs then?"

Again I get nothing but a silent, icy stare. "What can I offer you?"

"Nothing. You cannot offer me anything I want.

"There has to be something you want."

"What I desire, you cannot grant."

"Please." He seems completely unaffected by my pleas.

"I am begging you.... Please don't hurt them."

"I also have no use for your supplicating."

"You're a fucking asshole," I yell as he turns to walk away. He stops long enough to look over his shoulder as he sternly informs me.

"I am much worse than that."

Chapter Nine: Alone

Death Summer 2023

AS MUCH AS I did not want to be affected by her desperate pleas, I was. Consequently, and much to the chagrin of Nevil and his band of miscreants, I returned the children unharmed to their families. I tried to dissuade any thoughts that I granted their release because of her; I cannot say I accomplished this. So, to ensure no retaliation would be taken against Avalon, I instructed Xander to watch over her and her companion. He did not seem averse to the assignment. I believe he may care more for the one named Suki than he wants to admit, which is good because if I do not return, I trust he will continue watching over the tiny one and Avalon.

Realizing that my affection for this mortal has severely compromised my mission, I leave, hoping that with enough time and prayers, my father will hear my requests and grant me an audience. The thought of returning to my previous post brings a rush of emotions; some evoke relief while others are bittersweet.

Retreating deep into the uninhabited hills surrounding the town where I left my army, I begin my painstaking wait for my father to hear my appeal and call me home.

Avalon

After I screamed at Death in front of his entire horde, I thought for sure no one would ever hear from me again — yet here I am. Alive. Well. And still refusing to adhere to their frivolous demands.

Xander and Suki continue to skirt their growing attraction for one another, but one good thing has come from their little affair: it provides her with the security I cannot give her. Which leaves me time to concentrate on an escape plan.

It is high time for me to hit the road. I can't imagine it could get any better, especially since Death disappeared shortly after I found the kids. The longer he stays away, the more likely dissension will begin to form within the ranks, and one thing is for sure, I don't want to be anywhere around here when Nevil decides he's done following Xander's orders.

"Hey, A, what are you up to today?"

"Not sure. I have to check the board." The board is all the jobs that need to be completed. Every day, they expect us to line up like fucking cattle and wait to see what bullshit job we have been assigned. Nevil's bright idea.

The funny thing is I never see his name or any of his little cronies on the damn list, and to add insult to injury, the people who lived within this community, the ones who never asked for us to invade their world, are the people who are always listed first.

The other thing I have noticed is that the redheaded girl, who I have since learned is Cammie, the very girl I risked my ass to save in the basement from Bob, is not as sweet and innocent as I thought she was. It seems she enjoys being passed around among Nevil, Steven, and, to my astonishment, Bob. Hell, I heard rumors she offers her services to any of the men in his ranks. Such a fucking shame she doesn't hold more value in herself than this, but who am I other than the idiot who has to watch their back because I stuck my neck out for her.

"Alright, come on, let's go scope it out together. Here's hoping they added a get busy with Xander task." She may be wiggling her brows, but I can assure you I'm rolling my eyes while I do my best not to laugh.

"Oh, but only if I'm the only one assigned to that particular task. I might have to knife a bitch if she thinks otherwise."

"Suk, if you like him so much, why don't you just tell him?"

"A, I get that you're...." she drops her volume and pulls her lips back as she sucks air between her teeth before continuing. "...not very experienced, but we don't chase men."

"I'm confused. How is telling the guy you like, who also seems to like you, the truth, chasing him?" I ask while scratching my head.

"You have so much to learn in the art of seduction."

"Yeah, because taking those lessons from a former barista is the best way to learn this art?"

"I have game, Avalon. Game you've never seen before," she tells me with a swish of her hips and a toss of her hair.

"Didn't it take you like four months to work up enough confidence to ask out the tech guy before all this happened?"

"Art. Of. Seduction."

"Art. Of. Never. Getting, Laid." I mimic back. This has her slamming her hands on her hips as she scowls in my direction. Shaking my head at her theatrics, I drape my arm around her shoulder and lead her toward the job board.

"Oh, yay." Suki squeals when she sees they have assigned her to kitchen duty. She has always loved to cook, so this is more like a reward than the punishment I'm sure I'll discover my name by.

"Son of a bitch," I grumble

"How in the hell did you manage to pull ditch duty so many times this week?"

"Just lucky like that, I guess." Ditch duty is essentially going outside the walls and clearing the debris that is collecting in the trench surrounding the town. It's arduous, stinky, sweaty work, and since several others within the horde could easily handle this shit, they should assign it to someone else since I have more than taken my turn. I took my turn, Suki's turn, not to mention Nevil and his band of misfit's turn. Hell, I took half of the camp's freaking turn. This is utter bullshit that I have gotten stuck with this shit seven times in as many days.

This is a two-person job, but when I hear the voice of the girl they assigned to work with me, I think I would rather struggle through the day by myself.

"Hello, Avalon."

An exasperated sigh slips out before I can stop it. "Hello, Cammie."

"I'm told you're like the ditch person around here, and since I have never had to do this job, I'm hoping I can count on you to show me the ropes." Of course, it doesn't take long to figure out that showing her the ropes means I do all the work while she sunbathes. I would be fine with this if she didn't insist on rambling about stupid shit.

Progress is going much slower than it should, but since I'm the only one doing anything by the time the sun has moved low on the western horizon, I have barely cleared halfway around the settlement.

"Oh, hey you." Having to listen to Cammie's singsong voice all day long is driving me batshit crazy. Especially since this loon seems to think she's fucking Snow White and talks to every bird, rodent, or four-legged mammal who has the misfortune of stumbling across us. It's not until I hear the response that I whip my head in her direction.

"Nice work, Cam. Now, why don't you head back inside? We have business with this one."

Fucking hell. My day just went from bad to worse in the blink of an eye. Having Nevil, Steven, and Bob all looming over me, especially since I know no one is around to help me if this goes the way they want, has my heart instantly jumping into my throat.

"Okay, babe. See you later?" Nevil grunts before jerking his head in the direction he intends for Cammie to go.

"Seriously, you're just going to leave?" She shrugs her shoulders as she twists a strand of hair around her finger before she turns on her heels, going in the direction Nevil pointed. Leaving me alone with the men who want to break me. Literally and figuratively.

Marcelle Valentine

"Time to answer for your crimes, bitch." Bob snarls while Nevil looks on.

Death

After days of meditation, or it could have been weeks since I had no recollection of the passage of time during my long wait, my father finally granted me an audience.

"Have you completed your task so soon?"

"No. I fear I have failed you in my assigned duty." His silent response is enough for me to understand I need to further elaborate on this statement.

"I worry I can no longer judge them fairly."

"Why? What could possibly have swayed you from your obligation?"

Dropping my eyes, too ashamed to admit that one human, a female mortal, is the sole reason I have presented to ask my father to release me from this task.

Dealing with these mortals is vastly different from the ones circling the rim between life and death. The only thing I need to do for them is to wait, watch and deliver, yet the ones who still believe their lives hold meaning, who can yet feel the sun upon their faces. These mortals are difficult. Until I met her, I felt no sympathy or remorse; knowing I planned to eradicate their existence held no more importance than an ant scurrying underfoot. To, at long last, remove the ones my father regarded with such high esteem. Until she changed everything; made me wish for.... for far more than I ever thought possible.

"I will not release you from this. Your task is to determine whether or not they are worthy of redemption. You will remain among the mortals until you have the answer I require."

"But—"

"This is not a request, nor is this matter up for further debate. You will return, and the next time I see you, it will be to pardon or condemn the ones you have walked among. Do we understand one another?"

"Yes, lord."

The hills surrounding me blink back into focus. The air has grown much cooler in my absence, further confirming I have been gone much longer than I thought.

Upon returning to the town my army once surrounded, I discovered half the numbers I had before. Xander is trying to hold everything together, and Apple is not the same being she was when I left. It seems much has changed during my quest to have another assigned in my stead. Unfortunately, none of it is for the better.

Avalon

Shit—shit—shit and double shit, I am in big fuckin trouble here.

"You really didn't think your bullshit antics would go unanswered forever, did you?"

"I guess whether or not my actions were bullshit would all come down to who you ask." I need to learn the value of a filter or keep a healthy stock of medical supplies close at hand.

"Well, since I'm the one standing here, my opinion is the only one that matters." I guess Nevil's the one who plans on doing all the talking today. It shouldn't surprise me since he believes he's their leader. Leader of the assholes, what a great thing to strive for.

"It would appear that way. So, what's it gonna be then? Let me guess, three against one?"

"You should have learned the value of keeping that fuckin trap of yours closed."

"I've never been all that great with keeping my mouth closed."

One side of his mouth curls up into a smirk while his eyes narrow on me. I can't say which bothers me more, watching a man's expression transition into pure evil or Bob's lust-filled eyes. And don't even get me started with Steven, who is currently tapping the side of his leg with the same damn whip they used on Dave and Ryan.

My eyes dart from left to right, hoping to see any means of escape. All I need is one small path, one break in their focus, but my chance never comes. Nevil is the first to pounce, landing a blow to the side of my head. The impact sends me stumbling but does not put me down as I imagine he was counting on.

Another blow and my head snaps back, slamming painfully into the wall behind me. Not wanting to give these assholes an ounce of satisfaction, I choke down the yelp caused by the impact. Nevil lifts his foot to kick me in my stomach, which is apparently his favorite means of assault. I am amazed he can get his leg as high as he does for such a big man.

I know I need to stay on my feet if I have any hope of surviving this, and if I am on the receiving end of his boot, there is no way I stand any chance of accomplishing that. With this thought repeating through my head, I twist at the last second, narrowly avoiding the bone-jarring kick he tried to deliver.

Seeing an opportunity, I scramble out of the ditch and sprint in the direction I figure other people will be. If I can get close enough, someone is bound to hear me scream. As much as I despise showing weakness, the thought of being found dead in a ditch is something I hate more.

With my flight reaction fully engaged, I foolishly believe I can still make it until the snap of a whip, followed by searing pain, buckles my legs. Nevil is on me before I can recover. The beating escalates from there. They have no fear of repercussions because these three men fully intend to end my life tonight. I can't believe after everything I have survived, all the horrors, all the abuses, this is what will finally put an end to this shitty fucking life. Three idiots who didn't have the guts to face me one-on-one.

When Nevil is done punching and kicking me, they drag my limp frame to a tree to string me up so Steven can dole out his brand of justice. As horrible as Nevil's assault was, having my flesh ripped open repeatedly with each crack of the whip was infinitely more excruciating. More than once, I feel the world fade as everything goes fuzzy. My clothes cling to me from the blood soaking them, and each time Steven stops to reel his whip back to him, a drip can be heard in the silence. It doesn't take me long to realize the drops are coming from me.

"Beg for your life, bitch. Beg, and I might let you live." Turning my head as far as the throbbing pain will allow, I force my eyes open to look straight into his. Thinking he's won, believing he's broken me, as evident by the grin covering his face, he repeats, "Beg me, Avalon. Plead for your life."

Swallowing to force any amount of fluid I have left in my mouth down my ragged throat. Next, I run my tongue over my parched lips, desperate to add any moisture to them. I try to respond, but nothing comes out. The pain is excruciating. I may only have one chance to answer him, so I take a second to clear my throat before muttering, "I don't fucking beg."

I know this may seem completely illogical when he offered me a chance, but the truth is, Nevil never planned on releasing me. When others find out what he did to me, many would flee for fear of facing the same, let alone if or when Death returns, he would have to answer for his blatant disregard of his previous order that all punishments are for him to decide. No, it's clear neither Nevil, Steven, nor Bob ever intended to let me walk away from this, so I have no intention of giving them what they want.

"Think of this as a lesson from the horseman himself since he plans on wiping the useless fucking assholes from our world. We decided to help him by ridding the planet of one worthless bitch." Nevil snarls directly into my ear.

Bob walks over and yanks my head back, and of the three, I know his brand of justice will by far be the worse. If any of them can break me, without a doubt, he will come the closest to achieving it.

"My turn, bitch, and I have no intention of being gentle." His confession sends a shiver ripping through me, causing the mangled flesh on my back to make me damn near scream from the pain, yet it is the knowledge of what he intends to do, killing every piece of my already tattered soul. I wish I could say my life blinked out before he ripped my pants down; I can't. Yet thankfully, darkness overtakes me, so I am blissfully unaware of the vile act he plans to commit against me.

After they had each extracted their own brand of justice and removed the shackles used to hold me in place, the three men tossed me down the hillside to die alone, like the piece of trash they kept calling me.

Bloody and bruised.... Flesh ripped and bones shattered.... Entirely alone.

But still not broken.

Chapter Ten: Raven

But the one who endures to the end will be saved. Matthew 24:13.

Avalon Summer 2023

NOT YET. THE LESSON has not yet been learned, little lamb. The command is spoken like a thought passing through my head. Not so different from my own thoughts when I talk to myself, but unlike my thoughts, this voice causes a nagging little itch deep inside. I try to shake it away, only my body refuses to comply.

"Avalon." I am semi-aware of hearing someone call my name.

"Avalon.... Can you hear me?" I am also vaguely cognizant of warmth spreading over my back.

"Avalon.... A.... If you can hear me, make a noise." It's Suki. Damn, but if my little friend isn't devoted.

Wait, didn't I die? I remember the assault, being chained, the whip, Bob's tongue on my face, and then being tossed down a ravine to die, but if I'm dead, why can I hear Suki calling for me? And if I've passed on, why do I hurt so goddamn bad? I guess these are questions to be answered at another time. Now I just want to answer the call of my friend.

Pushing with every ounce of strength, I drag myself from under the brush and leaves covering me. This is the best I can do. It's up to Suk now. If I am going to live, my only hope lies with my crazy friend.

I can hear them somewhere above me moving around. I try to stay conscious, believing if they come anywhere near me, I might be able to signal them, but the darkness has pushed in again.

The next time I wake, their shouts and calls are coming from further away. I am not too bullheaded to admit my heart drops as I realize they may not find me.

Darkness. Darkness is becoming my last companion. Is it sad that I find contentment here? I don't think so, making it easier for me to slip further within.

The caw of a raven startles me awake. Blinking away some of the haziness, I find it sitting on a rock while it watches me with cautious curiosity. Wouldn't it just be my dumb luck if this thing decides to make a meal of me while I'm still alive and unable to stop it? I recognize my chances of being found before he loses his hesitation and decides a free meal is worth the risk are slim, especially since I no longer hear my rescuers.

Darkness. I wonder if this time will be when it finally swallows me up. At least here in the dark, the pain recedes, which is a welcome relief.

Owww, shit. New pain flares, and this time my eyes don't snap wide; I have to drag them open. The fucking raven. His stomach must have finally won out because he now stands next to me. I swear this damn thing is waiting for something. Does it sense I have not yet died? Is it waiting to save me the pain of having more flesh torn from my body? The only thought repeated in my brain is, "Good bird. I promise not much longer, buddy."

I'm not afraid of the darkness, not anymore. Somehow I know if I open my eyes, the raven will be there waiting. Maybe he's here to carry my soul away. Do I believe this? I don't have any reason to disbelieve it, but carry it away to where? If I'm being honest, the almighty creator and I.... well, we haven't been on the best of terms for most of my life. Either way, the darkness is warm, welcoming, inviting, and I think I would like to stay here. I figure here is as good a place as any.

"Oh my God, I found her. A. We're coming. Xander, Dave, she's over here."

The darkness begins to slip away, and for the briefest second, I want to beckon it to come back for me. The raven's wings slapping the side of my face as he takes flight is what at long last causes my eyes to flutter against the light. I watch as my winged friend glides on the currents away from me. My thought now shifts to, "Maybe next time, my friend."

Morbid? Yes. Truthful? Absolutely. Born of necessity? Without a fucking doubt.

Darkness is pushing harder now. It is trying desperately to consume its trophy before it loses me, just as the raven did.

The next thing I am aware of is being lifted because the pain is so intense; if I could scream, I would. But it seems my vocal cords no longer wish to produce sound. The darkness may yet claim its prize.

*****

My next memory is waking up a week later in the makeshift medical facility. Which amounts to three beds, no curtains, a nurse, and a medical student who had yet to begin significant training when the world shifted.

Although he must know what he's doing since I can move my extremities, which I couldn't down at the bottom of the pit, the one Nevil, Steven, and Bob believed would become my tomb. Little did they know my buddy, the raven would prevent this simply by keeping me awake.

"Welcome back, Avalon." I try to speak, but much like the day they found me, it produces no sound.

"I imagine your throat is pretty dry. Here, let me get you something to help with that."

Finally, hell yes, I'd be willing to get up and dance a damn jig for a glass of water. When he returns with a damp washcloth, I feel like asking if he has short-term memory loss or some other affliction. He went to get me some water, not grab a rag for my head. Realization of why he did this rushes in when he wipes it across my mouth, letting the tiniest bit of fluid trickle in, and I instantly begin coughing.

"We'll have to take this slow. Once you can handle this, then I'll get you a small glass of water. Oral swabs or ice chips would be better, but we have to make do since they are no longer an option."

"Do you remember anything?" Do I remember? Is this guy kidding me? Of course, I remember everything... all while I shake my head no. Hey, I said I remember, which means I remember who did this to me and why. Since I have not lost my common sense, I am all too aware if Nevil finds out that I'm alive, awake, and have total recollection of what he and his band of assholes did to me, I don't have much of a chance of staying alive for long. Especially since I'm still laid up in this hospital bed and don't have a hope in hell of protecting myself from them. After my brush with death, I am kind of partial to living.

"Is there any chance her memory will come back?" I didn't realize Xander was sitting next to me, and I jumped at the sound of his voice.

"Maybe, maybe not; only time will tell." They continue to chat about my prognosis. I don't have any problem with this, but my head is pounding right now, so I would prefer if they took this conversation somewhere else because what I want is to go back to sleep.

I am beginning to drift off when Xander rests his hand on my shoulder, leaning closer to me so he can quietly deliver me a promise, one I have little doubt he means but zero doubt he will be able to keep.

"I know Nevil and his asshole followers are responsible for this, and I promise they will pay for doing this to you when I can prove it." I don't have the strength to acknowledge him or validate his belief; right now, the slow pull of sleep is overtaking me, and I know my new friend, the raven, will be waiting for me.

Later, when everyone is tucked in safe and warm in their beds for the night, I receive another visitor. And unlike Xander's presence, this one is completely unwanted.

"So it is true you somehow survived your *fall*." The way he says fall is meant to indicate the three of them had nothing to do with it. I want to tell him to go fuck himself but hold my tongue, opting to stare at him, hoping my expression conveys this: *I sure did. But why do you care since we have never liked one another?*

"You did fall because you're a fucking clumsy bitch, but it was nothing more than a freak accident. Wasn't it Avalon?" I fear my better judgment just flew out the damn window, and now fury rapidly replaces it as I narrow my eyes.

"I'm going to need an answer from you." What he does or does not want is too fucking bad because I refuse to answer this asshole.

"No? Don't want to cooperate? Shame. Well then, let's tackle this issue from another approach. You fell down the fucking ravine because you're a clumsy bitch, and if by chance you have any other memories from the night in question and have a pressing need to share this bullshit with anyone, then your little friend, what's her name again? Suki? Let's just say this time, I'll damn well make sure there is nothing left to be found. Followed by me removing your venomous tongue. Let's be honest; since you have no control over it, you'd probably be better off without it. Can never tell what kind of *pricks and assholes* you might run into during your travels." I think it's safe to assume he knows what my nickname for him and his band of thugs entails. "Are we clear about what happened now?"

Crystal clear.

*****

Over the next couple of weeks, I am slowly regaining my strength. Xander is busy running things, and when he is not doing this, he is trying to hunt down the evidence needed to prove his belief of who is responsible for my *accident*. Too bad he will never find it. Nevil, Steven, and Bob made sure of this.

After I left the medical center, Xander, along with the appointed leader of this little community, Ted, insisted I take one of the empty quarters within the walls. I could have argued until the cows came home; it made no difference. They would not relent, so until a few nights ago, I had a room right down the hall from Suk and Xander.

I imagine you're wondering what happened then. Simple. Nevil happened. Nevil and his band of misfits told me to pack my shit I was going back out with the rabble. I'll miss the bed almost as much as the energetic Suki.

Speaking of Suk, she was so furious with me for leaving she didn't talk to me for a week believing I left of my own accord. It was easier to let her be mad than to risk her finding out Nevil threatened to kill her, and he constantly held her over my head to keep me in line. This would have led to one thing for Xander and me — more fighting.

By the time Death returns, half his horde is gone, Xander is in over his head, and Nevil is completely out of control. But on the plus side, aside from the scars they left, I am back to normal. I can handle the scars; hell, they can join the ones I already had.

I admit seeing him stride into town after everything that happened; he no longer holds the same allure he did before. Now I just see him as the reason for the shit I went through.

I don't get stuck with ditch duty anymore, but my new job isn't much better. Fieldworker. This is basically farm work without the aid of any modern conveniences like a tractor, cultivator, or seeder. In this new world, you have a hoe and a horse who looks like he's on his last leg.

Today was particularly hard since the cool night air of Autumn is forcing us to harvest before we planned. Xander and Suki are officially together, ending any thought of us leaving the horde together. This is not to say that I plan on staying, because I don't; it simply means I will be on my own when I leave.

All morning I had to deal with Bob, and of course, he acted like a miserable prick the entire time. The way he looks at me leads me to believe a lick to my face was not the only offense he committed all those nights ago. This is a memory I am only too happy not to have to live with. What's the saying? Oh yeah, ignorance is bliss, at least where this is concerned.

When I finish this chore, I get to set up the tents for the poor unfortunate souls who will toil out here in the muck with the rest of the rabble while Nevil and his buddies live it up in a warm room with a comfortable bed. Even though there are numerous empty units we could sleep in, we lowly workers are not permitted to stay in them. Another of Nevil's decisions. We have lovely moth-bitten tents, and I just had to set up every one of them for the new arrivals by myself. Punishment for mouthing off yet again.

My buddy, the raven, also showed up today. I can't say this is the same bird, but I would like to think it is. Although I can't be sure if he keeps hanging around because he likes me or if he is waiting for his meal.

Tonight I have big plans with my new favorite couple. I'm reading the fourth book in the series I found, and the heroine is getting ready to travel through hell to save our hero.

"Ava," Dave yells as I shuffle towards my humble, shabby little shelter in what I like to call Tent City.

"Hey, Dave."

"Xander asked me to come get you."

"For what?"

"Didn't say, but I think it was at Death's request."

"No." I could give a shit less who is asking for me; they can all kiss my ass. I'm tired, hungry, in need of a bath, and I have no intention of going anywhere other than straight to my place for the night.

"No?"

"That's what I said, isn't it?"

"But, A."

"No, Dave."

"What am I supposed to tell them?"

"Whatever you want," I say as I pull back the flap to my tent. I begin to enter but stop midstep to provide a better response over my shoulder. "Actually, on second thought, tell them I said kiss my ass."

"Avalon, I can't—" I don't hear the rest of his argument because as much as I like Dave, I could give two shits about Death or his stupid order.

I'm sure it will come as no surprise that Death doesn't seem to understand simple courtesy like knocking. I was preparing to wash up and change out of these filthy clothes I had been wearing since digging in shit. I realize it's called fertilizer, but what is fertilizer other than processed shit?

Since Death doesn't have the courtesy of waiting until I invite him in, I feel no need to be the hospitable host. These clothes stink, and I want them off of me. I want to wash the stench of sweat from my body. I want to brush my teeth and fall into another world only my book can offer. I also have no shame as I continue pulling the clothes from my body. There's no point to it, really. He has made a point of repeatedly telling any who have tried to trade their body for his favor he has no interest in their putrid human flesh. So, fuck him. If he doesn't want to see this disgusting body, he can leave. After all, this is my freaking tent he just barged into uninvited and unannounced.

Looking at him through the reflection of the tiny mirror over my washbasin, I don't miss his eyes assessing the healing injuries inflicted by his number two.

"What happened?"

"Fell. I'm told I'm clumsy."

"Do not lie to me, mortal." Whipping around to face him, my chest heaving from the rage building within me. I mean, who the hell does this asshole think he is?

"Total klutz, apparently. In fact, I am so damn inept that I tossed my stupid ass right off the cliff down into a ravine." I'm sick of the damn questions. I'm sick of seeing Nevil peacock around here like he's the cock of the walk while Death disappears for months, and I don't have it in me to hide my frustration anymore. I may not come right out and say it, but I don't have to pretend like I'm an idiot either. When a low growl rumbles from deep in his chest as he takes several deliberate steps towards me, my damn mouth takes on a mind of its own as the last of my restraint shatters, and fury at what they did to me takes its place. I will protect Suki by not saying a name, but I cannot stop the words as they come tumbling out of my mouth in a rush.

"What do you want me to say here, Death? Do you want me to say I was in the wrong fucking place at the wrong damn time? Okay, I was in the wrong fucking place at the wrong damn time. Do you want me to say I didn't fall? Okay, I didn't fall. Do you want me to admit this was done by the hands of assholes? Okay, this was done by the hands of assholes. Are you looking for confirmation they beat me and left me for dead? Okay, they beat me and left me for dead. Are you fucking happy now?"

"They ripped you apart."

"Funny, isn't it?" The short, huffed laugh I give him has nothing to do with being amused.

"I find no humor in any of this."

"Oh, but wait, you haven't heard the punch line yet, so here you go.... I found you when mortals left you mangled and dying in that abandoned building. I nursed your ass back to health and protected you as you stitched your body back together, only to have you rip mine apart a year later as a thank you."

"You are mistaken, human; I did not do this to you."

"Yes, you did. It may not have been your whip, your blade, or your hand, but it was your will. Done in your goddamn name. All because you forced me to stay here and took no responsibility for the assholes you led. At least John and his gang left you in a building. No cushy fucking building for me. Nope, I was dumped into a pit and left to die in the dirt."

"Yet you did not die. Why is that?"

"Wow." I laugh sarcastically. "That's what you took away from this? Fantastic. Okay, I can pretend too; I've gotten pretty stellar at it. I guess we mortals are harder to kill than you thought, especially when you send inept assholes like the ones who beat me."

"Mind your tongue, mortal."

"Or you'll have it removed. Yeah—yeah, you all really need to come up with a better threat; the tongue one is getting old." I turn my back on him, returning to my sponge bath.

What I would give for a shower; an honest-to-goodness shower with warm water, shampoo, conditioner, and body wash. Damn, I miss my body wash.

I can feel his eyes lingering on the scars left by my previous life and the new ones doled out by his guards, but I'm done entertaining this rider of the apocalypse, so he can just sod off.

Chapter Eleven: What Comes Around

For he is God's servant for your good. But if you do wrong, be afraid, for he does not bear the sword in vain. For he is the servant of God, an avenger who carries out God's wrath on the wrongdoer. Romans 13:4

Death Autumn 2023

WHEN XANDER TOLD ME that Avalon had been involved in what she stated was nothing more than a fluke accident that left her on the brink of death, I admit it sent a rush of emotions through me. Had I been doing as my father asked rather than meditating as I waited for his call, I would have sensed her life was in peril. Knowing I could have protected her from such an atrocity causes an unfamiliar feeling to twist within me. Still, when he informed me he believed it was intentional, he just couldn't prove it left one outcome; I will look into this on my own.

Since it seems Xander has countless other outstanding issues which simply must be discussed with me immediately, he sent Dave to fetch her in my stead.

I do not need to tell you how infuriating it was when he returned alone and advised us she would not be coming. I am unsure why this woman refuses me when I give a simple command. Nor can I express the irritation coursing through me at being denied yet another request.

Given that my father refuses to relieve me of this damnable task, I will endure the job he has assigned me so I can fulfill his bidding with the hopes of returning to my rightful role. The last thing I should do if I wish to achieve this anytime soon is chase after this mortal.

Yet here I am, stalking through town on my way to see this frustrating woman. If my brothers could see me now. I imagine War would laugh, Pestilence would find it endearing, and Famine would call me a fool, which I can't say I disagree with.

Arriving at the building I assumed she would be staying in, I admit to being confused when Xander stopped me, advising that she had left the room granted to her, opting to return to the tents outside the walls. Yet another question to be answered. And before this night is done, I shall have them all.

Not waiting for her to acknowledge me, I storm inside her tent to find her nearly undressed. The instant my eyes settle on her back, I am left speechless.

Her back is more scar than flesh. While some I can clearly see are from a time long before I encountered Avalon, most are fresh, red, raw, intentional. Seeing her like this, I must swallow the growl twisting within me. I am aware she is watching me through the small mirror, yet if I say anything in this second while I am processing what she must have endured for this kind of damage, I fear I will not be able to control myself.

"What happened?"

"Fell. I'm told I'm clumsy." She lied. Does she not realize I can sense the deceit in her words?

"Do not lie to me, mortal."

"Total klutz, apparently. In fact, I am so damn inept that I tossed my stupid ass right off the cliff down into a ravine."

After waiting out her rant, Avalon admits someone did this to her; what is confusing is why she would believe I ordered this. I am astonished she could think I would condone such acts. I am aware I have killed, yet I do not torture. Death at my hand is quick, painless, efficient. This was.... Brutal.

The individuals who did this wanted to make an example of her to the rest. They tried to humiliate, disfigure, and dehumanize her in a way I have not seen for quite some time.

Why do these mortals believe it absolves them of their crime by claiming they did it in someone else's name? Much like the individuals from ancient times who claimed their atrocities were all done in the name of their God, these miscreants evoked mine.

A choice they will soon pay dearly for.

*****

"Summon everyone to the square." I snap at Xander as I storm past him.

"Is everything okay?"

"Summon. Everyone." If these mortals wish to test the boundaries I am willing to grant them, I shall prove how incredibly wrong they are. It is time for me to return to the task assigned by our creator, which includes assessing, deciding, and judging. Tonight they will learn this lesson well.

Investigating the area he advised they found her in, I located the tree she was bound to. The grass surrounding it is trampled down, yet the evidence of faint blood on the ground confirms it. I follow the path back to where the altercation began. The footprints have faded during my absence; however, I can make out the distinct tracks of three individuals while using my heightened senses. The size and span led me to believe it was three men, all around six feet.

Arriving at the edge of the ravine they threw her from, I am amazed she is still alive. A testament to the strength and fortitude this woman possesses. Launching into the air, I fly down into the pit where they believed she would meet her end. I easily locate the spot where she lay after dragging her battered body from where she landed. I know everything I need to know about what transpired. Only one more stop before I have my say.

By the time I arrive, every mortal within my horde and those who have sheltered us are gathered, waiting with bated breath. I surmise the ones who traveled with me believe I have had my fill of this town, and like all the others, it is time for me to pass judgment; in contrast, I find terror filling the eyes of the residents from here.

"Come here," I demand, leveling my gaze at Avalon. The mask of cool indifference she often wears slips away replaced instantly with panic. She shakes her head several times, forcing me to retrieve her. She swats my hand away each time I reach for her until I have had enough of her insolence. I guess she has not yet realized her resistance is futile.

I guide her through the crowd back to the selected spot to address them. Her head is dropped, shoulders slumped, and I find humiliation reflecting within those soulful eyes with each brief glance I receive.

"Who did it?" I snarl, knowing the one responsible is here. I have my belief, but I shall allow them to take responsibility and come forth of their own accord. A hushed murmur surrounds us.

I wait as they each discuss their belief regarding what I asked.

I watch as faces display sympathy, anger, accusation, and fear. Yet the guilty parties refuse to take responsibility for their action. If they had hoped to conceal their crime, they should not have used the same weapon from their previous transgression. A mistake they will soon regret ....

With the assessment and decision parts concluded, the sentencing phase will begin. Sadly for the guilty trio, I will deliver the same sentence they bestowed upon her.

Looking down at her, I know she hates every second of this. I can feel it as much as I can see it written all over her face. She hates having their eyes on her, hates being the center of attention, yet the one thing she despises above all else is the sorrowful looks filled with pity from the humans gathered to bear witness to my judgment.

Stalking in his direction, I stand before the mortal always at Nevil's side, Steven. He was not the brains behind the attack. No, that was most assuredly Nevil. He will pay for his role in her attack, along with the fidgeting fool standing next to him. Right now, I am solely addressing the one who ripped the flesh from her back.

If Steven knows I suspect him, he gives nothing away. Surely he has to realize I know it was him, yet he stands here looking around, waiting for the guilty culprit to step forward. He does this until the second I pull the whip from behind my back. His jaw twitches, and the pounding of his heart increases. Unwinding the device he used to torture her, his eyes grow wide as all the other mortals around him recede.

"This is what you used."

"I... No — no, it—it wasn't m—"

"You." I finish for him.

"Nev—Nevil?"

"There will be no aid coming for you."

"Guys?" The others wisely remain silent. "Duh—Death... I didn't... Nevil!"

"The difference between you and me is I do not need two others—" Nevil begins to interrupt, but one look from me has him quickly letting the words die before they ever tumble out of his treacherous mouth. "to punish you."

"Please. Please, Death, let me explain."

"Did you or your accomplices," I don't miss Bob's eyes darting in my direction when I say this, "grant her a chance to explain? No? Then why would you believe I will entertain anything you want to say?"

He opens his mouth to further protest, but I have heard all I will hear from him today or any day after. Flicking the whip, it snaps, finding its mark across Steven's face; his screams of pain echo through the camp. The only other sounds are the gasps coming from the members of my horde.

Marcelle Valentine

Snapping the whip again, I want this asshole to feel even an ounce of the pain they heaped upon her. The misery one can only experience when having their flesh ripped from their bones. Paralyzed by the fear of what I may do if he moves, Steven remains rooted in place until the tremble of his legs threatens to send him sprawling.

With one last crack of the whip, I snatch out, snapping his neck before dropping him to the ground to die in the dirt as he had hoped she would.

Steven will not find me waiting to take him to his lost loved ones. His is a life I hold no value in, so he can wander purgatory alone and lost in darkness for all eternity.

But I have two others who require my judgment, and they will soon understand Steven was the lucky one.

Avalon

When death calls me front and center, I am horrified, but even more so when he kills Steven for his role in my attack. I know Nevil will blame me for his death. If I hope to continue living, which I am somewhat partial to, I have little choice but to speed up my departure timeline.

I don't know where Death, Xander, Dave, and Ryan took Bob along with Death's former second-in-command, Nevil, nor do I care.

I know what needs to be done. I need to pack my shit and wait for the perfect time to run before I end up on the wrong side of Nevil's blade. I know I can't do it tonight because all eyes are on me but soon and only after I have a candid conversation with Suki. The last part of this statement is possible now. The running will come shortly.

Cautiously sneaking inside the same building Suki and Nevil both live in, I am on edge the entire time. Believing any second Nevil will come storming around the corner on the way to his room. The problem is, if he catches me here, I have nowhere to run or hide. Rounding the last corner before arriving at Suki's apartment, my chest is burning, my heart is pounding, and I realize I have been holding my breath for far too long, forcing me to release it with an audible exhale.

Using as much discretion as my shaking hand will allow, I quietly tap on the door, praying the entire time she is in there alone. Whenever I hear a door open, my head whips in the noise's direction, fully preparing to discover Nevil standing there.

"A? Oh my god, get in here." She squeals while pulling me into her place. I am still closing the door when she wraps me in a tight embrace. "I've missed you so much."

"I've missed you too."

"Then why did you move out? We could have been neighbors like we were before," she trails off. I know what she was going to say, just like before, as in before the world we knew tilted on its axis, causing everything in our world to shift and transform our lives for the foreseeable future. As in before we knew the horsemen of the apocalypse existed and the worst one, the one all the bible proclaimed would be the last to come, was actually the first.

"You know me, Suk. The tent works fine. I don't need—"

"A bed, four walls, a roof?"

"A lot." I'll let her ascertain the meaning behind my comment.

"I don't know anyone who would prefer sleeping on the hard-assed ground over a comfortable bed, but you go on and keep your secrets." I will Suk. I will guard them with my life and, in doing so, protect you from the asshole who will do anything to hurt me.

"Is it true, A? That jackass—" Suki's nickname for Nevil, although I still prefer sausage fingers. "and his band of dipshits are the ones who did this to you?"

And there it is; until now, Suki has never outright asked me if any particular person was the one who attacked me, so I never had to spew an untruth to her. Now I need to decide whether I lie to her for the first time, tell her the truth thereby risking her safety, or figure out something else. Because the straightforward fact is my little friend may be lots of things, but forgiving is not one of them. Especially when you hurt someone she loves. Even though we have never said this aloud, Suki is more family to me than my biological one ever was. Making my decision easy, I can't lie to her, but this doesn't mean I need to admit shit. I'm sure you want to know how I accomplish this. Simple.... I deflect.

"Suk, I need to tell you something."

"Okay," she says, taking my hand to lead me over to the small table in the corner. She has a good thing with Xander, one I know I can't ask her to give up. My choice, although painful, is simple. I have to go, but her place is here with him. I admit I am already mourning the loss of my friend and travel companion. "Can I get you anything?"

"No, Suk, I—"

"How have you been? I know I've been a shitty friend because I was butthurt when you left the building and didn't even talk to me about it first, but it doesn't excuse my behavior. So tell me the truth. How are you?"

I know I have no option here other than to rip off the band aid. Taking a deep breath, I blurt, "I'm leaving."

Suki's eyes double in size while her mouth falls open. Her shocked expression reminds me of one of the few things my mother told me that has stuck with me.... Close your mouth if you don't want flies making a home in there.... As ludicrous as it may be, I reach over to push her jaw up.

"What? Why?" she demands, jumping to her feet to give her more space to flail her arms while pacing around the room.

"It's time."

"Uhhhh, I beg to differ because, no it's not."

"Suk." This one word speaks volumes, instantly silencing any further protest from her. When she talks again, sadness has replaced the determined tone she had seconds ago.

"Why would you want us to leave here?"

"Not us. Just me. I'm leaving; your place is here now."

"But we're the two drunketeers." Something Suki came up with one night after we found and finished a bottle of cheap bourbon. She said we couldn't be musketeers since there were only two of us, or Mouseketeers because Walt used that one for his famous cheese-eating rodent. Hence, drunketeers were born.

"And we always will be. Just not in the same place anymore." The light from the flickering candle reveals the glistening unshed tears filling her eyes. I knew she would have a hard time with my decision. I mentally prepared myself for her screaming and yelling; however, I was definitely unprepared for tears. I am not equipped to deal with this emotion, and I hate this is something I did to her. "Besides, I think Xander would have something to say about you leaving. You know something like: *if you try, I will tie you to our damn bed, my little sex vixen.*"

"Sex Goddess," she corrects with a sniffling little laugh as she wipes the tears from her eyes.

"My mistake," I reply, bowing my head in mock humility. Suk ignores my previous objection, getting up to retrieve a bottle of wine and two glasses.

We sit quietly, enjoying the company and the sweetness of the alcohol; neither of us acknowledges that this will probably be the last time we do this together. When I toss back the last of the contents in my glass and begin to stand Suki places her hand on mine to stop me.

"When?"

"Soon."

"Will you come to say goodbye.... You know before?"

My short answer to this should be, of course, but the truth of the matter is I don't know if I will or not. When I do not respond, Suki knows she has her answer, making her jump up to hug me as she chokes back a sob.

Pulling back so I can look at the woman I have claimed as a sister, I realize what I am about to ask her is completely unfair; still, I know if I ask her for this, she will not betray me. "You can't tell anybody, not even Xander. Okay?"

She nods even though we both know if she did, it would prevent me from leaving because Xander would tell Death and everyone knows Death does not like losing numbers from his horde.

I gave her one more quick hug before spinning to go. If there was ever a time in my life I came close to crying, it was when she spoke next, "I'm glad Death killed that fucker, and

I hope he kills the other two bastards too. Only after he leaves them bloody, bruised, and broken, as they tried to do to you."

Not broken, Suki.... *Never broken.*

Chapter Twelve: Dream a little Dream

LEAVING SUKI'S PLACE WAS almost as nerve-racking as going there. I try to camouflage myself within the shadows until I am safely inside my tent, although calling a canvas tent safe is laughable.

Death has his sentries out in mass tonight, confirming there is no way I would get any further than the tree line before they rounded my ass up and dumped it either back in my tent, in jail, or on Death's doorstep. After seeing how pissed he was tonight, I have no desire to spend any one-on-one time with him. I mean, I always knew he was Death, but I had some romanticized view of him. Tonight he made it abundantly clear.... He is the bringer of death.

Grabbing my book, I try to slip into the world of demons, vampires, angels, and lycan. The problem is my mind keeps returning to Death and what happened tonight. I didn't ask him to do it. I certainly didn't tell him who attacked me. I have no idea why he would feel compelled to dole out any punishment to the ones who did this to me, least of all death. Especially since I seem to be the low chick on the totem pole around here.

Dropping the book beside me on the cot, I sigh before climbing out of bed to exit my little tent. The days are getting shorter and the nights colder. Before long, Death will either have to move us farther south or find all of us nobodies out here in tent city shelter indoors. Well, not me since I don't plan on being here much longer.

Pulling my sweater tighter around my body, hoping it will help block out some of the chills from the cool night air, I move further into tent city. Most nights, the residents are out here having a bonfire, but I don't see the telltale signs of the amber flames on the horizon. I hope it wasn't canceled because of me.

Standing here looking down at the charred wood left over from last night, I can't help but feel responsible for all this. I should have left a long time ago. I should have learned the value of a filter by now. After all, it was my cocky comments that set Nevil off to begin with. For Christ's sake, I made fun of the man's name. Who does shit like that?

I stay out there until my fingers are numb, my legs are shaking, and my teeth are chattering before I decide I have wallowed enough for one night.

I would like to tell you that entering my tent helped chase away the cold, but it didn't. It helped with the bite when the wind whipped up; unfortunately, it did little else. Kicking my shoes off and dropping my sweater where I stand, I slide into the sleeping bag, hoping it will not take long before I warm up or, at the very least, fall asleep.

If the chill in my bones was any indication, I would have sworn I had only been in bed a couple of minutes when the sound of movement had my eyes snapping open. My head has a heavy quality. The kind that only comes from being startled awake from a sound sleep. I immediately begin blinking my eyes, trying to adjust them to the absolute darkness. No matter how hard I try, I cannot get a sense of who is in the tent with me. But make no mistake, I can feel their presence. It is not until the clouds move away from the moon that I receive the faintest sliver of light, and who I find sitting there ramps the pace of my heart up drastically.

"Death?"

"Yes."

"What—what are you doing here?" I stammer as I sit up. Didn't we do this once before? Does a wet dream count for a once before, or does it only count if it really happened? And why am I debating this shit right now when the being who just so cavalierly killed someone is watching me sleep?

"I wanted to make sure you are okay, Apple."

"Avalon." With my correction, I can barely make out his head tilt in the low light.

"I want you to know they will never hurt you again. I'm sorry I wasn't here to stop them."

"What did you do with Nevil and Bob?"

"Punished them."

"How?" I don't know why it matters to me, especially after these assholes had no problem leaving me to die.... It just feels like an unanswered question, not knowing.

"They yet live if this is what you want to know."

"For how long?"

"For Bob, I imagine not long; Nevil will last much longer."

"Why?"

"This is a question I do not understand."

"Why would you punish them?"

"Because they hurt...." He trails off.

When I realize he has no intention of finishing his sentence, I sit up and move to the side of the bed. Bringing me closer to him as I ask. "Me? Because they hurt me?"

"Yes," he replies, running the pads of his fingers over my cheek. His admission brings me fully to my feet. Despite my reaction, I remain frozen in place while Death stays seated. It is one of the few times he has ever had to look up at me. "I'm sorry if you believe I would condone what they did or that I would ever want someone to hurt you."

"Isn't that exactly what you do?"

"Never, Apple. Until tonight, I have never done anything like what they did to you."

"Avalon." This time when I correct him, I can barely make out the hint of a smile tipping those perfectly kissable lips.

What the hell? No, Avalon. Absolutely fucking not. I will not be going there again.

Death reaches out to take my hand in his, and even after being under the covers, his hand envelops mine in warmth; beautiful, luscious, wonderful warmth. But it's not only my hand heating up. My entire body feels the effects of being this close to him.

"There is something about you I am drawn to. I wish I could explain it. I yearn to understand it myself. When I am not near you, I long to be, and when you are close, I crave your touch. These are emotions I am ill-equipped to deal with." He stands to guide me closer. When I do not try to resist his advances, he brings his lips down to mine while he holds me firmly in his embrace. An act that chases away the last remnants of the cold.

Backing him up until his legs strike the chair, he sits down, bringing me with him until I straddle his legs. I can't say if I removed his shirt first or if he removed mine, nor do I care. The only thought playing on repeat is how much I love being here. In this tent, in his arms, wrapped around this man, every cell in my body is lighting up, every atom is dancing, every molecule truly awake.

He carefully removes my bra before marveling at my breast; the intensity of his gaze causes my nipples to harden. His tongue slides over his lips as if he is envisioning what it would taste like to run his tongue over one of the stiff peaks. Seeing him like this has me biting my lip. The act is my only hope of stopping the low moan trying to escape me.

He drags my hips forward, pressing me down against his growing erection before he slides me back again, resulting in the most delectable friction. Further increasing the heat coursing through my body until it settles between my thighs.

I am desperate to feel his skin against mine, his erection sliding over my slick folds. Not wanting to waste another second, I press my lips to his as I slide off his lap. His hands immediately try to return me to my previous position. Pulling back, I take a moment to enjoy the sight before me. His eyes are alight with desire, his jaw flexing and releasing in anticipation of what I may do next, and the way his muscles jump and tighten under my touch is extremely arousing.

Sliding my pants off, I guide his hands over the lace of the last piece of clothing I have on. His sudden shift from sitting to standing has me taking a step back while I continue encouraging him to remove them. I want to feel his hand skimming over my legs when he slides them down.

His lips trail from my mouth to my ear so he can whisper, "Beautiful."

And then he's gone.

I am back in my cot, fully clothed, wrapped within the sleeping bag, chair across the tent where it always sits but with heat still pooling deep inside me, aching to be released.

"Not again, goddamn it," I yell to my empty tent.

*****

My night was agonizingly long. No matter how hard I tried to erase the memory of his hands gliding over my skin, the taste of his lips on mine, and the glorious heat of his body wrapped around mine, I couldn't. As the first rays of dawn try to break through the shadowy gloom caused by the sprinkle of rain hitting my tent, I decide enough is enough and climb out of bed for the last time.

Gathering the supplies I will need and the tattered books I have repeatedly read, I take one last look around the place I have called home for far too long. Cautiously peering through the flaps meant to act as a door, I leave my little tent behind and silently slip out of tent city. I would love to take one of them with me, especially since the nights are becoming unbearably cold; I won't because they belong to Death's horde, not me.

The chill in the air is further compounded by the steady drizzle from a mid-October rain. At least it is not snowing, but I know it is coming soon. If I hope to still be alive next year, I either have to move south or find shelter to survive these long, unforgiving winter months.

Directly outside the gate, I stop to take one last look at the building holding the only friend I have in this world. I will miss her laugh, her smile, her gentle heart, but mostly I will miss her wit, her snark.... Her. I'll miss her.

"Stay safe, Suk. I love you."

When I turn to begin my trek away from this quaint community, I find my newest friend, the raven, watching my departure. I wonder if he'll follow me. Will he become my only friend, or will he simply become my constant reminder of time running out?

The fastest way out of here is also the one place I have avoided since the night they cornered me. The closer I get to the spot they tied me to that tree, a sickening dread invades every part of my body.

"They cannot control me. I will not give them any further power over my actions," I say to the empty woods surrounding the path I follow, but the words do not chase away the demons filling the trees around this place. The caw of the raven does what nothing else could. It is almost like he is telling me I'm not alone, and this finally gets my damn feet moving again.

One more bend in the road, and I will come face to face with the place I thought I would find my end. My heart has begun hammering in my chest, pumping blood at a frenzied pace until the only thing I can hear is the beat in my ears, but with this comes the endorphins.

"Get your shit together, Avalon. How in the hell will you ever survive on your own if you can't even walk down a damn road?" Albeit a road filled with horror, yet a road nonetheless.

When I round the corner, I freeze, my legs falter, and I end up on my ass in the mud. I cannot believe who I find, "Bob?"

Chapter Thirteen: Mistakes

Avalon Late Autumn 2023

$\mathscr{E}$VEN AFTER ALL THESE weeks, the horror I found along that path still haunts my dreams. I have no idea how long I stood there staring at Bob's mangled corpse, knowing his punishment directly related to my actions and some of the choices I made. If I had covered up or willingly gone with Dave when he asked, none of this would have happened. He deserved to be punished for what he did, but this.... I'm not so sure the punishment fits the crime. The penalty he suffered for his role in what happened that night.

What bothered me the most was that I knew Death must have suspected what I had imagined this entire time: Bob raped me that night in the woods. Or is it possible he forced him to confess? Or was this what Death thought would hurt Bob the most? I will never know for certain what he did to me, and Bob can't tell anyone any longer because what I found the day I left was Bob tied to the same tree they strapped me to, stripped bare, genitals removed and draped around his neck. Head held an unnatural angle. His face beaten so severely that if not for the tattoo he loved to show off, I'm not confident I would have recognized him. The glassy, wide eye stare filled with the misery he experienced in his final moments, agony permanently etched on his face…. Dead

I don't know if there is anyone still alive to mourn him. I can't imagine him as a father, a husband, or a son, although I realize the last has to be true. Even the evilest, most vile humans ever to have walked this planet had people who loved them. Could someone be out there wondering where he is, if he made it, praying he will return to them someday? So one part of me feels sorry for him because of the choices he made, yet a deeper, darker part of me takes pleasure in believing he got exactly what he deserved. Does this make me just as wicked as he was? Possibly. Probably. But I can live with it.

The time I spent with Death's hordes did not grant me a glimpse of how far the world had fallen around us. The bands of roving outlaws have flourished during the time we stayed within the community. They now own most of the roadways and do not allow you to travel them for free. Cutting across the countryside isn't any better since the four-legged predators roamed there.

I stumbled across a tiny cabin far enough away from the streets the bandits don't screw with me but close enough to a small community that I can walk there for supplies when I need them.

The place is a three-room cottage, the main living area, a bedroom, and a bathroom that I managed to convert to make it as functional as possible in this post-Death world. It's not much, but it has four walls and a roof. The windows are mostly intact. I boarded up the ones with holes in them to help stop the cold air from creeping inside. The working fireplace helps keep the place warm as the days get colder. There is plenty of work to keep me busy all day, but the long, lonely nights are much harder to endure.

Since leaving the horde, I haven't had any more erotic dreams with Death starring in the lead role. I admit this makes me just a little bit sad. Although come to think of it, I haven't had any dreams at all since leaving him. I guess the key requirement for having a dream is sleeping, and I don't do much of that either.

The raven followed me for several days until he grew tired of the constant rain and the biting cold. It has been unseasonably frigid this year, and I suppose he flew off for greener pastures. He hasn't returned since then. So, I am truly alone.

I guess this is the path my life was always supposed to take. Avalon versus the world, much like I always have. It's been the theme of my life since I was young. Hell, I should be used to it by now.... Then why do I miss the noise from tent city so damn much?

Death

I knew I never should have gone to her that night. As I watched her standing alone beside the remains of the burnout bonfire unlit by my army tonight, I knew she was conflicted. Avalon was used to being alone, yet she found a certain solace within my ranks. Although I cannot say why since she was brutalized by men within my horde. Men who vowed to follow me then used it against her when they claimed my task as the reason for their offense.

I remained outside her tent, patiently waiting until I heard her breath become steady; only then did I slip into the cramped space she had been living in. I sat there for close to an hour, watching her slumber. I have never taken the time to realize the simplistic beauty this act represents. To live in a world they created, losing oneself to a reality they imagined, to transport your essence to another realm. A part of me envies these mortals' ability to do this, yet another sin to add to my growing list. To simply lay my head down and become whoever I wanted, possibly the man who could fulfill her every desire. This is something I am fascinated with. I do not require rest to keep my body going as a mortal does; perhaps one day, I shall have to try.

I could not stop myself as I slipped into her dream. My altruistic reasoning was to apologize for what they did to her, yet I would be remiss if I did not admit I was hoping to feel her lips upon my own. Unlike the last time I invaded her dreams, I tell myself I will not touch her this time. Each time she corrects my perceived misspoken name for her, I smile slightly more. One day I will have to tell her why I call her this; for now, I enjoy the flash of excitement held within her eyes each time I say it.

Had I known the effect my actions would have on Avalon, I would have remained within my tent, merely thinking of her. Instead, I am surrounded by the shattered trinkets the mortals who come seeking asylum have bestowed upon me as Dave slowly backs away. Rage is consuming me from the inside.

"You're sure?" Xander asks as he moves between the man who risked my vengeance to deliver this information and me; however if I am being truthful, this is my fault, not his.

"Yeah, her tent is cleared of all her personal possessions." He replies as he takes another step back. His terrified eyes are glued to my every movement.

"When?" I growl even though I realize this single-worded question will require further explanation. I turn my back to Dave, trying to rein in the fury building within me.

"I—I just.... Cam-came—"

"No, when did she leave?" I roar, sweeping the remaining items from the tabletop. The crash, compiled with my shouts, has everything around us fall silent. Even the birds have gone quiet, fearful their calls may further rile my ire. I hear him mutter shit several times, and I know he must have dreaded having to be the one to deliver this news to me.

"How long?" I grit through teeth clenched so tightly I fear they may shatter.

"I don't know."

"Did I not assign the task of protecting her to you?" Yet it is I who chased her away; my anger is misdirected.

"Yes."

"Then I shall only ask this last time. How. Long?"

Dave clears his throat and takes several more steps back before telling me, "No one has seen her for days."

"You should leave. Now!" My wings have erupted as my gaze watches him through the mirror.

"Sir." He does not hesitate any longer, fearing what I may do. He turns before scrambling out of my tent.

"It's not his—"

"I know," I snap, interrupting Xander, not wanting to hear him say the words I already know are true.

"But you're still angry."

"At myself. He was nothing more than the unfortunate messenger."

"Are we letting her go?" My barely contained fury must be clear as my eyes flick to his since he is now the one who is backing away with his hands raised submissively.

"I will have the horde tear down camp immediately."

"No."

"But—"

"I said no. The days grow short, and soon winter will be upon us. I do not believe the weaker ones who travel with the horde will survive on the road. I will find her myself." Strapping my baldric around me, I slide my sword into place. Prior to exiting the tent, I look over my shoulder to give him one final directive.

"Bring everyone within the city walls.... None are to be left to toil in tents any longer. We will make our supplies available to the entire community."

"And if they refuse to let the rest of your followers in?"

"Then take the city by force."

*****

Having no idea which direction she traveled has made this task infinitely more difficult. I do not possess the ability to track her; this is a gift granted to my brother, War. If he were awake, I could ask him to use it to find her.

Although this is not ideal while on this plane or during my long wait in purgatory, I can sense all life as it fades away from them. So at least I can locate her if she is in trouble.

Mercifully, the frigid temperatures have driven most mortals indoors, and the few I do come across grant me a wide berth. Leaving only the clacking from my horse's hooves against the road, along with the rhythmic lilting of his breath to fill the absence of all other sounds.

This is how I always imagined my task: me atop my steed, traveling from one city to the next, passing judgment, toppling their world, then moving on. I never envisioned I would be leading an army of the forgotten.

At first, I told myself I was collecting them for my brother. War would need them for his role in the sentence we will deliver, yet somewhere along the way, this shifted. I cannot say I found value in all of them, but most.... Most were not inherently wicked. Perhaps I have judged them too harshly.

"Hey asshole," a whistle followed by the whoosh of an arrow cutting through the air has me leaning back to avoid the incoming projectile.

"The next one will not miss. So allow me to tell you how this is going to work. Get off the fucking horse and lay the goddamn sword on the ground along with your coat. Then you can start walking back in the direction you came from. Maybe I'll let you keep your pathetic life if you do it. Ya know, on second thought, I'll take those boots too."

My horse exhales as he stomps his front leg. I give an incredulous snort as my response. If this cretin believes I will give him anything, he will soon be sorely disappointed. Another arrow is nocked, but the one holding the bow makes the wise decision not to release it. He will need it soon if they continue this misguided assault.

I realize because my tunic's hood is pulled up, concealing my face, they may not have made the connection of who they threaten; this is a mistake they will soon regret.

"He's not getting down."

"I have eyes."

"What do you want me to do?" Their murmured conversation carries over to me on the wind as if they were standing before me.

Having deemed them unimportant to warrant my full attention, I keep my gaze focused on the road I fully intend to proceed down. There is only one I wish to see, and she is not among them. I remain seated on my horse, whose agitation is increasing by the second for having his master threatened. They are welcome to attempt to take him from me; they will quickly find out that he will only accept one rider. He is an extension of me, as much a part of this task as I am.

"I said get the fuc—fuck down," the man repeats, although much of his confident conviction has slipped away.

"No." My single-worded response is all they will get.

"We will take them from you."

"You are welcome to try."

This time when the arrow flies toward me, the hand that released it is anything but steady, and it slices a narrow line across my cheek.

"What the fuck? I never told you to release another arrow," their makeshift leader hisses. I had hoped they would realize their folly and allow me on my way without further harassment, but I guess they will require a lesson in good manners.

Marcelle Valentine

My horse's breathing becomes ragged, increasing the snort he offers as a warning of the death coming their way. The world echoes around us from the impact when my booted foot slams to the ground. Sliding the hood back, I give them the first glimpse of who they have the misfortune of meeting this day. Their faces grow ashen as the realization of who they just crossed comes to light.

Reaching up, I pull my sword from the baldric. I could kill the bandits with a word; however, I am a fair being and will allow them an opportunity. If these mortals can defeat me, they can take whatever they want.... At least for a time.

Chapter Fourteen: Loss

MY SUPPLIES ARE DWINDLING. I am down to a couple jars of canned venison, some late-summer vegetables, and three apples. I will have to make the short trek into town. It's never a good idea to leave your shit unguarded since the damn gangs of assholes are moving closer this way. A farmer who lives somewhere north of my little cabin often stops to give me updates when he and his family travel into town to sell their stock.

He has always allowed me to barter with them for my needed supplies. I give them pelts from the small game I trap, and they provide me with food. It's a system that has worked well for both of us, making my trips into town a rarity. I hate leaving my stuff vulnerable and at the mercy of the assholes who travel these back roads. I don't have much and prefer to keep the meager possessions I do have.

My depleted supplies are because I have not seen the young family for several weeks now, making me fear for their safety. I know I have delayed as long as possible, leaving me with no choice but to travel into town. I hid what I had deemed most important, yet still left out valuable supplies. My hope is if someone stumbles across my place, they will take what I left lying around and forgo any intense search of my home.

Due to last night's heavy snowfall, my trek into town is slower than I like. When I finally arrive inside the gated community, I negotiate for some of the necessary supplies I require. I don't miss the quiet conversation regarding the gangs and how they have become increasingly brutal while stalking the roads around us. The young couple's stall is noticeably abandoned.

"Excuse me, can you tell me when the last time the young family who is normally at this stall was in?" I ask an older gentleman who lives within the town borders.

"I'm afraid they have not been here for a while."

"Three weeks. It's been three weeks since Claire and Ben came in. I sure hope nothing happened to them." Another woman interjects.

"Does anyone know where they live?"

"Their farm is about seven clicks northeast of here." A younger, well-built man says as he tosses the deer slung over his shoulder onto the butcher's table. I'm almost positive his name is Jake.

"Seven clicks?"

"Sorry, retired military. It's about four and a half miles northeast of here, but if you're thinking about going there, I wouldn't."

"Why not?" I ask, loading my supplies into the sled I brought with me. Jake tilts his head, giving me a questioning look. I can't tell if his expression is one of concern or irritation.

"Because it's overrun by a gang of worthless pricks."

"Well, shit."

They repeatedly try to convince me it is no longer safe for me at my little cottage and that I should move into town, but I like my little house. I am getting used to the quiet again. Yet what I find most appealing is the seclusion it offers. I'm better alone because the truth is people tend to get hurt around me.

And, of course, I am a complete idiot because I ignored all his advice. I had to wait until the next morning to make my trek to their farm. I can hear Jake's warning echoing through my head while cautiously inspecting the farmhouse Ben and Claire live in.

The house is still. I would expect to hear movement or their young child's cries, but it's eerily silent. Swallowing down my growing apprehension, I carefully open the door and sneak inside. I know if they are here, I will have a lot of explaining to do, but I'll cross that bridge when I get there.

One room after another reveals more of the same, which is a whole lot of nothing. It's like they never lived here. When I get to the last bedroom, I find the first and only signs of a struggle, and if all the blood is anything to go by, this doesn't bode well for the young family.

"You fucking idiot. Who told you to do that?" Shouts followed by the front door slamming open causes me to jump. The heavy thuds of footsteps suggest more than one man down there. I'm completely screwed because there is no way out of here other than down the stairs, and if I had to guess based on their drifting voices, I would say they are all in the same area the stairs descend to.

Realizing my chance of escaping unnoticed is rapidly dissipating, I seek an alternate route, and my only option seems to be the window. Sliding it open, I look down and realize the drop is further than I anticipated. As I prepare to drop two stories, I make the mistake of reaching out to steady myself as I climb through the window and end up knocking a lamp on the bedside table to the floor.

The argument downstairs instantly stops, replaced with the certainty of approaching footsteps. I would have preferred to lower myself out the window, but now there is not enough time; as a result, I whip my legs through and push off the ledge as the first man reaches the top of the stairs. My landing is awkward, causing pain to shoot up my leg.

"Grab that bitch," he yells while staring down at me from the window I leapt from. Pushing up to my feet, I hobble towards the woods as fast as my injured ankle allows. I barely get inside the tree line when someone tackles me from behind. My head smashes painfully against the frozen ground. Hands tangle in my hair as the one who caught me repeatedly slams my head down.

"Who fucking sent you?" His screams are feral. Coming face to face with these assholes, I understand what fate befell Ben, Claire, and their adorable little baby. I am not ashamed to admit the baby hurts more than anything else.

"I said who fuckin—" his words cut off, and the weight from his body is gone. My head is swimming in confusion from the repeated blows, and I find it increasingly difficult to maintain focus as darkness pushes in on me.

"No." I am only vaguely aware of his screams, and if I didn't know any better, I would say they were filled with agony, but who would be so stupid as to willingly come into the lion's den? Well, besides myself. This is my last thought as darkness overcomes me.

I have brief periods when I am aware. Aware of something wrapping around me, powerful arms. Arms made for one thing destruction, yet they cradle me gently. My eyes flutter, but the glaring sunlight blinds me, and before I can adjust, I slip back into the darkness.

Softness replaces the hard planes I was resting against only moments ago. Familiar fragrances invade my senses. Home. I'm in my little cottage, safe and warm in my bed. Dream? Yes, this must have been a dream, one I played the hero in but more importantly, one in which Death did not make an erotic appearance.

The sound of movement startles me awake. My head hurts, and my body aches, but I know my last memory was correct. I'm home. Pulling the covers under my chin to cocoon myself completely within them, I can only hope that the aching in my bones will be gone when I wake up.

I plan to sleep as long as is needed until the noise that originally woke me returns. Forcing my eyes open, I turn my head towards where it came from. Shock courses through me at who I find waiting.

"Hello, Apple."

*****

Son of a bitch, somehow he tracked me down and is sitting in a chair next to my bed watching me sleep.... Wait a minute, this is all very familiar. Could this be another vivid dream? I could pinch myself, but my throbbing head works just as well.

Pressing my fingers to the wound over my eye, the intensity of the searing pain confirms there is no way this is a dream. Of all the times I have wished my dreams were reality, this was not one of them. Damn it.

"Death? But how…. How did you find me?"

"I am no mere mortal." He confirms, shifting closer to me.

"Which means?" I question, pulling away.

"Your soul called out to me."

"My soul called you?" His lack of response is all the confirmation I require.

"How the hell did my soul call you?" My question comes out in a rush as I leap out of bed. An act which results in my ankle throbbing and the dizziness I felt earlier returns in full force. Both cause me to sway on my feet. Thankfully, Death reaches out to steady me before I end up on my ass.

"Why did you leave?"

"I asked you a question first."

"Do not play games with me. I asked you a question." His barked response leaves little doubt I am pushing my luck with him.

"Because I am not meant to live a happy little life among others. Now answer my question."

"I am Death, Avalon, the reaper of souls. What did you think this meant?"

"I don't fucking know," I shriek, putting my hand on my head. When he reaches out for me this time, I recoil. I need a second to process what he said. If Death can sense my soul, he will always be able to find me. I certainly didn't react this way for the reasons he thinks.

"Do I frighten you?"

"No," I answer a little too hastily.

"No?"

"I'll admit I was confused and, to be honest, shocked you reacted the way you did. But it takes much more than what you did to scare me."

"We shall remain here until you have recovered, then we will return—"

"No."

"This was not a request."

"I don't give a shit. I'm not going back."

"You should not be so keen to push me on this issue."

"What are you gonna do? Kill me. You tried that already once. It didn't work out in your favor, so let's move on, shall we?"

"You push your luck, mortal," he snarls, storming directly in front of me.

"Here's a little hint for you if you want to make a mortal comply, you should have something I want more than their freedom, and there's nothing you can take from me, asshole."

"Avalon." His growl confirms I am pushing this issue too far.

"Death." My mimicked response brings him directly into my space. I attempt to step away from him, but my bed prohibits further retreat, and I wind up on my ass in front of him, but I have no intention of staying here. First, I don't want him towering over me like he is, and second, I do not plan to have his—ahem—man parts in line with my face.

"I will only tell you this one more time. I did not make any attempt on your life. I have no need nor desire." Wait, the only time he told me this was in my dream. Right? I am fairly confident he only ever told me this during a dream. "As I said, we will remain here until you are fully healed, but once you are, we *will* return."

My guess is he only found me because the asshole who took over Ben and Claire's farm was trying to kill me.

Speaking of the assholes, I wonder what happened to them. No doubt they met the same fate Steven and Bob did. I can't say I'm sorry, especially since it seems they hurt Ben's family. I refuse to let my thought drift back to the bloody bedroom or what awful fate may have befallen them. My only hope is whatever it was, they went fast and with as little pain as possible.

"You should rest now. The sooner you heal, the faster we can be on our way."

Or the faster I can give you the slip. This thought no sooner materializes when Death spins to settle his eyes on me. He had been leaving, but now he returns to the chair to watch me. You have got to be fucking kidding me. Is he seriously going to sit there and watch me sleep? No effing way.

"You can go now."

"I think I will remain here to.... Protect you; since you seem to find so much trouble along the way."

"Protect me from what? The cold air seeping through the cracked windows, the rodents, the lumpy mattress. There is no one around for miles. Where the hell am I going to go? Not to mention my ankle sure as shit can't handle running through the ass deep snow outside."

"Still, I think it would be prudent to stand guard."

"Stand guard?" I repeat, tossing the covers back before sliding between them. "I think I can manage without you 'guarding' me."

Death's eyes follow my movements as I wiggle around, trying to find a comfortable spot. When he realized I was watching him, he immediately dropped his eyes and turned his head to look out the window. Is he embarrassed? Who knew he was capable of this emotion? This gives me an idea of how I can get his ass out of here.

"Unless you would like to join me, that is?" I say as I lift the covers and pat the spot next to me on the bed.

"What game are you playing?"

"Who said anything about a game? I merely thought it might be nice to have a warm body next to mine on such a cold winter night." I move my hand from the bed to my abdomen, sensually running my fingers back and forth over the sliver of exposed skin. His eyes follow my every movement. When he abruptly stands, I'm unsure if I made the right decision. I mean, what the hell will I do if he takes me up on my offer?

My hand stills as I wait to see what he intends to do. He remains at the edge of the bed for several seconds before storming out of the room without another word. The sound of the front door slamming shut confirms he has left the house entirely.

"Score one for Avalon," I mutter. Here's the thing though, as much as I want to pretend I did it to chase him away, there was a moment when I was unsure if I wanted him to go or stay more, so I'm glad he made the decision for me.

Death

Marcelle Valentine

This woman is infuriating. She goes against everything I have come to expect when dealing with these mortals. First, she stuck her neck out for someone she didn't know. She is taken captive to be offered to me as a tribute. Then she survives Nevil's attack. When everyone else seems to avoid danger, this mortal runs straight towards it. She has an innate ability to look past what I am and what my being here means. But what surprises me the most is how she has made me look at mortals in a new light.

I question if my father put her here as a test. She certainly seems to have the ability to escape death, escape me. One might say she has a charmed life, yet if you look at her, you can sense she has survived more than my arrival.

All this aside, she is far too dangerous for me to stay close to. She represents temptation. Besides, living as a mortal is not a part of my assignment. Stalking off the porch, my faithful companion approaches. He has been my one constant since all this began.

"Do you understand this world any better than I, old friend?" My horse's snorted exhaled response sends tendrils of misty smoke from his nostrils, twisting and swirling through the air. This clear sky and frigid temperature would ordinarily necessitate any living creature to seek refuge from the cold; however, like me, my horse is anything but normal.

He paws the ground while nodding his head. I know he is nearly as eager to be on the road as I am. He has a strong sense of duty. First and foremost to me, with our mission a close second. He will not waiver; he will not rest until I have fulfilled our creator's request. Why can't she be more like him? It would certainly make things easier for me. He nudges my arm as if to tell me I know the answer to this question.

When her soul called out to me tonight, it filled me with an overwhelming sense of dread. For the first time in my existence, I feared for a mortal's safety. Afraid I would not arrive in time. The thought of watching her cross over causes tightness to form in my chest, a sensation I have only experienced since I found her clenched in the arms of the man who thought to kill me. An insignificant mortal she risked her life to protect me from. The notion of never seeing her again is a confusing one.

"My friend, I need you to watch over her for an hour. Will you do this for me?" His snort is all the answer I need. While he would prefer to be on the road again, he will do as I asked.

Letting my wings appear, I rub his forehead and muzzle before patting his shoulders; stepping back to give myself enough room, I take flight. I know he will stay with her as long as I am gone, and I plan to use this time to clear my head.

Chapter Fifteen: Ghost

I DO NOT KNOW WHERE he disappeared to. The only thing I know for sure is he is not outside my house any longer. I stayed in bed for what felt like an eternity, expecting him to slam back through the door at any second. When it didn't happen, I got up to search for him. Moving from one window to the next, I can't say where he went, only that I am confident he left. I also understand he will not be gone for long since his horse still stands in front of the cottage.

The howling wind shakes the loose panes of glass in the window, and I admit to feeling bad for the horse. The poor thing has to be cold out there. Especially since he doesn't have anything to shelter him. Hell, he doesn't even have a blanket. I should go out there and at least try to make him more comfortable.

Or.... I could use this time to put some distance between me and the reaper.

One extremely hard gust of wind has me looking back outside at the horse. I feel like an ass, but running wins out, or actually, a hobbling limp wins out since my ankle still cannot bear my weight. I wrap my injured limb to provide it some extra support and throw on as many layers as possible, hoping they can protect me from the harsh elements I will soon endure.

Grabbing my dash bag from under my bed, I take one last look outside before quietly sliding open one of the back windows to climb through. I know what you think; what the hell is a dash bag? It's my quick escape emergency bag, something I have kept under my bed since a time in my life when I was too young to have even known what a dash bag is. I did tell you my life hasn't been easy.

Thankfully, it is snowing hard enough that I know it will cover my tracks, making it impossible for him to follow me. And now I know he can only find me when I am on the brink of death, so avoiding previously owned family farmhouses repurposed into a bandit hangout would be ideal.

I also understand many people will be confused about why I am leaving; after all, Death has done nothing to hurt me. Honestly, he's been nothing but decent to me. Demanding, overbearing, and unrelenting at times... but decent all the same. My simple answer for fleeing is I hate to be caged. He may not confine me in the traditional sense of the word, but I am also not free. After leaving the last home I lived where someone told me what to do, I swore I would never let anybody have that kind of control over me again. Even if that someone is one of the four horsemen, hell, especially when that someone is one of the harbingers of the fucking apocalypse.

Any exposed skin freezes within minutes of being out in the elements. Thankfully, when I get to a thicker part of the woods, it helps block out the worst of the winds and allows me to hear the snapping of twigs behind me. Shit. Did he come back and realize I left or were the bandits watching the house biding their time until they could exact their vengeance? I hide behind a large rock as whoever is out there moves closer.

Whoever is following me stops before they come into view. This confirms whoever it is, they are definitely here for me. There is no point in staying here. They are as aware of where I'm hiding as I am of where they are standing. Cautiously stepping around the rock I am concealed behind, I come face to face with Death's horse, but no Death.

"What are you do—doing here?" I stutter through a shiver.

"Go back," I say, knowing the last thing I want is Death thinking I stole his damn horse. When he continues to stand there, I try another tactic.

"Shoo…. Ya…. Giddy up." He doesn't seem to care. I just used every word and sound I have ever heard when watching a western. Sighing, I turn and start moving through the woods again, hoping he will tire of following me and decide to return to his rider, but neither of these things happens.

Two hours later, the horse is still following, never letting me get too far ahead yet not allowing me near it. We keep this pace until the cold has me shaking so violently my legs are having difficulty keeping me upright, and my teeth chatter so hard they may break. I think this causes the horse to take pity on me as he moves closer.

"If I did-didn't know any bet—better, I would s—say you are trying to kee—keeppp me war—warm. Is that wah—what you're do—doing.... try—trying to keep me war—warm?" I didn't really expect him to answer me. I don't have my head in the clouds living some fantasy, but until a year ago, I would have said Death was nothing more than a story. Yet here we are living a new existence because of him while I am being followed by his horse. If he's smart enough to track me, who am I to say he can't speak. Perhaps he has stage fright; maybe he is Ed's less talkative brother Fred. We all know how much the horse named Ed liked to talk on that show from the '60s; maybe Fred is the quiet one.

"Is th-that ya—your name Fah-Fah-Fred?" He does not look at me, merely matching his steps with mine.

"Nah-no? I ah—agree. Your cl-closer to a noo-noodle." The horse's snort tells me he hates his name. We walk in silence for several minutes. I admit having him here with me is somehow comforting.

"Mah-mar-marsh—mellow?" This not only gets a snort but a stomp of his foot, and I certainly don't believe he's fluffy in any sense of the word.

"S-so that's a nah—no. Oh-okay, wah-what about Go—Ghost?" This does not cause the typical snort or foot stomp. Do we have a winner?

"Ghost ha-huh? Wah—well, oh-okay." Taking a chance, I reach up and place my hand against his neck. I would expect him to be cold, but he's not. I'm not saying he's warm, yet nowhere near as icy as I had expected. We walk side by side with my hand resting on his mane for a while before a realization hits me. Even if Death cannot track me, I bet he can follow his horse. Shit! Stopping, I focus on the horse studying his face for a second.

"Why are ya—you fah—following meee? Your rah—rider will be loo—looking for ya—you."

"Unlike you, he is doing what I asked him to do." Turning, I find Death standing behind me.

"You havvvve gah—gah—got to b—be shitting mah—me."

"Even after all the years I have spent on this plane, I still do not understand this sentiment. No, Avalon, I am not *shitting* you."

"It's rhe—rhetorical, asshole."

"Then why say it?"

"Dramatic eff—effect," I retort.

"Mortals."

"Hor—horsemen." I tried to sound as indignant as he did, but mine didn't quite have the bite with my teeth chattering so violently.

"Let's go."

"Up yours." It's the first sentence I manage to say without stuttering.

"This was not a request," he snaps as he storms over to where I am standing. I try to back away, but his horse blocks my retreat. Allowing him to grasp my arm. Unfortunately, before I can stop him, he has my hands bound and is tossing me over his horse's rump like a sack of potatoes.

Is being treated like this humiliating? Hell yes.

Thankfully, no one is around to witness this shit, apart from the asshole who put me here. Not to mention, being flung over his horse's ass like this has all the blood rushing to my head; on the upside, it disguises how mortifying this is.

To say I'm pissed doesn't even begin to cover it. In fact, I use words and phrases I didn't even know existed before tonight. I may have called him a pathetic turd fucker asshat more than once. But no matter how much I yell or curse, the pace we travel is like we are out for a pleasant Sunday ride.

By the time we get back, the chill of the night air is chased away by my tirade, and evidently, Death has had enough of my bluster. Without saying a word, he pulls me off the horse and tosses me over his shoulder before storming into my rundown little cottage. Bypassing the living room, he continues straight into my bedroom, where I fully expected him to flop me down on the bed, but rather than a comfy mattress, he plops my ass down on the hard floor and then ties me to the nonfunctioning radiator.

"It seems this relic still has a use." Yanking on the ropes, he apparently wants to test them to ensure they will not break, allowing me to slip away yet again, ignoring my irate rant the entire time. Instead, he opted to collapse down on the bed. You know the same bed I asked him if he wanted to join me in only hours ago.

"You can't fucking keep me here."

"It seems not only can I, but that I am."

"I swear to god."

"Do not take my father's name in vain, and let me make this perfectly clear, Avalon. The next time you attempt something like this, I will chain you to me."

"Bullshit."

"You only need to try it to discover the truth." I know he means it. The asshole will have no issues tying me to him, which silences any further protest.

After sitting on the floor until the tingling sensation in my frozen limbs from being out of the cold subsides, and my ass starts to hurt from the hard surface, I discover the blade he overlooked in my bag. The same dagger I stole from Bob shortly after we arrived in Death's camp. I quietly push up before tiptoeing to his sleeping form with the blade poised and ready to strike. The rope he used to tie me to the radiator is just long enough to allow me to reach the bed. A mistake he will soon regret.

With my hands trembling, I seem momentarily frozen in place. My first mistake was in putting the edge against his neck. I should have plunged the blade into his black heart. My second mistake was hesitating when I took in his sleeping face.

"Go ahead," his voice makes me jump. I did not realize he was awake since his eyes remained closed and his body relaxed as if I was not preparing to kill him.

"I am."

"Then why haven't you dragged the blade across my throat, finally taking your justice? And why does your hand tremble like you are unsure of your decision?"

"I will kill you, reaper!"

"And how do you know if you take one of God's chosen, he will not strike you down?"

"A calculated risk, but one I am willing to take."

"Yet your hand remains still."

"Do you really want to see your life end so fast? Are you ready to die already?"

Faster than I can register what is happening, he grabs the hand holding the dagger against his neck and flips me onto my back on the bed. The worst part is now he is on top of me, and I know I just lost my opportunity. I can't imagine he will give me another one.

The weight of his body pressed down on mine, his thighs nested firmly between mine. If someone walked in right now, they might mistake our position for that of lovers. Except for my hand holding the dagger, now pressed to my throat. He stares down at me; something flickers in his eyes before he calmly asks, "I could ask you the same."

"For as long as I can remember."

Death

I have heard mortals proclaim they are ready to die, but something in her eyes informs me her statement is more than mere words said in the heat of the moment; she truly does not care if she lives to see another day. To her, living or dying seems to be one and the same.

Which begs the question.... What happened to her before I came here?

I have already told you she has numerous scars covering her back, and if I'm not mistaken, the one time she stood before me undressed, I believe I saw what appeared to be the letter C carved on her abdomen.

Pushing off her, I slide the blade into the back of my pants. She is so adamant about not returning with me; perhaps it is only fair to ask her why.

"Apple," her eyes narrow before she can utter the heated rebuke I am certain she is preparing to unleash; I raise my hands and correct, "Avalon, I have no desire to fight with you."

"Then maybe you should have left me where you found me," she huffs as she hastily readjusts on the bed, so her back is now pressed against the wall with her knees pulled up to her chest.

"You would not have survived the night."

"I'm stronger than you think."

"Will you tell me why you do not wish to return with me?"

"I already have."

"Why do you believe you are not meant to be happy?"

"Who the hell said I'm not happy?" Sometimes speaking with her is akin to chasing shadows. She often answers a question with a question without ever actually answering any of them.

"You said you were not meant to live a happy little life."

"Jesus, do you remember every damn thing someone says?"

"It is one of my abilities, yes."

"Well, it's a shitty one. You should see if you can get a refund for it. Maybe trade it in on wings that work."

"What do you mean?"

"Well, what the hell is the point of having wings if you can't fly?"

"I can fly."

"Wait the hell a minute, you mean to tell me we could have flown back here, and instead, you opted to toss me on the back of your horse like a sack of shit before meandering our way back to this shitty little cabin?"

"I felt the ride would do you good."

"You are such an asshole."

"Among other things."

"I thought there were supposed to be four of you. What did the other three get sick of your sparkling personality too?"

A low guttural growl escapes as I try to contain the rage she so easily evokes in me. "Tread carefully, human, or you may find there are worse things than my sparkling personality."

"Did I strike a nerve?"

"I am trying to understand—"

"I bet War is a ton of fun, isn't he? Personality for miles. He's the horseman everyone wants to be around. Can we visit him?"

"My brothers still sleep. Until the time the lamb is directed to break the seal that will release them, they will continue slumbering, and you, little Apple, should not be so keen on meeting them."

Chapter Sixteen: Time To Go

$\mathcal{D}$EATH STORMING OUT AFTER telling me about the other horseman is a sure sign I pushed things too far, and the worst part is he really didn't deserve my contemptuous attitude all night. Yes, I left. Yes, he came to find me. Yes, he wanted me to return, but when he asked why I didn't want to go back with him, instead of explaining why I was better off on my own, I acted like a damn child.

Way to go, Avalon. Real goddamn mature.

Over the next week, while my ankle continued to heal, Death and I hardly spoke to one another. I should have apologized straight away, but with each passing day, it has become more difficult until the entire situation has made talking awkward and uncomfortable. You can never understand what it is like to live in the same space as another person and never say a single word to them. In many ways, it is warmer outside than it is within the walls of this cottage, and it's damn near freezing outside. Here's hoping what I am preparing to do will go a long way to set things straight between us again, or at the very least, thaw the freeze.

"Thanatos?" I figured calling him by his other name is as good a place to start with this apology as any, but the only response I receive is his patented, indifferent stare.

"Okay, I deserve that," I murmur, followed by a forced exhale. For a moment, I contemplate scrapping the whole damn idea. He may refuse to accept anything from me. Hell, after the way I behaved, can I really blame him? Before my nerves make me chicken out, I let my words come out in a rush as I shove the wrapped gift out towards him. "I got you something."

His eyes drop from my face to my outstretched hand. They linger there before gliding back up to meet mine again, but he makes no move to accept or reject the gift.

"I'm sorry for how I acted before, particularly what I said. It was uncalled for. Will you please accept this?"

"Why?"

"Because when I saw it, I thought about you. Because I'm willing to bet no one has ever given you something without hoping for something in return and because it's Christmas."

"Christmas? You realize I do not celebrate this day as many mortals do."

"I know. Regardless...." I take a step toward him, laying the gift in his hand. "I want you to have it."

His eyes focus on the gift while I impatiently wait for him to open it. I don't think I have previously witnessed someone with the restraint he shows, allowing an unopened gift to remain for so long. He sighs before tearing open the only thing I could find to wrap the box in, an old faded piece of newspaper. When he finally opens it, he stares at what he discovers for several moments, while I am beginning to believe this whole thing was a terrible idea.

"It's a...."

"Compass." Why I feel the need to confirm what he can obviously see is beyond me.

"I am aware. What I do not understand is why you would believe I need it."

"In case you lose your way," I reach out to turn the compass over so he can see the engraving which reads: *To always find your way home.* When he stares at me without responding, I briefly contemplate walking away to bury my head in the sand, or I guess it would actually be snow, but I elect to push on instead.

"I get the distinct feeling you would prefer to be doing anything other than what they have asked you to do. I just wanted to remind you not to lose yourself along the way."

After several tense seconds of his steely gaze assessing me, he finally looks down at the gift I gave him, his thumb running over the words engraved on the back.

Did I lie to him about thinking of him when I saw it? Not really. I did think of him, but it was more like, 'oh, maybe I can use this to stay one step ahead of him' kind of thought. I didn't lie about my belief that he would rather not be here. Far too often, I catch a glimpse of him looking at the sky with so much sadness in those beautiful eyes; it's heartbreaking. So, for this reason, I believe the compass was always meant for him.

And yeah, I'll chastise myself later for associating any part of him with the word beauty. Even if it is true. I can't allow myself to feel this way about him.

"I don't have anything to give to you."

"I didn't give it to you hoping for anything in return." Death closes his hand around the compass. His abrupt change from sitting to standing has me stepping away from him.

"We are leaving tomorrow," he advises walking towards the door; right before exiting, he hesitates, "Thank you for the gift."

"You're—" he doesn't wait to hear the rest, "welcome." I finish saying to the empty room.

"That went swell," I mutter sarcastically.

Death

Yet again, she confounds me. In what reality does the one being judged remind the being who is deciding your fate not to lose themselves. Isn't this precisely what most mortals want for me... to lose my way? I realize she is different from most souls. The truth is, she is unlike many of the beings from my own realm. Unique and rare would best describe her.

Looking at the compass, I flip it repeatedly. Watching as the needle tries to right itself with every rotation. How astute Avalon must be to realize I am conflicted. I wonder if she understands she is the reason for my turmoil?

Marcelle Valentine

My original plan was to remain here at this habitat until the weather got warmer, but after the week we have had, I think it may be prudent to be on our way. It will take weeks of travel to return to the settlement. My initial plan was to leave this morning when the weather was clear, yet after the kindness she showed, how can I demand this of her today?

My horse nudging my arm pulls my attention.

"Hello, my old friend. Maybe you can explain her actions to me?"

He whinnies, bobbing his head before he paws at the ground.

"I suppose she is as much of an enigma to you as she is to me."

Running my thumb over the smooth surface of the compass, I wish I had something to give her in turn.

"Perhaps we may discover one of those books she likes so much during our return trip." His snort confirms what I already know: she deserves so much more than a book found on the side of the road.

"I'm open to suggestions since you believe you can do better."

I stay outside, watching the clouds skim across the bright blue sky. It's the first time in days the sky is not gray and snow is not falling. I remain beside my horse, enjoying this day's splendor until the door to her dwelling, or as she calls it, her cottage opens.

"I was hoping we could talk," Avalon says as she comes to stand next to me. Her arms are hugged around her chest, trying to hold the cold at bay. She is not like me since winter's chill does not affect me as it does with her kind, resulting in her shivering within seconds. Turning, I wait for her to say whatever it is she is risking hypothermia for.

"I have a proposition for you?"

"You do? What would it be?"

"I will willingly go with you, but I have a request."

"Which is?"

"I ask that we do not return to your horde, at least not right away."

"Why not?"

"Let me show you what humanity is really about. You have only ever seen the worst of it. Let me demonstrate what we can do if given the opportunity."

"And if I agree, what will happen if you cannot deliver on your promise?"

"I'll go back to the horde, and you have my word I won't run again." She turns to face me, waiting to see whether I will accept her offer. I would be within my right to deny this, yet what she offers does align with my goal.

"What do you say, Thanatos? Do we have a deal?"

"We leave tomorrow," her shoulders slump, believing I have rejected her offer until I continue. "Where will we be heading?"

Her beaming smile lights up her entire face. "Southeast."

"You should go inside."

"Actually, my lesson starts now."

"Meaning?"

"I need you to come in too," she replies softly, taking my hand to bring me back inside. I allow her to lead me, and when we enter, I discover a small feast spread across the table.

"What's this?"

"Christmas dinner."

"You realize I do not require any of this to sustain myself?"

"But you can eat?"

"Am I physically capable of such trivialities? Yes. It is simply not a necessity."

"Great, this is about enjoying the day while eating ridiculous amounts of food, not about necessity."

"This is what you consider a ridiculous amount of food?"

"Hey, I improvised," she grins at me before taking her seat. "I used the rest of the supplies I had in the house."

"You didn't think it prudent to retain some of these for our travels. While I do not require food, if I am not mistaken you still do."

"I do," she mumbles around the bite of the fruit she had shoved in her mouth. "I'll worry about that tomorrow. Today is about living in the moment."

We spent the rest of the day sampling the different dishes she prepared, and to my great surprise, I enjoyed every second of it. Even if most of the food was inedible, the company was.... Pleasant. A welcome change of pace from our constant bickering. After finishing, she packed her clothes and the few things she deemed too valuable to leave behind. The books I have often seen her reading for one. She will uphold her promise to go with me willingly, and I will fulfill mine by allowing her to show me what this world has to offer.

Avalon

Okay, somehow, I managed to convince one of the riders of the apocalypse to give me a chance to change his outlook on us. Now I just have to figure out how to do it. Here's hoping I can come up with something fast. Until then, I'll have to improvise. The problem with this approach is finding something noteworthy enough to sway an unbending force.

Last night I packed as much as I could into my little bag before sleeping in a warm bed for what may be the last time, at least for a while. This morning I filled my belly with the leftovers from Christmas dinner last night, and now I am pulling on my heavy parka, preparing to hit the road with my two new travel companions, Death and his horse.

Walking outside, I take one last look at my little cottage. The day is crystal clear and cold as hell; that is if hell is cold. Maybe I could ask Death. If anyone can answer this, I'm willing to bet he can.

By midmorning, we are on the road, and as requested, Death is heading Southeast. Why did I pick this direction? Simple. I want to go south since it's warmer and east because if I fail in this endeavor and the world truly ends, I want to stand on the beach one more time. Let the water splash against me as the sand covers my feet. I wanna listen to the waves crashing against the shore, smell the salt in the air and listen to the gulls crying as they glide on the currents.

Is this selfish? Yes. Would every other human do the same if they truly knew what he was capable of? Hell yes.

I walk next to his horse for close to an hour. Death offered to let me ride also, but I didn't think it was fair for the horse to be forced to carry two riders. Our pace may be slower than he would like, but he stopped arguing with me shortly after we left the cottage.

My choices for what roads we traveled were deliberate since I knew we would come across fewer towns this way. Fewer towns mean scarce people and less possibilities for dumbass humans to fuck up my plan by doing the stupid shit we tend to do when we don't understand something. You know, the kind of ignorant shit that would give him a reason to eradicate them. I don't have to tell you how nervous I was when the first community came into view.

Hoping to further conceal his identity, he pulls the hood of his tunic up to hide his face. I don't know how many people out there know what he looks like, but there's no point in taking any chances.

"So, first opportunity, Avalon, what would you like to show me," Death says, climbing down from his horse.

Shit, does he expect me to just pull these random acts of kindness out of my ass? Thankfully, the first thing I see is a group of kids playing together. Some chase others through the snow, some make snowmen or snow angels, while others....

"What are they doing?"

"Playing."

"Why?"

"Because it's fun."

"This is considered fun?"

He watches as several of the youngest among the group exhale their breath, giggling as they watch the vapor appear. The mist carried from their warm breath into the cold air produces a vapor resembling smoke.

"Why do they do this?"

"It's something they don't understand or can explain at their young age."

"Mortals have many phenomena; this is not one of them."

"Not for an adult, but for a child. It's magical... and seeing the magic through their eyes is beautiful."

I quietly slip away, letting him watch the children so he can form his own opinion as I grab a few supplies, and then we're back on the road. Thank God we leave the place the same way we found it.

I'm not too bullheaded to admit how tired my legs are from the constant walking. I do not miss the exasperated huff Death lets out when I stumble. Like I can help the fact that my legs are tired or that I'm freezing my ass off. As I shake my stiff legs, trying to loosen them up, he takes me by surprise when he leans over to scoop me up and deposit me behind him on the horse. The relief of being off my feet is instant, but I hate making the horse work this hard. Maybe it will not be too hard on his horse if I ride for a bit and then get back down.

"Tell me something you like about being mortal."

"What? You want me to narrow my life down to one thing?"

"Isn't that precisely what this excursion is about? Convincing me of humanity's worth."

"Yeah, but—"

"If you cannot think of one thing, tell me how you plan on proving this."

"Okay. One thing." Racking my brain for anything that would satisfy his inquiry, I'm irritated when I can't think of anything to say; there are far too few things I like about my life. Leaving me with few options other than telling him something general. Maybe not so much of what I find appealing but what most people do.

"People like—"

Marcelle Valentine

"I did not ask about all mortals; I asked specifically about you." He says, looking at me over his shoulder.

"Ahhh — well — I guess," I stumble, not knowing what to say now. When Death shakes his head and turns to face the road again, I blurt, "Blueberry."

"Blueberry. I understand this may be a foreign concept, but humans cannot claim blueberries as something to prove their worth; this was not a human accomplishment. You are not off to an encouraging start, Avalon."

"Yeah, well, you didn't let me finish."

"Pardon me. By all means, please proceed with how blueberries may yet convince me of the value humanity has to offer."

"First, I said blueberry, not blueberries." Death turns on his horse to look at me. His expression conveys how idiotic he believes I may be.

"You do realize these are one and the same."

"Do you want to hear this or not?"

He rolls his eyes, further irritating me, so I snap, "Dial back the skepticism for a second."

Death lifts his hand, indicating I should proceed, and I swear I see the hint of a grin before he turns away, "Okay, Apple, I should like to hear how you rationalize they are not the same since they are."

"No, they are not. Blueberries would be the fruit; blueberry is the singular act of kindness my elderly neighbor could offer when I was a little girl."

He gives me a side-eyed glance while saying, "Proceed."

"When I was between the ages of four and six, my parents moved us to a dilapidated shithole in the heart of drug country. It was there I met Ms. Deniker. She was this sweet old lady who had resided there long before the area fell to

198

gangs and drugs. When she realized my parents didn't.... that I didn't have much to eat, she started leaving a homemade blueberry muffin outside her door every morning. At first, I thought I was stealing it, but one morning when I crept out of the apartment to grab the muffin, she opened the door and asked if I would like to eat my breakfast with her instead of alone in my apartment. After this, I went there every morning. For a year and a half, I spent almost every morning with her until one day, the muffin wasn't there, and she didn't come to answer the door when I knocked. I waited in the hallway outside her apartment all day, but she never came; the truth is she never would again. Some good-for-nothing, worthless asshole decided he deserved her social security more than she did. He broke into her house the night before and stabbed her for four hundred dollars. I never forgot about Ms. Deniker or the blueberry muffins. So you see, Death, this little old lady who barely had enough to feed herself, made sure the scrawny little girl next door had something to eat even if it meant she went without."

His eyes meet mine, holding my gaze until I can no longer stand the compassion I see swirling within them, forcing me to look away. I guess my one thing must have been enough because he doesn't say anything else. I didn't have the heart to confess the good-for-nothing, worthless son-of-a-bitch just so happened to be my father. His way of repaying the kindness she showed his little girl. After this, we ride in silence, with him thinking about whatever a horseman of the apocalypse thinks about and me trying to remember Ms. Deniker's kind face. And this is how it goes until the cold seeps in, and I cannot stop the trembling of my legs.

"Why do you keep moving like that?"

"Like wh—what?"

"Are you cold?"

"I'll be oh—okay." Death looks over his shoulder. Before I can protest any further, he twists, grabs me, and plops me on the horse in front of him. If this isn't enough, he pulls me back against him to wrap me inside his coat. The very coat he is still wearing. Enveloping me in the most wonderful warmth.

"You should have said something, Apple."

"I didn't think it would matter." He exhales with more force than necessary before he clicks his tongue to speed Ghost up. Clearly, I pissed him off. After riding for several minutes in silence, I take a chance to ask a question I have long wondered about. Here's hoping he will answer me.

"You've called me Apple for a long time. Why?"

"It is fitting."

"How?" This question goes unanswered. Rather than let the awkward silence persist, I push the issue.

"So it's something you call everyone." This is not a question as much as a declaration to myself.

"No."

"No?"

"No, it is fitting for your name."

"Bullshit, you called me Apple long before you knew my name."

"Have I?"

"I suppose I might as well tell you we met long before they brought me to you as an...."

"Offering?"

"I was trying to think of something less degrading but okay before they handed me over to you as an offering; you called me this, and you didn't know my name."

"Truly?"

"It was during our first interaction, not after I joined your horde, so I think you are mistaken."

"Correct, and this was when you told me."

"No, I think I would remember doing something like that."

"Apparently, my memory is better than yours, Apple."

"I beg to differ. I know you don't remember this, but you've called me Apple since we first met. It was when we were up on the roof of my apartment building. So you didn't associate it with my name because I hadn't told you it was Avalon yet."

"I heard you say it."

"When?"

"When you sheltered me."

"Sheltered you?" What the hell. Does he know I rescued him?

"From the one you called John. You said your name while I was recovering." Son of a bitch.

"You remember me?"

"Of course I do."

"Why the hell didn't you say anything?"

"You did not ask."

"I didn't…. ask? I didn't think I had to. When you remember someone, it's customary to acknowledge them or… something. It's common courtesy, Death."

"I shall keep that in mind if this should occur in the future."

"Oh, Jesus, give me strength," I mutter, rubbing my head, trying to stem off the headache beginning.

"As I stated, I do not call all mortals Apple. Is that what you thought?"

"I have no damn idea," I snap, looking at him over my shoulder.

"I can assure you I do not."

"Okay, we'll come back to the remembering me this whole time without acknowledging it thing later, but for conversation's sake, explain why I would have said my name?"

"I cannot explain why."

"Let's put your photographic memory to work. What the hell did I say?" I ask as I run through the course of that night and cannot come up with a single instance of me saying my name.

"Would you like the first time or subsequent admissions?"

"I'm talking about the first day we met."

"As am I."

"Let's go with the first one, smartass."

"I quote, 'This is what you get for sticking your nose where it doesn't belong, Avalon. Next time, I'll just leave you out there to die at the hands of John and his band of misfits,' does this help with your memories?" Hearing him repeat what I said, my commentary comes back to me in a rush. Oh. Fuck. Did I say anything else? Shit, shit-shit, shit.

"Why the look of horror, Avalon?" He asks with a cocky grin. Cheeky fucking bastard knows why I am damn near shitting my pants. I want to scream, *Oh, I don't know, maybe because I can't remember if I voiced how attractive I thought you were or merely thought about it.* No, this is definitely something I should keep to myself. No point in saying something he may not be aware of, so I simply roll my eyes with a shake of my head. I swear I can feel the slight movement of his chest against my back.

Great, now he's laughing at me.

Chapter Seventeen: Scars

WE CONTINUED TRAVELING, WITH Avalon doing her best to prove their worth, hoping I would return to my father and convince him not to begin their judgment. Avalon has more than proven her worth; astonishing as this may be, she has shown me they are not all like the fools I encountered when I first arrived.

If I change my mind about humanity and somehow convince my father to show mercy, I wonder if any of them will ever know we only spared them because of her, because of Avalon.

The compass she gifted to me is something I have grown very fond of. I keep it in my pocket and find my fingers skimming over it anytime I long for my old life. The action brings me comfort and back to what I am here for. But mostly, it brings me back to her.

We have traveled most of the day without seeing another soul along the road. As the day progresses, I feel her begin to relax behind me. I realize she is often on edge, worried about what will happen if we cross paths with other travelers. Only a handful of times did I have to end the lives of the being we came into contact with.

They did not deserve her mercy before or sadness after; she could not sense their intentions. I could. Many only wanted to steal our belongings, but the worst of them planned to rob us, kill me and take her so they could pass her around among them until she was nothing more than the shell of the woman she is today. This is something I will never allow.

As the day progresses to evening, the wind shifts, and I realize a late winter storm will soon be upon us. Spurring my horse, I need to find a place to shelter us for the night. The further we travel, I chastise myself for not stopping sooner, and as the bite of the frigid air brings heavy snow with it, I worry I may not find a place in time to keep her from freezing. Unfortunately, there is only so much my body heat can do to help warm her. She needs to be protected from the elements. Indoors. Out of this blustery wind and driving snow.

Avalon's head pressed against my back, paired with her shaking frame, confirms she is not faring well.

Leaning forward, I give my horse instructions. "Find me something, my old friend. And make haste."

Praying I may yet offer her some insulation from the storm. I twist on my horse, giving up the reins, knowing my companion will do precisely what I have asked of him. This being to find me something to get her out of the storm.

"Wh—what are you do—doing?"

"Keeping you from freezing to death," I reply. Placing her legs over mine lets me pull her closer, which allows me to wrap my coat around her, further blocking the unforgiving, frigid winds. I have never experienced the sensation of being cold, nor did I realize a body could shake as violently as hers is right now. I admit this is unsettling, but it is not until the shaking ends I actually fear for her.

Fifteen minutes later, my horse stops. His snorts confirm he has found something. Looking over my shoulder, I discover a run-down cabin, but the windows appear mostly intact.

Sliding off, I pull her into my arms. She is so cold I do not risk setting her down for fear her legs will give out, electing to carry her inside. The cabin only has one area, but the fireplace is what my eyes focus on. This is what she needs. Placing her on the only piece of furniture not in shambles, a bed in the corner of the room. I get my first glimpse of her. I am astonished at what I found. Her skin is pale white, and her lips are deep blue. Her unmoving body has me rushing to start a fire.

Thirty minutes later, the cabin has warmed up significantly, and Avalon is finally awake. I know I will have to leave her here alone so that I can gather additional wood. The cabin only held enough supplies to start the fire, but this will soon burn out, permitting the coldness to seep back in.

Handing the cup of warm broth to her, I say, "I need to gather more wood. Will you be okay while I do this?"

"It's too cold. You shouldn't go out there."

"Apple, the cold does not affect me; I'll be fine. On the other hand, you will not, and as soon as this fire burns out, the temperature in the cabin will plummet. I need to gather wood to ensure this does not happen."

"I'm sorry to be such a burden."

"You do not have anything to apologize for. You did not cause the storm."

"Maybe you should have a talk with your dad. You know, tell him to give us a break, and that's about enough of this damn cold shit," she says with a slight grin.

"I'll be sure to mention it to him," I confirm as I stoke the flames once more. "Stay under the blanket. I will be back before this goes out."

"Yes, sir."

"Sir. I like it. Perhaps we should keep this moniker," I tell her as I attempt to keep a straight face.

"Yeah, just so you know, not going to happen, big guy."

*****

I could not have been gone any longer than fifteen minutes, but upon my return, I noticed my horse had left his post. The final instruction I delivered before I left was to watch over her. The fact that he's not here means something went wrong. Dropping the wood, I race toward the cabin noticing the multiple footprints in the snow.

"Avalon." Nothing. No response.

"Horse! Where are you?" I yell, but the howling winds prevent my shouts from carrying far. If Horse could hear me, I know he would find a way to respond. I am preparing to take flight when a noise from the cabin garners my full attention.

Busting through the door, I am shocked at what I find. A red-nosed Avalon is patting the horse I had left to guard her.

"Avalon?"

"What?" she looks up, seeing my eyes focused on the mammoth horse currently taking up half the room. "Now, before you go and get all pissy, I brought Ghost in because it's too cold to leave him out there."

"Ghost?"

"His name."

"You named my horse?"

"Well, someone needed to. How would you like it if people walked around calling you man all the time?"

"It would not matter because this is not what I am. Besides, I would like to point out that most people refer to me similarly."

"Similar to what?"

"My creation."

"Most people call you Death."

"And what precisely am I, Avalon?"

"Okay, point made. Damn, do I hate it when you get all logical and shit. Still, I hated calling him 'horse' all the time. So yes, I brought Ghost inside because it was too cold outside for any creature, even a horse belonging to Death."

"Apple, he is like me, unaffected by the elements."

"Well, the snow covering his mane and back would say otherwise."

After realizing I would not win this argument with her, I relented and agreed to allow my horse to remain inside with us. Returning to my discarded stack of wood, I gather the necessary supplies hoping it will be enough to last the night since it appears this storm will not be relenting anytime soon. To my utter amazement, my horse lies in the corner after Avalon returns to bed.

When I return to the cabin, I discover Avalon on the bed with the only blanket I found in the place, a tattered little scrap of cloth definitely not thick enough to keep her warm.

Avalon shuffles from the bed to where I am squatted, stoking the fire to keep it burning hot. We remain there quietly, sitting next to one another, watching the flames dancing wildly from the heavy winds outside until her eyes grow heavy. She seems reluctant to leave my side, so I pick her up and carry her over to the bed.

"Thank you," she says in a hushed tone.

"Are you okay?"

"Just cold still. The fire helps, but.... Actually, never mind, I'll be fine." Seeing her lying there shivering, I do the only thing one could do in this situation. I pull my coat off and tell her to move over before lying next to her. When she continues to shiver, I reach behind me, grasping the collar of my shirt to pull it over my head.

"What are you doing?" Avalon's tone belies her normal confident demeanor as concern weighs heavily in her voice.

"I understand this can help during times like this." I pause for a few seconds, wondering if I have made a mistake. Avalon reaches down to stop me as I begin to put it back on. She shocks me when she wiggles out of her pants. I try not to follow her movements, but I fail miserably. Inching closer, she does not stop until her head rests on my chest and her leg is draped over mine.

"Are you comfortable?"

"You're warm. I'm cold. That's all this is, so don't ruin it."

"Ruin what? I am not the one with my body slung over yours," I tease.

"Death."

"Yes, Apple."

"Be quiet."

Avalon

For the first time since the storm began, I'm warm. I'm comfortable, and sleep pulls me under almost immediately. My last recollection was of Death cradling me in his arms. The warm, safe embrace I have only ever felt around him.

Sometime in the middle of the night, a noise stirs me awake. Still held securely within his arms, I can't help the sense of contentment washing over me. This feels…. Right. Not many things in my life have elicited this type of reaction. But here. Now. I'm happy. Significantly more now since there was an actual bed in this cabin. Pressed against his body gives me more than enough heat to keep me cozy, which is a damn good thing since the fire is little more than embers.

Unsure of what originally woke me, the only sounds are coming from the rattling windowpanes and the soft snores of Death's horse. Who knew a horse could snore?

Is Thanatos sleeping? Does a rider of the apocalypse have to rest? Damn, you would think I would know this after all this time I've spent with him. I could look to see if he's sleeping, but I'm almost afraid to check. What if he doesn't and he catches me staring at him? Why does this man have to twist me up like this? After debating it for far too long, I realize he hasn't moved since I woke up, and if you consider the steady rise and fall of his chest, I would have to go with; yes, he sleeps.

My right hand still rests on the same spot I placed it on Thanatos's chest when I snuggled up against him earlier, is now itching to explore more. And I am not ashamed to admit it. I want to investigate every ridge and contour of a shirtless Death. His tone.... Muscled.... Firm chest, and as many times as I have imagined this, the fantasy did not do the reality justice.

Giving into my base desire, I allow my fingers to follow the lines of his chest down to his equally impressive abs. My hand only stills when I feel him tense under my touch.

I could pretend to be asleep or that my hand took on a mind of its own. Yeah, that's believable, Avalon. I can imagine it now. *No, really, Death, I was sound asleep. I did not know my hand was roaming down towards the promised land.* Yep, this is about as unbelievable as the horseman being nothing more than a fable.

Why the hell does he have to make me so damn nervous? The more important question I should be asking myself is, why the hell did I think doing this was a good idea in the first place? Swallowing down the fear and embarrassment within me, I take a chance to look up at Death, praying his movement was involuntary. I mean, he may still be asleep. Right?

Not a chance in hell since what I find is his gaze focused on me. I should feel foolish since I was the one who made the big stink that this was solely to help me stay warm, yet at the first opportunity, I'm the one taking things so far beyond the line of acceptable behavior I can't see it anymore.

His mesmerizing blue eyes burn bright in the dim room and beckon me to move closer. This is dangerous, and for the first time since he laid next to me, I understand I should have never taken my pants off. This is where the bad idea morphs into monumentally idiotic. What the hell was I thinking? I need distance. Freezing cold, squash this scorching heat building within me, distance before I do something I regret....

Apparently, my body either didn't get the memo or didn't agree with what my brain was screaming. At any rate, it definitely got the signals crossed since my lips have taken on a mind of their own and are now skimming against his.

"Apple?"

"Shhh." I know this is a bad idea, but for once in my life, I don't want to think. I want to live in this moment with the man who cared enough to tend to me all night.

The rush of excitement I experience when his hand comes to the side of my face is undeniable. Almost as much as when he rolls me onto my back. Those piercing blue eyes search my face. I wonder if he's judging me right now, trying to figure out if I'm worthy. If this is what he is doing, the short answer is probably not. No, not probably, definitely not.

I don't take my first breath until he lowers his lips to meet mine. The kiss starts soft, sweet, and sensual until his tongue sweeps over my lips; this singular act is enough to make me come unglued. Damn, but if his kiss isn't sinful. Perfectly. Undeniably. Deliciously wicked in all the best ways. I swear if this is another vivid fantasy, I will lose my mind because I can't live in a dream forever.

When he ends the kiss, he pulls me into his arms, holding me like he's afraid this isn't real. His lips press softly against my forehead. Before I can protest or try to take things further, he whispers, "Rest, Apple."

And darkness closes in around me.

*****

Light filtering through the dirty window brings me out of the haze from sleep. The first thought I am aware of is being alone in bed. Was it all a dream? Death in bed with me? Him shirtless? The kiss? Peeling my eyes open, I find the room empty. Not even Ghost is in the cabin any longer. So maybe none of it happened. It's probably best if it didn't because I'm not sure how any of this would work if it did. But that kiss, damn, even just the memory of it, sends heat pooling deep in my core. Now I don't know if I am more hopeful it was a dream or not. Throwing the cover aside, I get the first clue that maybe it wasn't all a figment of my imagination when I discover I'm not wearing pants.

Standing, I stretch my arms over my head; perhaps the better option would have been for me to put my damn pants back on because when Death enters the door, I am momentarily stunned. His eyes shift over my half-naked form. Unlike the last time I stood before him, this time my cheeks heat, burning bright from the red seeping into them. Because last time I had not just spent the night in his arms, nor were his eyes filled with the desperate desire I find in them now.

The desire melts away when his focus settles on the long-jagged lines running up my inner thighs from injuries inflicted on me by Calvin.

These are the only scars I feel ashamed of; the ones I know he put there as a reminder I belonged to him and always will. Of all the damage inflicted by his hand, these are the ones that make me feel weak and are a constant reminder of the child who could not protect herself from the monster who did not just stalk me in the dark. Where the rest of the scars I wear as a badge of honor, battle wounds to prove they could not break me, the scars there prove he came damn close.

Horror, shame, and humiliation now replace the shyness from our interaction last night as I grab my pants and pull them on. His booming voice startles me while I attempt to cover what I have never shown anyone before.

"Who did this to you?" Death demands as he stalks to where I am standing.

"Ghosts," I whisper.

"Do not push me on this, Avalon."

"What difference does it make?"

"Avalon," his growl echoes off the walls around us. Terrified he may yet drag this out of me, I do the one thing I do best, I deflect.

"Why does it even matter? After all, I am merely your prisoner. Besides, I don't know why you're bothered by them. You don't seem bothered by the ones you put on me. Don't tell me; let me guess: one was merely an abuse while the other was God's divine will."

"As I have already told you, I did not inflict those wounds on you, nor did I order it."

"And as I already said.... They did it in your name. So fucking drop it, Death," I snap before I storm out of the cabin. I am no sooner out the door when I feel his hand on my shoulder. Shaking it off, I am desperate to be anywhere but here. Anywhere he cannot look at me as he did in that cabin.

His reaction is to pick me up and launch us into the air when I continue struggling to break his grip on me. I don't think I need to tell you flying through the sky with nothing between me and falling to my death is.... Well, Death, the being, not the state of being, is mind-blowing.

Our progressions stop, and now I cannot say if I am more afraid of the flying part or the hovering. How long can Death's wings continue at the pace they beat to keep us here? After countless nerve-racking seconds, he brings his gaze back to mine.

"I could never hurt you, Avalon."

"Isn't that precisely why your father sent you here? What he created you to do?" The quiver in my response is not something I am accustomed to.

"Never." His quiet response is more a plea than a statement. He needs me to believe he would not and did not condone what Nevil, Steven, and Bob did. The thing is.... I already know. What I said was out of line and spoken more out of fear of him learning who this human before him truly is. A mortal woman with more than skeletons in her closet; there is a whole horde of monsters in that damn thing just waiting to pull me under.

"I'm sorry you didn't deserve what I said. I know you didn't have anything to do with what Nevil and his gang did to me."

"What happened to you? Tell me how you got the scars you try so hard to hide from the world."

"I wouldn't be hiding them if I told you, now would I?" I don't think Thanatos liked my answer; nevertheless, it's the best I can give him. I can deal with pain. Mountains of it have been heaped on me over most of my life. It's the shame of what he did that I can't handle. The thought of telling anyone, especially Thanatos, about my past.... About the things he did to me may very well be the thing that finally breaks me. While I am ashamed of the scars on my legs, the ones you can't see hurt the most.

"I promise you I'm okay," I pray he doesn't recognize the lie I told.

"And I promise you one way or another I will find out what happened to you and when I do.... I will make them all pay."

Chapter Eighteen: Lessons Learned

Avalon Early Spring 2024

I AM HAPPY TO have moved far enough south that the cold is no longer an issue. Only three times since the night in the cabin has Thanatos destroyed a community we stumbled upon, and most of the time, they attacked first. The last one was the hardest because, within the walls, I could hear the cries of children. I begged them not to fire on us, and when they refused to listen, I begged him not to retaliate, but when an arrow struck me, burying deep within my left shoulder, nothing I said could halt the inevitable.

The city fell in seconds. Reduced to rubble as I slumped against him. His screams of rage were the last sound I heard.

By the time I woke, dust covered my clothes while debris from the city, now in shambles, littered the world around me. I cried for only the second time since my mom coldly told me

Ms. Deniker had died. I reserve my tears for others, not me. Thanatos held me the entire time; never once did he tell me they didn't deserve them.

We may not have made it to the ocean, but sitting next to this lake is almost as nice. With my knees pulled up to my chest and arms wrapped around my legs, I rest my head against them as I think about how my life has changed since that fateful night he came into it.

Sitting at the water's edge, the only sounds around me are the chirping of the crickets, the clicking of the bats, and the lone croak of the bullfrog. After Thanatos stripped us of all the interruptions our advanced technologies brought, it left this.... The beauty and splendor most of us had forgotten about. Such a shame it took the world coming to an end for humanity to find it again. We have lost so much time.

"What are you doing, Apple?"

"Are you ever going to tell me why you call me that?"

"An answer for an answer."

Turning my head to look up at him, I wait for him to elaborate. The longer he stands looking over the water, I know he is waiting for me to ask. Sighing, I do just that. "What answer do you want from me?"

Tilting his head, he brings his full attention to me. "Will you tell me about the scars?"

Dropping my gaze back down to the water, I listen as it laps gently against the bank, and the lone frog calls out for his mate. I know as much as he wants me to give him this, I can't. I can never give him this confession. Never. Not to him because if I do it very well may not only break me; it may shatter me. I can't let him peek behind the wall I built to protect myself, nor hope he can lift me out of the hell my life has been.

Marcelle Valentine

Fighting to hold tears at bay. Tears I have never let fall. Not for the little girl I was. Not for the cynical woman I became because of Calvin. Not even for Janie, the little girl with the infectious smile.

Death sits next to me, but thankfully he allows the silence to prevail. We stay like this, me desperately trying to hold my nightmares at bay while Death deals with his own demons. After longer than I would have believed possible, I am the one to break the silence.

"I guess I couldn't deliver on my promise to show you all the good that humanity has to offer. We should return to your horde."

"Soon."

"Soon?"

"We will return in time, yet presently, I prefer to stay here for a while longer."

"I suppose I should give you some privacy then," I say as I pull my legs under me to stand.

"Won't you stay?"

"You want me to?"

He turns to look at me. I admit he shocks me when he runs his finger down the side of my face before tucking a strand of hair behind my ear. "Yes, very much so."

"But your horde—"

"Can wait. There is no place else I would rather be than right here with you."

*****

"What do we have here?" The unexpected voice cuts through the quiet disturbing the calm settled around us. Jumping to my feet, I spin to find several men standing there. Thanatos seems unaffected by their sudden arrival since he remains seated on the rock we had shared, with his focus directed out over the lake.

"You need to keep walking," I advise.

"Or what?"

"Please don't ask that. There has already been enough death and destruction today."

"Hey, asshole. You just gonna sit there and let your girl do all the talking?" Stepping to block their view of Thanatos, I try again to reason with these idiots.

"Your window for reconsidering your actions is closing. If you don't want to meet your maker, I will ask you one more time—" The blade of a large knife glistens as he taps it against his leg.

"Don't do this, please."

"Hear that guys? The bitch here knows how to beg." He says with a laugh as he twists to look at the equally dumbass men standing behind him. Turning his focus back on me, his tongue darts out, licking his teeth. His disgusting. Rotten. Teeth. And the shiver passing through me when I see him do this has Thanatos straightening behind me.

"Tell me, little lady, do you like to beg?" Should I continue trying to convince these men to leave us alone, or Thanatos not to kill them? Probably not. They sure as hell wouldn't be doing the same if the roles were reversed. Especially since I can see where his eyes are focused, and it's not on my face.

"He's going to kill you." Can't these idiots sense who they have stumbled upon?

"Nah, I don't think he's gonna do shit. Besides, I think I would rather like hearing you beg while on your knees. Preferably with my cock—"

Thanatos has heard enough of their shit if the low growl accompanied by him coming to full height is any indication. I spin, placing my hand on his chest. If this were any other day, I would have presented these assholes to him with a flourish of my hands, but the cries of those children still haunt me.

"Thanatos, please," my muttered soft pleas bring his eyes down to me. "They're not worth it."

"Yeah, Thannie, why don't you put your ass back down on that rock while I show her what a real man is about, or if you prefer, I can put your ass back down there and then fuck your bitch next to you so you can watch. Hell, maybe you can learn a trick or two on how to properly please the hot piece of ass. On the upside, her begging you to walk away may save you from getting the beat down of your miserable fucking life."

"This is what you are trying to save, Apple."

"Not them, Thanatos. Everyone else," I say, placing my hand on his face.

"Apple? Is that your name, sweet thing? So, tell me, Apple, are you more Red Delicious or Grannie Smith? When I first taste, should I expect sour, or will you be as sweet as you look? I'm betting on sweet. What do you fellas think?" Quite a few of them laugh, some of them respond with their thoughts on the subject, and I know none of them will live to see tomorrow.

Closing my eyes, I realize nothing I can say will shut this man up, and Thanatos is not going to willingly walk away after the shit he's said.

Grasping my arm firmly, the last chance these idiots had just slipped away as Thanatos moves me behind him.

"Oh, look at the big man, guys." The laugh coming from them is infuriating. "What are you going to do, big guy? There are ten of us and one of you."

"You will require significantly more. I shall await your return here, allowing you to rally others or give you the chance my companion has tried so hard to convince you to take."

"Big fucking mistake, asshole. I'm going to gut you. It's too bad you won't get to watch when I fuck her, particularly since you wanted to pretend like the big man and fantasize you have any hope in hell of protecting her. Just know now I will not go easy on the bitch."

Thanatos pushes me back several steps, allowing his wings to erupt. This stops the talkative one in his tracks as the laughs of his comrades fall silent.

"What the fuck are you?"

"I have many names, one you have already heard, but my other titles include Death or the pale rider. What I am is the horsemen sent to judge you."

"Stay back, or I'll.... I'll—"

"Kill me? You do not possess the power to kill me, but rest assured, I will reap your souls before the last dusting of the twilight has slipped away."

Marcelle Valentine

Death

Their first mistake was believing they could win against me. Their second and, quite honestly, biggest misstep was in threatening Avalon. Marching towards the leader of this rabble, he tries to prove he is unaffected by my looming presence, but the urine stain forming on his pants would suggest otherwise.

If this simpleton believed the wretch who followed him would be of any help, he is woefully mistaken since most of them began slinking away the instant they realized who they threatened. No matter, they will not get far.

Launching into the air, I scoop the ones fleeing under each arm before soaring high into the sky. Once we are at an altitude I know they will not survive; I release my grasp, allowing them to fall, screaming, back to the ground and their inevitable death.

Landing behind the remaining group of wide-eyed men, they watch my every move. Having seen what happened to the ones who ran, the remaining men stay rooted in place.

"We are not ah—afraid of you. You can't come to our world—"

"Your world."

"Yes," his first feeble attempt was ridiculous, while his second proves how weak and pathetic he truly is. "That's what I said."

"Truly?"

"Yeah, asshole, and today we take it back. Isn't that right, guys?" he says, swatting the arm of the man closest to him before pushing another from behind.

"N—no," the remaining men around him mutter as they avert their eyes.

"Now, what will you do? It seems your following of misfits have abandoned you."

"I'll.... I'll," he grunts, looking around as he contemplates his next move. When he bolts, I realize my mistake because he dashed straight toward a cornered Avalon. Proving he is everything I believed him to be, he cowers behind Avalon with a knife pressed to her throat. I see the instant he decides to kill her; the flash in his eyes is undeniable. I wonder if he sees the change in mine.

Rushing faster than their mortal eyes can follow, I snatch his hand from her throat as I rip him away from the one soul I could not imagine this world without. I silenced his pointless begging when I slammed my hand into his throat. The hit knocks him to the ground as much as it steals his next breath. I will deal with him in a moment. At present, he can remain where he landed. Perhaps he will be more comfortable there while he continues gasping for air. He's not going anywhere, and if he decides to flee, I can easily track him.

Every man before me jumps when I whistle, calling my horse to remove Apple from here. I cannot say what frightened them. I suppose it could be staring death in my eyes. My horse heeds my call as he barrels through the few men who unwisely remained.

"Please," the one who likes to talk begs. Slamming my foot down on his leg ensures he cannot flee while I deal with Avalon. The snapping of bones is only muffled by his screams of pain.

"Protect her, my old friend." With my directive delivered, he thunders over to Avalon, who looks reluctant to leave. I gently assist her when she makes no move to climb on his back.

"Thanatos, please come with me."

"Soon, Apple. Take her to Safety." I say, patting his flank, which sends him trotting away as Avalon watches over her shoulder until they disappear from view. With Avalon safely out of the fray, I turn my attention back to the mortal desperately trying to drag himself away. Sadly for him, his night has only just begun.

Chapter Nineteen: Who

WORD MUST HAVE GOTTEN out after our last encounter because people avoid us at all costs. When they see us riding up on Ghost, they run in the opposite direction. He no longer hides who he is because there are no more lessons for me to teach him. I suppose it's a good thing I gave up on the idea of proving our worth the day he destroyed the city since there are few options left for me to prove this any longer.

We never spoke about what happened to the men who threatened us the night we sat by the lake. Truthfully, I didn't want to know. Thankfully, he didn't have an overwhelming desire to share. I also don't understand why we are still heading southeast rather than back to his horde. It's almost like he doesn't care if he returns to them or not. He seems content to continue traveling with Ghost and me.

We are currently staying in a hotel that would have advertised its five-star facility rating back when these things mattered. Each unit is a suite with a jacuzzi; too bad they no longer work. The hotel has a gym with every piece of equipment you could ever want, a boutique, three restaurants, a spa, and a filthy pool. Before the world shifted, I could never imagine staying in a place like this. And now I'm staying in a freaking penthouse because this is what death wants. As nice as it was the first night to sleep in utter luxury, I miss staying in little cabins with Ghost nearby.

Sadly, we have also never re-explored the kiss we shared all those weeks ago. I think this is partly because I'm unsure if it truly happened or if it was another vivid dream. And let's face it, I would rather die than ask him.

Today Thanatos seems antsy, pacing around, mumbling in a language I do not understand. His eyes seek mine from time to time. Each time our eyes meet, I get the distinct feeling he wants to say something, but when I'm sure he is getting ready to tell me what the hell has him so rattled, he merely exhales before returning to his pacing.

The mood in the room makes it difficult to enjoy my favorite book. When I have finally had enough of his shitty attitude, I close my story, place it on the table, clear my throat and say, "Is something wrong?"

His response to my inquiry is to pick up the book and flip through the pages before he returns it to the same place I set it, only to pick it back up again.

"This is utter nonsense."

"What do you mean?"

"This book is pure nonsense; it would never happen.

"If I wanted real, I would read non-fiction. I happen to love it."

"I suppose this is for the best because it is all fanciful."

"Since a horseman of the fuckin Apocalypse is standing in the room with me right now, I am beginning to question how fictional these paranormal fantasy stories really are."

"Our creator would grant no being this much power."

"He's not all-powerful. He's more like the executioner of the other supernatural beings. Something you should be able to get behind." His eyes shift to me; apparently, he doesn't care for me comparing him to the male character in the series.

"I believe the author was merely attempting to hide his true worth," he says before muttering. "Although I saw right through it.

Eyeing him suspiciously, I slowly reply, "He isn't all-powerful. He can die—"

Interrupting me, he quickly informs me, "Only if he deems it so."

"Uh-huh."

"Do you disagree?"

"No."

"Then why the look of skepticism?"

"I'm just wondering how you know so much about the books in this series?"

He huffs as he runs his fingers through his hair before storming over to the window.

"Death, did you read my books?" I try to hide my amusement, thinking about him reading my smutty paranormal romance series, but I do a shitty job, and it leeches out with my question.

"I wanted to know why they held so much appeal to you."

"Appeal?"

"Yes, well, it seems every time I see you, you're reading one of them, so...."

"Uh-huh." I bite my lower lip, trying to stifle the giggle threatening to escape me.

"We should discuss something else," he declares as he places the book on the table next to where he is standing.

"Okay, what would you like to talk about?" I ask, pursing my lips to halt the grin growing faster than I can hide.

"Where would you like to travel next?"

"I thought you would want to return to the others now."

"In due time," he mumbles, yet his eyes and fingers remain on the book.

"Where would you—" He cuts me off, asking in a rush.

"Do mortals truly enjoy the things he did to the female in your story?"

"Things? You're going to have to give me more than *the things*," I state with air quotes.

"There are times when they are alone." He looks at me with a hopeful expression, and while I am fairly certain what he is referring to, I can't let him off the hook too easily.

"Wait, you read the smutty parts too?"

"Call it curiosity."

"Did it make you feel all warm and tingly?"

"Apple," the way he says my nickname is meant as a warning, but this is way too much fun to stop now.

"You did, and I'm willing to bet it did stir something in your nether regions."

"Nether region?"

"You know your...." clearing my throat, I point at the well-endowed penis hidden under his clothes. How do I know the size of what I'm pointing at? It is all thanks to him storming into the bathroom the other night without knocking or wearing a stitch of clothing. So, I am all too aware of what he has concealed down there. And let me tell you, he has nothing to be ashamed of. Mmmm-mmm-mm.

He sighs as he looks up at the ceiling. "Can you not just answer one of my questions without adding your own commentary?"

"Probably not."

"Never mind. Forget I asked." an exasperated sigh escapes him as he rubs his forehead.

"Are you asking if all humans like it or just women?"

"I guess females."

"You want to know if women like what Logan did to Kenna when they were in bed?"

"Not just in bed; it seems the shower had a starring role as well." I bite my lip to stifle the laugh he evokes. As funny as I find the entire exchange, the look he gives suggests he does not. I finally let him off the hook when I tell him what he wants to know.

"You have no idea how much most women enjoy it." He seems to contemplate what I just told him before he nods and turns to leave. Pausing at the door, he looks back over at me, and like earlier, I swear he looks like he wants to say something else, but after a couple of seconds, Thanatos dips his chin, thanks me, and leaves me to ponder when the hell he had time to read my book without me knowing.

*****

Thanatos woke me up early the next morning. I'm not sure when he came back into the suite. I fell asleep waiting for him.

For the first time since we started this little journey of ours, Thanatos is the one picking our path, and I admit the closer we get to Charlotte, the more anxious I become. This will be the largest city we've entered during this trip.... Actually, it's the biggest city I've been in since those good and honorable men of Cambridge handed me over to him.

"Do you really think this is the best idea?" He doesn't answer. I'm not sure what the hell is going on, but aside from Thanatos telling me we had to go, he hasn't said anything else to me all day.

"Earth to Death," I mock, poking him in his back. Nothing. I don't even get his patented over-the-shoulder glare. I'm unsure if I did something to piss him off, but the silent treatment needs to stop.

"What the hell crawled up your ass?" I snap.

"I can assure you nothing has crawled anywhere within this form."

"Whoa, he speaks. I see you didn't forget how to talk." He exhales but does not reply.

"Are you pissed at me or something?"

"Or something," he mumbles.

"Are you trying to start a fight with me?" When he does not respond, I've had enough of his shit. Fortunately, our pace is slow enough that I can swing my leg over the side of Ghost and drop to the ground. Unfortunately, I don't land as gracefully as I envisioned since I end up on my ass. Death is preparing to jump down, but when I spring to my feet, he changes his mind and remains on Ghost.

For the next hour, we traveled in silence, with Thanatos perched on his horse while I walked on the other side of the road. I get that I probably shouldn't have laughed when he asked me those questions, but it still doesn't mean I'm alright with him treating me like shit. It reminds me of my early days with his horde.

When the first skyscraper of Charlotte crests the horizon, the apprehension I've felt since I realized where he was traveling resurfaces with the added bonus of dread. Something deep inside keeps telling me this is all about to go horribly wrong. And if I have learned anything throughout my life, it's that I should never ignore my intuition.

Death

I accept veering in the direction of this place was not an ideal course of action since I am dealing with more emotions than I am accustomed to. And with these new feelings consuming me, I am not using my best judgment. Hence the reason I have this mortal by his throat suspended before me. If the color of his face is any sign, I would have to say he has only seconds left before his pathetic life slips away.

What was the nature of his crime? I witnessed him strike another. A female who was begging him to forgive her. When we rounded the corner, we found her on her hands and knees, pleading with someone unworthy of her desperation. In this new world, many mortals, especially females, feel they need to be in the safety of others. Thus far, Avalon is the only exception I have found for this simple truth. Where most mortals only find security within a group, she only feels safe when she is not.

Does his action merit a response? At first, it did not, but now it does.

Does the punishment fit the crime? It didn't until apple attempted to intercede on the woman's behalf. He didn't take kindly to her interference.

"Death, what the hell are you doing?" Avalon yells as she grabs my arm.

"Delivering justice."

"This isn't justice; this is anything but justice."

"If you dislike the method by which I deliver my sentence, then you should walk away," I snap, knowing I don't mean it. I know I am only pushing this hard because I am ill-equipped to process the emotions surging within me. All feelings she provokes.

"Stop," she yells as she continues her attempts to free the dying man. "You don't even know what happened." I know she is right. While he is not an innocent man, he is also not inherently wicked, nor does he deserve the harshness of my reaction simply for approaching Avalon.

Tossing him aside, I snarl, "Be thankful she was here to save you, mortal."

The man staggers to his feet, grasping his damaged throat, sucking in one lungful of air after another of the oxygen I deprived him of. Avalon positions herself between the wounded man and me, and only when he has disappeared from view does she spin back around to face me. The fury I find in those steely eyes confirms she will not let this go.

"What. The. Hell. Is the matter with you?"

"This is what I am, Avalon. As you have pointed out countless times, I am here for no reason other than to judge the mortals of this realm."

"Then judge me."

"No."

"Why?"

"I said no."

"Bullshit. Tell me why you are so willing to judge him but not me."

"Because they are unworthy," I yell, stalking toward her.

"Neither am I."

"They are insignificant."

"So am I. I've already told you once I'm nobody."

"Do not press this matter any further."

"Fuck you, Thanatos! Judge me." My wings explode behind me, a direct result of the fury coursing through me by her request. My attempt to end this standoff as I remove the last space between us does not have the desired effect because she does not falter or wane in her request. How Avalon can stand here utterly unaffected by my presence is a new phenomenon. I have never had anyone stand their ground against me. Not even my brothers will oppose me when I am teetering on the edge as I am now. The brink of destruction she continues to shove me toward, and when I reach it, no one will survive.

"You should not wish for my judgment so fucking hard, Apple."

"You can't have it both ways, Death. If you think humanity isn't worth saving, then you don't think I am either," she replies with as much force as I spoke.

"You are nothing like them," I growl.

"I'm exactly like the rest of them. No, actually, I'm fuckin worse."

How she can believe this is something I will never understand. Hearing her say this has the fury I felt all morning slipping away. I take several tentative steps in her direction, hoping she will not misread my advance. To my utter amazement, she remains rooted in place, allowing me to place my hand on her face as I tell her, "You are the best of them."

"Really? Because I'm pretty sure you wouldn't say that if you had any idea what I have done. What I'm capable of." Some of the fire drops from her response, yet she is no less determined to confess her imagined atrocities.

"Enlighten me," I breathe.

"I've committed the worst of the sins. The Grand-motherfuckin-daddy of them all."

Confused, I step away from her. With my brows furrowed and eyes narrowed, I wait for Avalon to explain what crime she believes she has committed. Her apprehension of revealing whatever long-hidden secret she's alluding to is apparent from her closed eyes and slow, methodical breaths. With a final deep exhale, she snaps her eyes open, looks directly into mine, then blurts something I was ill-prepared for, "I killed someone."

"What did you say?"

"Yeah. So, if you plan on eradicating humanity because you have deemed them wanting, then I should be the first to face your judgment."

"Avalon," I growl, needing a second to absorb what she just told me.

"No, it's well past the time I face my judgment, so do your worst. Pass your goddamn judgment, and let's get on with the punishment part."

"You should not push me about this right now," I hiss through gritted teeth as I try to come to terms with what I was sent here to do and wanting to protect this woman from everything. Even if the everything includes my creator.... And by extension me.

With a shake of her head and a humorless little laugh, she continues pushing when she should hold her tongue.

"You either have to judge me, or you have to forgive all of us. Anything else is hypocritical and confirms God is what I have always believed him to be, an asshole tyrant with an ant farm. And we mortals are nothing more than the insignificant bugs he put in the colony," she snaps before storming off.

*****

Confusion, anger, and refusal to accept what she told me delayed me from stopping her when she walked away from me, and now I am frantically trying to find her. I want answers to my lingering questions. I will not accept she killed someone without provocation. She is not evil. I meant what I said to her; I still stand by it: she is truly the best of them.

"Avalon!" I yell into the empty streets. Every passing second she is alone in this god-forsaken shit-hole metropolis does nothing to help the mounting trepidation within me. Until I am prepared to tear this world apart to find her.

"Avalon, where are you?"

"There!" The first voice penetrates the quiet of this city I should have never come to.

"It's him." The second calls almost immediately after. Looking towards the rooftops, I try to pinpoint where the shouts are coming from as I release my wings, preparing myself for whatever they have planned. The heavy haze from the steady rainfall limits visibility. Additionally, had I not been so preoccupied with my thoughts of Avalon, I would have sensed them long before they could have seen me coming.

The zip of something whisking past my head has me spinning at the last second; however, I did not move fast enough.

The second arrow they fired pierces my chest as I reach up to pull it out; a third, fourth, then fifth soar in my direction, each finding its mark. One in my arm, my stomach, and my thigh. As I release the first roar, I look up only to discover the volley of arrows they intend to end me with flying in my direction.

Chapter Twenty: Not Ready

Then shall the dust return to the earth as it was:
and the spirit shall return unto God who gave it.
Ecclesiastes 12:7

Avalon Spring 2024

THE CHEERS COMING FROM somewhere in the city
are startling. I haven't heard this sound since a time that
predates the arrival of the horseman, a rider who has me
beyond furious, back to a time when stadiums were filled to
capacity with people cheering on their favorite sports team.

I want to get the hell out of this damn city. I knew coming
here was a horrible idea, but like the village idiot, I elected to
ignore all the alarm bells blaring in my head and follow him
into this hell on earth. Had I kept going straight when he

veered left, we would never have come here because for everything people believe him to be, none of them understand how loyal he is. For that reason alone, he would have followed me... or picked my ass up and dumped it on the horse before riding away. I guess this is as much a possibility as following me could be. The one thing I'm certain of is he would not have left me.

The longer I roam through the city streets, the more I realize the ones who made their home here are not the kind of people who would escape Death's radar. Drugs are used openly on the street, as well as people engaging in various sex acts; hell, I even stumble across the same chick who was begging the guy Death almost killed on her knees with another man's junk buried in her mouth.

This place is disgusting, with trash littering most of the city streets. I was here before, and I can tell you this place is nothing like it was then. Sadly, much of the beautiful architecture is long destroyed.

When the banking industry fell, Charlotte was hit hard. Gone are the museums, sports teams, and amusement parks. The metropolis once known for being the City of Churches is no more as these all stand vacant, unkempt, and a reminder of how much we didn't know. The place I once thought of as the epitome of where I would live if I could, has been erased in a few short years. Replaced by this den of depravity.

Another round of cheers echoes off the buildings. Like last time, the sudden outburst startles me. Since the shift occurred, nothing good can happen when a rowdy crowd gathers. Their shouts of encouragement have the tiny hairs on the back of my neck on edge as my dread mounts with each step I take. Something tells me remaining in this city could be detrimental to our health.

Damn it, of all times to have a fight and storm away from Thanatos, now was not the best time to do this. Pausing, I look behind me, expecting to see him perched upon Ghost as they trot down the middle of the road. Any second now, he's going to come around the corner pissed I left the safety he can provide. Any damn second.

As much as I want to be as far away from this place as possible, when a fresh round of applause followed by roars of approval echoes off the buildings surrounding me, I know something is terribly wrong. Why the hell hasn't Death or Ghost found me yet? One of them should have by now. The longer I stand here with this nagging feeling, the reality of why he's not here sinks in.

With my heart hammering in my chest, I cautiously make my way to the area the raucous sounds are coming from.

"Just a quick look," I tell myself. "Then I can get my ass out of here and catch up with Death. Just one quick peek—"

The words die on my tongue when I see why they are cheering. They have Death strung up by his neck with his arms extended to shoulder level and his feet tied together. I swallow hard, hoping to push the bile creeping up my throat back down as the horror of seeing him crucified registers. Arrows litter the lot behind him, but the number buried in his body has my heart sinking.

The one leading the brutal attack drops his arm, and another barrage of arrows sails at him. Each time one hits its mark, the crowd's cheers grow wild. Death makes no move to end their assault, nor does he try to protect himself.

The image of him lying on the ground the first night I met him comes rushing back to me, but this.... This is so much worse. His head slumps forward as rivers of blood steadily fall to the ground beneath him. The wings he normally holds proudly behind him sag behind his back. Clumps of feathers are missing, caked in mud, with the ends coated in thick blood.

They have captured Ghost as well. He is bound so they can whip him repeatedly without the fear of him fighting back, but he gets in one good hit when he kicks out his hind legs, knocking one prick currently hitting him several feet away. I admit the crunch of bones shattering is a satisfying sound.

"Let's make sure these fuckers receive our message loud and clear. We mortals are not to be fucked with," the leader roars, pulling something from the waistband of his pants. The flash of steel confirms Thanatos may soon live the same nightmare he did before. Yet his intentions are much worse than plunging the blade inside him. Walking behind, he grabs Death's wing and slowly begins sawing the knife through it.

The anguished cries of pain from my horseman send my heart racing as a new reality crashes around me.... Thanatos is awake, and he's suffering through their torture. Just as I prepare to rush out to protect him, someone yanks me back behind the wall I only barely had time to step around.

Panic seizes me as a hand slams across my mouth, stifling the scream I was prepared to release.

"Don't." I continue to struggle against the brawny arms surrounding me.

"Please, I won't hurt you, but they will kill you if you go out there. If for no other reason than to make him watch." When most of the fight has left me, he continues.

"I'm going to take my hand off your mouth. If you scream, we're both dead." His hand slides away as the arm he has gripped around my chest releases me. Spinning, I shove the random guy wanting to put some distance between us. His hands shoot up, hoping to show he has no intention of touching me again. Damn good thing because if he does, he won't like my response.

He takes numerous steps away from me, putting enough space between us I no longer feel threatened. Eyeing him suspiciously, I wait for him to explain why he would care if they killed me, beat me, or left me to live with the knowledge of what humanity did to him.

"The guy leading this spectacle is a sadistic prick who grew up a few blocks from me. He got involved with a gang, killed a couple people, and found his ass sitting in prison until the world fell to shit, and some idiot let him out. He came home demanding allegiance from anyone unfortunate enough to still live here; he's the worst kind of survivor. If you storm out there, he will make you wish you were never born."

"I won't just stand here and let them continue to torture them."

"They are already dead." Does this idiot not understand who they have down there? I don't think there is a person alive who could kill him, and Ghost is not a normal horse either. I have no doubt they can and will survive this.

"Thanks for your concern, but I have no intention of walking away from them," I say as I turn to find something I can use as a weapon.

"Maybe someday you'll thank me." This is the last thing I hear him say before something hits the back of my head hard enough to cause flashes of blinding white light to appear before my eyes. Then nothing.

*****

Water dripping on my face slowly brings me back to the world around me. I'm lying on a dirt cake floor in a room below street level. The small window near the ceiling reveals the day has slipped away to night, and the steady rain outside compounds the night's foreboding darkness. For the first time in my life, I wish it was light.

Two years ago, I would have said this was a perfect night, but now I can't shake the sense of déjà vu overwhelming me as I realize Thanatos needed my help again. Unlike then, this time, I may have failed him. Pushing up to my hands and knees, I have to know what became of them. The problem is the room is spinning as a wave of nausea twists my stomach into knots. I wince as I place my hand against the bump throbbing on the back of my head.

Using the wall to help me to my feet, I stumble as the world shifts dramatically.

"Get your shit together, A," I mutter as I shuffle along the wall, searching for anything I can use to get the hell out of here. When I find a door, I don't have much hope that this will be how I escape. No way in hell would my captor make it this easy, figuring when I twist the knob, I will be woefully disappointed to find the damn thing locked. Imagine my surprise when it opens. Now the only thing left is to find my horseman, so I can learn his outcome.

The rain has almost stopped by the time I weave my way back to where they held him. The area, once filled with cheering assholes, is now deserted except for Ghost, who has been bound and left to watch his rider suffer, and the lone idiot left to watch over them.

"You fuckers think you can come here and kill us," he slurs before taking a long swig from the bottle he's holding.

Looking for anything I might use as a weapon, the only thing I find close at hand is a jagged rock.

Sticking to the shadows the second I pick it up, I regret having done it when my hand encounters a sticky substance. The coppery scent confirms what I already know; it is blood, and since Thanatos and Ghost are the only two bleeding, it had to come from one of them. A wave of nausea threatens to give away my location as I fight to keep the retching at bay. Unable to hold anything that was used to hurt them, I drop the damn thing, followed immediately by me scrubbing my hand down the front of my jeans. At least something must be on my side tonight because the dumbass guard is more concerned with getting drunk than actually guarding, so the noise from the rock falling goes unnoticed.

"Well, we showed you," his growl comes out more ridiculous than menacing as he stumbles slightly closer to Ghost, who is bound and lying on his side. If this asshole is the only thing standing between me and saving them, I would have to say my odds substantially improved.

Realizing I can no longer hide in the shadows, I take one last look to ensure no one else is lingering in the area. With his back to me, the time to act isn't going to get any better than it is right now.

Creeping towards him at a painfully slow pace, I only pause when he shifts. He's fumbling with something, but it's not until the unmistakable sound of a zipper pulling down I realize what he's preparing to do. Rage surges through me the instant I hear him pissing.

It's not the act infuriating me; it's the knowledge of where he is directing it.... At Ghost, who is struggling to come to his feet. No longer caring if he hears me, I charge at the asshole, intending to make him regret his choices. Kicking my leg out, he reels forward, falling over Ghost's colossal frame. Not wanting to allow him the opportunity to recover, I leap on his back and twist my hands in his hair as I repeatedly slam his face against the ground. I don't stop until his body goes limp under me.

When I'm sure he will not attack me the second I release him, I slip off his back and work to bring my ragged breathing under control. As anxious as I'm sure Ghost is to be free, he patiently waits for me to compose myself.

Not sure my legs will support me, I crawl over to untie the rope secured around his neck first, but the knots are pulled too tight, making me realize that if I want to free him, I will have to find something to cut them away.

"I'll be right back," I whisper. All my plans come to a screeching halt when I spin and find another asshole standing directly behind me. But not just any asshole. It's the one Death held by his throat shortly after we arrived here, making me instantly regret interfering when Thanatos wanted to pass judgment on him. Before I can react, he slams his fist into my jaw, sending me flopping in a heap on the other side of Ghost.

The only good that has come from the surprise attack is I landed on my back, which allowed me to bring my knees up at the last second as he tried to pounce on me. A mistake he will soon regret as his crotch slams directly into them. Not one to waste an opportunity, I slam the heel of my hand into his nose. The initial joy I have when the crunch confirms I broke it is short-lived when he delivers his retribution for my assault.

The flashes of white light and intense pain from his punch begin the moment he makes contact. His hands choking off any chance of taking a breath almost takes the last of the fight out of me, but when Ghost struggles against his binding, the asshole makes the cardinal mistake in an altercation, he turns his back on his opponent all so he can snarl at Ghost, "Shut the fuck up you miserable pri—"

Slamming my head into his jaw dislodges him. The fist that follows knocks him on his back, and the snap from his neck as he lands awkwardly against Ghost confirms he's dead.

As crazy as this may sound, I'm pretty sure Ghost saved me, not only when he pulled his attention away from me but when he shifted his legs just as the man fell. Guaranteeing the guy would fall against them, thereby ensuring this asshole would not be a problem anymore. Not for me or any other poor soul unlucky enough to cross paths with him.

Gasping for air, I know I can't linger here long since I have no clue when the next curious observer might arrive. The only upside to this asshole stumbling in when he did is the knife attached to his belt, which is precisely what I need to release Ghost.

The forced snorts coming from Ghost confirm they tortured him too. Cutting away the ropes they used to tie him up, he wastes no time returning to his feet as the pain in my head causes another wave of dizziness. As much as I can sense his desire to get to his rider, he remains next to me as I reach my hand out for anything to steady me. Luckily for me, the thing my hand crashes against is none other than my favorite horse, Ghost. Without his unnatural intellect and quick intervention, I would have face planted. Him saving my ass seems to be an ongoing theme tonight.

Knowing I cannot delay this any longer, Ghost and I slowly approach Thanatos. His mangled body is still riddled with arrows. Long jagged wounds cover his torso, and the asshole who tortured him didn't take off one wing; he removed both.

The blood surrounding him is disconcerting. How much blood can a supernatural being lose and still regenerate? I mean, it's been hours since I discovered what the cheers were all about, and he looks worse now than he did then.

I count fifty-seven arrows embedded in his flesh. Fifty-seven projectiles proving these cowardly bastards had no intention of fighting fair. Fifty-seven reasons to hate them and wish them all horrific deaths. Fifty-seven points to prove humanity is as bad as he believes. Removing each one as carefully as I can, the one in the middle of his chest scares me the most. Taking a deep breath, I yank it out, praying I didn't just make a horrible mistake by doing this.

One at a time, I began cutting away the ropes used to hold him in place as they carried out their atrocities. He sways as I release each limb, but there are no voluntary movements; there are no sounds other than the wind rustling the leaves in the trees.

"Thanatos, please be okay," I whisper before I cut the last line. His body slumps forward and crashes into mine, sending us both sprawling to the ground. Wrapping my arms around him, I will my breathing to slow down. I tell myself he can't die, that the low-life pricks who did this to him do not possess the power to end him. That he is so still because his body is trying to heal. I promise myself his heart has not stopped beating forever; I merely can't feel it right now because my own is pounding so wildly.

"Please don't leave me.... I — I need you."

Hugging him tighter against me, I do something I have never done before, not for my parents, not for Janie, not even for myself. I plead for his creator or anyone else who could be listening now to help him. With the last of my waning strength, I roll him off me to begin assessing my horseman's injuries.

Reaching for his face, I run my fingers over his cold skin. When he does not respond to the contact, the fear I have felt since waking up morphs into an overwhelming panic. Knowing I need to get him out of here before they return, I look for any place I can drag him. It needs to be far enough they won't find us but close enough that I can pull him there, all while trying to keep the world from tilting under me because of the knock I took to my head.

Ten to one, I have a concussion. As I rub the lump on my head, I think I'd like nothing more than to find the asshole who thought he was doing me a favor and show him how wrong he was. Massaging my temples, hoping to curtail the throbbing pain and clear some of the confusion, I need to devise a plan. I assume these assholes aren't done with him yet, and as long as they continue torturing him, Thanatos has no chance of regenerating. As I debate what I'm going to do, Ghost nudges me.

"Hang on, buddy," I quietly tell him, afraid any noise I make will bring a wave of angry people rushing back here to finish what they started.

I could take him back to the room I woke up in, but I dismissed this almost as fast, realizing the guy who hit me may yet be involved with the others. Okay, maybe we don't go down; we go up instead.

Standing up to better view our surroundings my eyes scan the high-rise buildings dotting the skyline. There is no electricity which means no elevators. Suki is hundreds of miles away from here, and Thanatos has suffered substantially more damage than last time.

Marcelle Valentine

Again Ghost nudges my arm, and instinctually I reach out to caress his nose. He lets me know this is not what he wants when he snorts before lowering himself next to Thanatos. The realization he wants to help get his rider to safety smacks me almost as hard as the hit I took earlier.

Seeing him lying on the ground, covered in dirt and blood, unaware of what is happening, an absolute certainty settles over me. I am not ready to lose him.

Chapter Twenty-One: The Real Monsters

GHOST REMAINED ON THE ground without moving until I had Thanatos draped over his back. Taking his reins, I'm not sure if he'll come with me or bolt the second I have him secured, carrying his rider as far away from this place as he can get. Here's hoping I'm fast enough to keep up if he does.

But he doesn't bolt. Instead, he rises to his feet as carefully as possible so as not to jostle his precious cargo. Doing what I have seen Death do to get Ghost moving, I click my tongue several times, prompting him to follow. I send a silent prayer of thanks when he does precisely what I ask of him; follow me. Ghost normally doesn't listen to anyone other than

Thanatos, so I don't think I need to tell you how relieved I am to have him silently trailing close behind me. I guess he knows I am trying to save his rider.

My plan is to get us all out of this shithole and as far away as I can manage before I find something to shelter us while he heals. Weaving through the city streets, I do my best to restrain all thoughts that someone will look out their window or come around a corner and discover us at any second. I have so much adrenaline coursing through me my limbs are tingling as my pulse pounds, further increasing the pain in my head.

The sounds of voices carry through the deserted streets. I don't know if they are out on patrol or late-night partiers. Either way, most of them regale the others with tales of how they took down the horseman. One idiot mockingly declares his pussy ass cried like a baby.

"Fucking liar," I mouth, afraid they might hear me if I say it out loud. And as much as I would like to call him out on his bullshit, I want to protect Thanatos more.

Progress is slower than I like, but on every path I choose, I discover more of the same; assholes whooping it up about the fall of my horseman, forcing us to hide or change direction to avoid them. Each time we have to backtrack, I can't help but worry I am wasting precious seconds, seconds that may decide my horseman's outcome.

Ghost silently keeps pace with me. When I move, he moves. When I stop, he stops. When I hold my breath trying to hear what direction the voices are coming from, I swear he does too. I don't think I take my first real breath until the high rises are nothing more than a speck in the distance.

We nearly made it out of the city when they raised the first red flag that Death was gone. Shouts and sirens rang through the air. I know we have never been closer to being caught than at this moment. But like my knight in shining armor, Ghost moved in front of me, waiting for me to mount him. Understanding this is our best chance of survival, I wedge my foot in the stirrup as I try unsuccessfully to hoist myself up on his back. The days spent on the road, getting knocked out, and witnessing Thanatos being tortured, compile together to zap the last of my strength.

"It's alright, big guy; I can run if necessary. Just get him somewhere safe." Ghost snorts. Damn if this horse isn't exactly like his rider. They both have no issues letting me know when they are annoyed with me, but right now, I don't have the strength to pull myself up there, so he's just going to have to get over it.

Lowering himself to the ground, he waits for me to climb on. Taking one last look over my shoulder, I positioned myself behind Thanatos. Holding the reins with one hand while keeping him from sliding off with the other, Ghost comes to full height before racing away into the night.

*****

It is nearly dawn when Ghost finds us a suitable place to stay. A little hovel far enough off the road any passerby would easily miss. Which is fine by me after everything we went through when we met the last humans in Charlotte.

With the first rays of dawn making an appearance, it becomes painfully obvious during my haste to escape that god-forsaken place I went the wrong way. I can't tell you where Thanatos wanted to go, only it wasn't the direction I took us in. Damn it, we lost ground, and not just a little because at the pace Ghost was running, I'm willing to bet it was a lot.

Sliding off him, I'm thankful to find there are only four steps I will have to haul him up. Ghost dispels any notion I will have to drag Thanatos anywhere when he climbs the first two steps waiting patiently for me to open the door to allow him access to carry his rider inside.

When we have him positioned on the couch, I carefully remove the remnants of his destroyed clothes before assessing the wounds.

An hour later, I have done everything I can for him, and my eyes are too damn heavy to keep them open any longer. Not wanting to be far in case he wakes up or needs something, I lay on the floor next to his makeshift hospital bed and let sleep carry me away.

This is how we do things over the next forty-eight hours, with repeat cycles of me either inspecting his injuries, cleaning his wounds, bandaging the ones healing slower, or sitting next to him as I wait to see if he'll wake up. There may have been some begging followed by bargaining with a certain almighty creator mixed in there too.

On the third day, I awake to find the most beautiful and terrifying sight I have ever seen.

Death in all his glory, brilliant blue eyes sparkling with the life they tried so hard to steal, wings proudly held behind him, yet with his armor and body covered in blood.

"You're injured," he says softly, running his thumb over the still healing split in my bottom lip.

"I'll be okay. Are you—"

"Fully restored." The sigh of relief I exhale is something I neither want to hide nor could even if I tried. Until this moment, I truly was not sure if he would recover or not. Unlike the last time, this time, he never moved while I took care of him.

"You saved me. Again."

"I did."

"Why did you do it, Apple?"

Hearing him call me this again brings a surge of emotions, some pleasant and some painful. Pleasant since I wasn't sure if I would ever listen to him say it again. Painful because he won't tell me why he refers to me as this or what it means. Which leaves me to assume it means nothing. Even though he told me he doesn't call all mortals this, it's possible I didn't ask the right question. Perhaps the question I should have asked is if this is the nickname he gives all women. A term of endearment he uses when he is trying to.... Trying to what? Be nice, put them at ease, flirt? Okay, definitely not flirt since he has made it abundantly clear he has no interest in all things naughty, but oh-so fun. Leaving me one option, he only says it to put people at ease. It is much harder to be on guard with someone when they call you something like this. His questioning stare tells me I have been living in my thoughts for far too long again.

"It was the right thing to do."

"Is this your standard response when you save someone?"

"I don't follow."

"This is the same thing you said to me on your roof all those months ago. So, I will ask again, is this your standard response or one you hold solely for me?"

"I still find it hard to believe you remember me."

"Of course, I remember you. Do you truly believe I could forget the woman who rescued me? Well, now I guess it would be more accurate to say saved me twice."

"I just don't understand.... Why you never said anything? Never let on that you knew me. Why?"

"What do you believe the others would have said or done if they had realized not only do I know you but owe you a great deal?"

"Nothing. They would do nothing."

"They would do everything. People would either hold it against you or try to hold you against me, hoping I would grant whatever they wish for."

"I'm sure they all know I don't hold that kind of sway over y—" before I can finish, he appears directly before me. And like previous encounters, his eyes shift from the deep blue they normally are to a color much closer to resembling a crystal.

"I wouldn't be so certain of this."

Swallowing hard, I try to redirect the conversation to the memories I recall. "Besides, you told me you were repaying me by letting me leave the city. Which, by the way, didn't work out so well."

"I disagree with this sentiment." Not ready to acknowledge what he said, I point to the blood I know doesn't belong to him.

"Did you...."

"Go back?"

"Yes."

"I did."

"And?"

"Charlotte and its inhabitants are no more." I can't blame him for this. In fact, there is a part of me happy to hear those assholes will never hurt anyone again, but at what cost did their annihilation come? Not just to humanity as a whole... but to my horseman as well.

Death

The arrow responsible for my fall was the one that pierced my heart. Volley after volley of arrows rained down on me, assuring they completely removed me from the fight. When they ran out of their projectiles, they ripped them back out of me before returning to their fun. When they grew tired of attacking from a distance, they hung me so each could take a turn jamming their knife into me. Ghost made it to within ten feet of me when the surging crowd surrounded him before dragging him to the ground.

During one fleeting moment when I was conscious, I thought I saw Avalon, but the next second, she was gone. A figment of my imagination or a wish to see her one last time should they accomplish what they set out to do.

The agony I felt as they tore my wings from my body was indescribable. This is a pain I pray I never have to experience again. After they finished with me, I only had brief periods of recollection. I remember the rain soaking me. I remember nightfall and Avalon reemerging. As someone snuck up behind her, I recall feeling powerless. I remember Apple counting every arrow as she pulled them from my body. The sensation of being held in her embrace and when she was wrestling to get my mangled, bloody torso across Ghost's back. Memories of pain as she led us out of the city and moments of relief upon realizing she had succeeded. There are flashes of her tending to my wounds and sleeping beside me while I healed. But mostly, there is nothing, just darkness filled with agony as my body stitched itself back together. Piece by piece, wound after wound, I regained my strength, and when I was fully recovered, I returned to show them the mistake they had made.

These foolish souls who thought they could kill Death. I am the embodiment of what they wanted to achieve, and what these humans do not understand is I grow stronger with each of their failed attempts.

Humanity's saving grace is the one soul who cared enough to help me. The one who whispered her soft pleas begging for my survival. For me to fight. For me to stay with her. The only soul, my horse, would heed their call. Avalon, a living, breathing mystical heart, and while she may not be the isle of Apples, the place where humanity lost their way, where they chose to forgo their innocence, she is the one being who has done the impossible.... She has turned me from my task.

Chapter Twenty-Two: Janie

Avalon Spring 2024

WE LEFT THE LITTLE cottage after he was confident I had my strength back and could travel. Something feels like it has changed between us. I don't miss the lingering looks he gives me, the softness of his touch as he cares for me, or the husky, sexy timbre of his voice every time he's close to me.

Yes, something has changed.

Should this bother me? Probably.

Does it? No.

Especially since I realize over the last couple of weeks, I have referred to him as my horseman on more than one occasion. I'm not sure if any of it is true, least of all the him being mine part, but the shift between us is undeniable. Or maybe it's just me. It could be just me.

"We should stop here to replenish supplies for you." Ever since our time in Charlotte, I haven't liked the idea of staying in any city, town, settlement, community, or camp. Let's just make this easy. I don't particularly like going into any areas where we may encounter other people.

When Thanatos confessed they overtook him while he was searching for me, I felt like a royal shit. Had I only stayed with him rather than storming off, it's possible none of it would have happened. He keeps telling me it's also possible they would have taken us both captive. Let me make this clear.... I don't believe it. If I had been there, he would not have fallen. Those assholes would never have gotten the upper hand against him if he wasn't distracted. I'm the reason he suffered, and no amount of him denying this will change my mind.

"I think we'll be fine for a while longer. Let's keep going."

"Avalon, nothing will happen to us."

"You can't know that."

"Come on, Apple, let's get this over with and be on our way." Groaning, I proceed inside. If some asshole wants to take a shot at him, they will have to go through me first. Which I understand is stupid since I cannot regenerate like the man I am trying to protect.

I guess he must sense my apprehension, but I'm not sure his reaction is making it any better. Death's hand on my lower back as he leads me from one area to the next is equal parts comforting and confusing.

We've made it through the entire structure, and with only one room left, I think I finally release some of the tension building between my shoulders. I'm happy we found most of the supplies I needed, although I wouldn't pass up another bottle or two of water if we were fortunate enough to find them.

Fear coils low in my belly the instant we walk through the door and find someone else already there. Shifting my eyes nervously around the space, I search for anyone poised to shoot their first arrow in his direction.

"Damn, if you all ain't a sight for sore eyes. I haven't run across another soul for days." The woman appears to be alone. Her fingers dig incessantly at the crook of her arm, an act I am all too familiar with, having witnessed my own parents do this every time they were jonesing for their next fix. "You all wouldn't have a little brown sugar, would you?" her eyes focused mainly on Thanatos.

"What did you say?" I snap upon hearing this for the first time since I was a kid.

"Come on now, I'm in a bad way. I'll do whatever you want, honey pie." Staring at her with blind horror all the blood drains from my face, and the world closes in around me. Suddenly, there is not enough oxygen in this room. With my mouth gaped open, I desperately try to suck in any air I can as my heart rate ramps frantically. Frozen with the certainty of who this person is, I watch as she shuffles toward Death, although I'm willing to bet she thought it was sexy. I wish I could tell her to stay the fuck away from him, but my body seems to be rebelling against what my mind has already figured out, and nothing wants to cooperate with me.

"I'll make you feel real good, baby." She whispers seductively to Thanatos, whose eyes are assessing me.

"I have no desire for anything you have to offer, human." His cool, indifferent response is directed at her, yet his eyes intently watch the range of emotions I imagine are playing out on my face.

The woman turns to assess me like I'm her competition. Her next comment solidifies what my mind has been telling me since she first looked at me. "Close your mouth if you don't want flies making a home in there."

Son of a fucking bitch. How is it possible that the one person in this world I have wished dead countless times would be the one soul I stumble across? A better question is, how in the hell is she still alive? When she reaches out for him this time, he slaps her hand away.

"Do not place your hands on me again," Thanatos's growl is anything but human. Cowering, she backs into the corner, digging jagged scratch marks on her already mangled skin.

My mother is nothing more than a skeletal version of her former self. The years and drug use have not been kind to her. I can't say how it's possible since I was barely twelve when they traded me away for a high that lasted them the afternoon, which I can assure you is a whole lot less than the agony I suffered by the one they gave me to, but recognition flickers in her eyes.

"Wait, don't I know you?" she asks cautiously. Shaking my head wildly. I deny the truth, hoping to keep Thanatos in the dark that this vile woman is my mother even though I want to scream: *Yes, I'm the kid you squeezed out twenty-seven years ago. Only to use, abuse, and hand over to a psychopath for a dime bag.*

"Avalon?" Nope. There is no goddamn fucking way in hell she could still be alive. I refuse to accept it. Refuse to believe she could still be alive when so many others have perished.

"Avalon Mercy, is that you? It is you, isn't it, baby?" Mercy. A goddamn twisted joke of a middle name since neither my parents nor the asshole they sold me to showed me an ounce of it, but they had no problem making me beg for it every day I was with them.

My eyes move over this person who brought me into the world. The only thing she ever did for me. A kindness I would have preferred not to have been awarded. At twenty-seven, I have seen more shit than many other people ever have. In all honesty, my parents never should have had kids; they valued the drugs they shot in their veins more than they ever did me.

The man who claimed me wasn't any better. This fucker abused me in ways I will never fully recover from. But even with all the twisted shit he did to me, when he killed the only person I ever cared for back then, right in front of me, was the worst moment I had experienced until then.

A girl who was barely thirteen and the only person I considered family. Punishment for allowing a boy at school to touch me. Not sexually either; hell, I was so withdrawn growing up that I practically melted into the background. This, in part, is the reason I found the boy offering me a hand in the first place. He didn't see me; truthfully, no one did back then. He was goofing around with his buddies, probably hoping to impress the giggling girls watching him. As he spun, kicking his leg out to show them some karate moves, I discovered the hard way I was in the wrong place at the wrong time.

Like always, I rarely lifted my eyes from the ground resulting in him knocking me flat on my ass. Normally in any other situation, and had it been any other boy, they would have just laughed or snapped at me to watch where I was going. They all turned their noses up to me. I wasn't worthy of simple courtesy. After all, I was the weird kid whose clothes were twice the size of my slight frame, hair too often unwashed, unkempt, and hanging across my face, anything to further hide me away from prying eyes. Prying eyes that may see the bruises often left by Calvin. Showers or bathing were a luxury Calvin only afforded me when he decided he wanted a piece of my skinny ass, as he so eloquently put it. Janie is the only reason I didn't run or seek my school counselor's help to stop what he was doing to me.

Janie was the last unfortunate soul whose parents would trade off to Calvin as payment for the drugs. Her pathetic parents fought over the stash as they rushed out the door. Chasing the dragon was more important than even a glance back in their daughter's direction, the innocent soul they handed over to the fuckin' boogeyman. I will never forget how he looked at her the first night they abandoned her there. As she cowered in the corner crying, Cal was deciding when he would bed her. I decided no matter what happened to me or how bad that bastard could make things, I had to protect her from the monster who believed he owned us.

Calvin cared little for life, well, apart from his own. He did not fear the police or what might happen to him if they discovered what he had done. So, for Janie's sake, I kept my head down and my mouth shut until that one fateful day when a boy I didn't even know by name knocked me down. He was not like the other assholes; he had a gentle way about him. He never teased me or threw things at me like so many of the other kids had. I made for an easy target for any asshole trying to prove his manliness. After putting me on my ass, he stopped and offered his hand to me, apologizing for not paying attention. This is where my mistake began because as the young man was looking me over to ensure he did not hurt me, Calvin was watching everything from the parking lot.

My punishment, the last one he would ever dole out, was the worst beating I had ever experienced. Not fully satisfied I had learned my lesson, Cal grabbed the knife from Janie's plate and plunged it into her heart. The memory of her shocked expression and desperate eyes still haunts me today. The worst part is cold, closed-off Avalon couldn't even muster a tear for her the entire time I watched the life drain out of her face. As the light left her eyes and they faded from a beautiful blue to a dull gray, he raped me for the last time. I returned the favor he bestowed on Janie that night when I drove the blade, still coated in her blood, through the empty space where his heart should be.

Without waiting, I ran for my life. At seventeen, the thought of being homeless was infinitely more appealing than the one I had lived thus far. To this day, I don't know if he lived or died from the wound I inflicted. I can't say I care one way or the other. With this last act of self-preservation, I changed. Steel covered my emotions, and ice filled my veins. Never again would I be a victim, nor would I hide. I entered his house as a meek child and left an uncaring adult. All thanks to the parents who were meant to protect me.

And now, after all this time, the one being I had hoped I would never see again is cowering in the presence of Death. I don't know if she thought he would spare her simply because I was traveling with him; if so, she is mistaken. It is the one time I am happy for him to be unrelenting in his assigned task.

"Avalon, honey, it's me, momma."

"You are not my mother." The words erupt from me. My heated response does nothing to waylay his growing belief she is exactly what she claims to be. I hate sharing any amount of DNA with this vile woman, but contributing this one thing required for all life to exist does not make you a mother or a father.

"Baby girl," a nickname she gave me at a young age when she tried to butter me up so I would *be nice* to the men who came to visit.

"Don't call me that either," I hiss, trying to stop the tremble of my hands as rage slowly leaks through my system, poisoning me as it goes. Closing me off even further than I already am.

"Ava, it's really me. I'm your momma." Her words have lost much of the conviction they had earlier. She mumbles as she slowly pushes herself back upright with her hands reaching out. For what? For me? Fuck that! I can't say why she thought I would welcome her with open arms. What I can tell you is like the reaper watching us; I sure as shit have no intention of allowing her to touch me either.

Watching this pathetic woman, I realize she gave me a gift of sorts. She made me someone strong enough to face Death himself without begging on my knees. Her lessons, though hard taught, were learned well. Turning, I feel no need to remain in her presence, just like when I was a child; she has nothing left to offer me. The only lessons she could teach me were doled out long ago.

"Avalon, honey," I have no desire to remain in her presence for one more second, nor do I care to listen to anything she has to say.

It's not until Death speaks that I hesitate. "What would you have me do with her?"

With my hand on the doorknob, I take several deep breaths. Calvin's evil sadistic grin flashed through my mind, but the memory of Janie's smiling face alone seals her fate. Turning my head slightly, I reply, "Whatever you want."

Her screams are cut off as I shut the door behind me. I know I should regret letting him reap the soul of the woman who gave birth to me. Let me assure you I do not. My only regret is I couldn't save Janie and that fucking infectious smile of hers.

Chapter Twenty-Three: I Don't Believe You

Death Late Spring 2024

AVALON DISCOVERING HER MOTHER alive left more questions than answers, although I now understand where her strength comes from. She had no choice but to grow up quickly, and when the woman touched me, I felt some of what Avalon's life had been like. After I reaped her mother's soul, I was provided with all the memories they both hid away. I saw every despicable and horrible thing her parents did to her. If I could revive her only so I could carry her away to the gates of hell myself, I would. She deserves no less. I do not push Avalon for answers; I believe she has earned the right to disclose only what she wants to tell me.

One name weighed heavily on her mother's thoughts; a man named Calvin. Someone her mother cared for more than her own daughter. Her mother would do anything to please him, hoping one day he would take her to be his wife, but as Avalon grew, his eyes turned from the mother to the scared little girl no one protected. Unlike most mothers, this heinous woman handed her only daughter over to him, hoping to win Calvin's favor.

Since the day we discovered her mother, Avalon's desire to be close to me has increased, especially at night. Often, we start in separate beds, or when no bed is available, the bedrolls we sleep in, only to have her climb into mine. Each time, my response is to pull her into my waiting arms. My soothing soft whispers tell her she is safe with me while I stroke her hair. I hope I offer her some comfort, even if only for a few hours.

Roughly a month after the events in that warehouse, Avalon has slowly returned to the woman I have come to care for more than I should. Which makes lying next to her every night difficult. I long to run my fingers over her soft skin, to commit to memory every dip, every curve, every scar. I often think of the first time I invaded her dreams. I want to hear her say my name as she did that night in her tent.

I came closer to giving into this all-consuming desire the night I sheltered her from the cold, but in the end, I realized her affection had also shifted. Avalon deserves so much more than a rider who will someday be called home. If I could give it to her, I would. Unfortunately, I am not capable of granting this, and I will not take what I cannot keep.

For the first time in my long existence, I find myself wishing for a different path, for a mortal life. A human life I could share with Avalon until time and age reap my soul before claiming hers.

Marcelle Valentine

I am certain our maker never intended for me to develop feelings for one of his other children. We, and by we, I mean his divine non-mortal creations, are meant to love them all equally, judge them fairly, and reap only when he is assured they are no longer redeemable. But I know as long as Avalon lives, I cannot do as he has instructed because this one soul proves I do not treat them as equals. Which explains why Ghost wants to remain with her since he is merely an extension of me.

Watching as she slips into the peace she only finds during sleep and only when in my arms, I realize it is too late for me to halt these emotions. If I hope to fulfill my father's request, I must tread carefully around her. Therefore, I have no damn idea why I am preparing to ask her the following question....

Avalon

Death has been more subdued than normal. Making me question if he is still longing to return to his previous life. Maybe seeing my mother was the tipping point in his decision; we, in fact, are not worthy. I guess my side trip was a horrific failure, and when his brothers wake, I wonder if they will take me out first for failing or leave me until the end to witness our fall.

I've thought about her a couple times since that day. I have to wonder what happened to the woman who gave birth to me in her life to turn her into the cold, drug-addicted monster I knew. I thought about asking Thanatos what fate he chose for her a few times, but honestly, I don't care enough about her.

Since we are still riding southeast, I can only assume he doesn't want to return to his horde. Based on our location, if I had to guess, we should arrive at the eastern seaboard within the week. I can't say I'm disappointed knowing I will get my wish to see the ocean one more time, and I would be lying if I didn't admit that I find the thought of doing this with Thanatos appealing.

Everything about today has been less about talking and more about self-contemplation, but the first thing he says to me since we climbed on Ghost shatters our peaceful existence.

"Would you enjoy what he does to his mate?"

"What?" I admit to being extremely confused by his question. I do not know who he's talking about or what they did. So, I'm unsure how to answer him.

He lifts my book. "I am referring to this?"

When the hell did he take my book? I swear I put it in my bag before we set out this morning. Running through our entire day, I rack my brain trying to figure out exactly when he could have taken it right up until he says, "Well?"

Is he trying to make me uncomfortable, or is he just trying to see if he can get a rise out of me? Well, I hate to tell him this, but I don't rattle easily. Squaring my shoulders, I blurt, "Death, are you asking me if I like sex?"

"Once again, you answer a question with a question, Apple."

Okay, so he has no intention of answering me. So maybe my question rattled him. With a devilish grin tipping my lips, I give him an answer even if it is not what he seeks, "I'm no virgin if that's what you are asking."

"I did not ask if you have ever engaged in a physical act with a mortal man," He advises while turning in his saddle, his eyes boring into mine. If I didn't know any better, I would say he doesn't want to hear about me having sex with other men. Jealous. Jealousy is the best way to describe how he is looking at me. Which is ridiculous. What the hell does he have to be jealous of? "I asked if you would like the things described in your book to be done to you. If the crumpled pages are anything to go by, I would say you spent most of your time rereading the passages describing these acts."

"Scrutinized the pages, did you?"

"Avalon," he growls

"Thanatos," I growl right back, but it may have been tinged with a hint of amusement.

"If you are attempting to start a fight merely to avoid answering my question, you could just say you do not wish to answer."

"Okay, I do not wish to answer." The tick in Thanatos's jaw displays exactly how much I can get under his skin. But I notice he hasn't turned away yet. Still, I should take pity on the poor guy and give him some credit; most men could give a shit less what a woman wants in the bedroom. Which begs the question, why is he so curious?

"I thought you had no interest in our putrid flesh." I swallow hard, trying not to show my interest in knowing the answer to this question. To determine if his stance regarding mortals, specifically sex with a human, is different now.

"Who said this has changed?"

"Then why — why ask?" My stutter giving away this is not what I was hoping to hear. Damn it to hell; why does his response bother me so much? It shouldn't; since the night of the winter storm, he has not given me any sign he has any desire to be with me. Even so, I guess I always held out hope that night was not a dream. With his response, my lingering question has at long last been revealed.

"I believe I have my answer," he says, tilting his head.

"I didn't say shit."

"You didn't have to. Your dilated eyes, flushed skin, shallow breaths, and pounding heart all tell me what I want to know."

"Which is?"

Death leans closer to me. His lips brush along my ear, and his warm breath against my neck has a shiver passing through me.

"Not only would you like it, but you have also thought about it more than once." Fuckin hell, please tell me he doesn't know he had the starring role.

"Nah-uh." Oh, real goddamn convincing, Avalon. Why don't you just stomp your foot while you're at it? Throw a little temper tantrum because they would all be about as believable as this pathetic attempt to deny what he just said. I would have been better off keeping my damn mouth shut.

With his mouth still pressed against the shell of my ear, he calls me out on my bullshit answer, "I do not believe you."

Squirming uncomfortably behind Thanatos, his next action does little to help with this when he twists to pull me in front of him. Trying to swallow down the range of emotions swelling in me, I ask, "Why did you do that?"

"Because I enjoy having you close, Apple." His warm breath tickles my neck, and his powerful arms bracing me firmly against his chest, has my heart racing. Now I have more questions than answers.

"I was right behind you."

"And as much as I like the feel of your arms wrapped around me," he leans forward, his lips hovering centimeters from the spot I want him to kiss. "I wanted you right here because having you in my arms is infinitely more gratifying."

My sharp inhale causes a slight chuckle from him. But I don't miss how he pulls me closer against his firm body. While I try to dissect the turn of events our conversation took, I can't help thinking how much I agree.... I like being here too.

*****

For the first time since the world changed, I'm content. I am staying in a mansion which is another brand new experience. Okay, calling the place a mansion might be a stretch, but it is the nicest house I've ever been in, let alone slept in. Made nicer by the delicious meal Thanatos and I prepared, followed by a bath with warm water in an actual bath. This would not have been possible without Thanatos lugging bucket after bucket of water from the fire we started to cook the food upstairs. And since the bath is one of those huge made-for-two tubs, it takes multiple trips to fill it.

Having learned his lesson a while back, Thanatos knocks before pushing the door open.

"Sorry to interrupt. I just wanted to ask if you need the water warmed up or if it's still warm enough?"

"It's fine," I say, but can't stop the smile from appearing.

"Just fine?" Seeing him leaning against the door frame with his head tilted, coupled with that sexy voice of his, makes me painfully aware of how underdressed I am, or he might be overdressed. Damn, why does he have to twist me up?

A thin layer of bubbles is the only thing hiding my naked body from his watchful eyes. Hell, who's to say he can't see through them anyway? I mean, let's face it, he is anything but human.

"Better than fine; it's the nicest bath I've had in years."

"I'm pleased I could provide you with this." He straightens to leave, and I realize this is the last thing I want him to do.

"Have you ever.... I mean, do you even have to...."

"Apple, are you asking if I bathe?" he inquires, leaning back against the frame, his muscular arms crossed over his sculpted chest. The material, pulled taut against it, shows every ridge and every flex of a muscle when he moves.

"Yeah, I guess I am."

"This body is not unlike your own while I am on your plane, so to answer your question. Yes, Apple, I do bathe."

"I suppose it was a silly question."

"No." I chuckle at his single-worded, sexy-as-hell answer. His eyes linger on the water right about where my breasts are located.

"Well, I'll leave you to it." He tells me, pushing away from the frame, and this time I know he'll leave unless I come up with something to make him stay. I may regret my next statement, but I can't think about it right now, or I will chicken out.

"Or you could...." I slide back, pulling my knees up to make room for him.

"What are you asking me, Avalon?" His eyes linger on the bubbles. If I didn't know any better, I would say he is trying to pull a Moses. Only instead of parting the red sea bubbles seems to be his goal, but that is just ridiculous. I am suddenly very aware I just asked one of the horsemen to join me for a bath, which leaves me feeling silly, to say the least. But what's done is done, causing me to swallow back the uncertainty creeping up inside me. Deciding the worse he can do is reject me, I lift my eyes to meet his. Making my decision, I will not retract my offer; I square my shoulders. What's the saying? In for a penny, in for a pound. With any luck, no one will be around to collect that pound of flesh.

"I guess I was asking if you would like to join me. We are two grown adults; I think we can handle sitting in the same space as one another. Don't you?" His eyes flash, and when they meet mine again, they shine as bright as the stars on a cloudless night. There is a split second I believe he will storm out of the room, but when he removes his shirt, I don't know if I'm more excited or dumbstruck.

I turn my head, pretending something outside the window has just garnered my undivided attention, but in reality, I didn't want to be caught gawking at his body as I have in the past. The thud startles me when he drops his boots to the ground, yet I still refuse to look over at him. I can faintly make out his reflection in the window. What I discover is him standing with his hands resting on his hips while looking up at the ceiling. Is he asking for strength? Forgiveness? Or is he realizing how stupid this whole idea really is? Based on the mildly pained expression reflected back to me, I would have to say it's the latter.

Closing my eyes, I allow the first pang of disappointment to materialize. I am just preparing to force a laugh while yelling something equally stupid like, *I got you*, before rushing out of the bath when the water shifts around me. It rises higher until it sloshes over the side of the tub, and I feel one leg brush against my hip. With my arms still hugging my knees, I rest my head on top of them. Desperate to know if he is as nervous as I am, I take a chance to glance in his direction.

"Feels nice, doesn't it?" He tilts his head, allowing his eyes to follow the contours of what skin he can see, the hint of a smile tipping the corner of his lips. His back is resting against the tub, arms are lounging on the rim. Since a fair amount of water sloshed over the side when he joined me, I recognize if he abruptly stands up, the bubbles will no longer cover my breath, leaving me exposed. But right now, I don't care because his chest is out on display, and this time, my eyes are the ones following each line I find there.

Realizing how awkward the situation can become, I clear my throat and try to change the subject from being together, naked, in a bath. Only a few feet separate my body from his. Did I mention together? Naked? In the same tub? I take a deep breath, hoping to steady the tremble in my voice before asking my next question. An attempt I fail at rather miserably when it comes out in a rush.

"Where are we heading next?"

"Southeast."

"So, the same direction we have been heading the entire time," I laugh.

"It is the direction you asked me to travel in. Is it not?"

"It is. You realize we will not be able to travel any further at some point?" His jaw clenches for a second before relaxing when I elaborate. "Because we will run out of land to continue going east. If my calculations are correct, we are not that far from the Atlantic Ocean."

"They are correct."

"So I guess what I was asking is what happens then?"

"Why do mortals like sitting in their own filth?" Okay, so he isn't going to tell me. To be honest, he hasn't said much about his plans for several days now, which is unusual. Normally, he has no problem telling me these things. But if he wants to hold some things secret, who am I to balk? Hell, I have kept my entire existence a secret from everyone I know. So rather than push my question, I respond to his.

"Ummm, I don't think most of us do?" My response is more question than answer since I'm unsure what he meant by his inquiry.

"Isn't that precisely what we are doing now, sitting in water used to wash away the grime and sweat from the day?"

"Oh. Well, most people who linger in the tub do it more to relax than wash away the day's grime." I guess I never thought of it like that, but he has a point.

"You find this relaxing?"

"It can be."

"How?"

"The warm water eases tense muscles. If you add bath salts or oils, the aroma can be calming. Having someone else bathe you can be...." I trail off, not wanting to tell him: sensual, arousing. Nope, it's best to let him form his opinion on what this last part could mean all by himself.

But it seems my comment has garnered his full attention. "Have you ever had someone bathe you?"

"No."

"Why not?"

"Truthfully, I never liked having my hair done or going for massages, manicures, pedicures. None of it really."

"Why?"

"I don't do well with people in my personal space," his eyes soften. Does he understand my past is directly related to my aversion to these things? A question I would prefer not to have the answer to, so rather than allowing it to hang in the air providing him the opportunity to ask, I say, "but under the right conditions.... It can be nice."

"I shall have to take your word for it."

"You've never had anyone do these things for you before?"

"I am Death, Avalon. Most mortals avoid me or at the very least give me a wide berth," I think back to the times with the horde, and I realize he's right. No one, not even Xander, ever intentionally went into his space. "Those who do generally are not long in this world."

"Except me?"

"Except you."

"Why? I mean, why me?" I have often wondered about this; the issue is I never had the guts to ask, but since he brought it up, it's now or never.

"You are the anomaly."

"Anomaly. I don't think I like being abnormal." I respond with a laugh.

"Not abnormal, different, unique, and being either of these is not a bad thing, Apple."

"I'll have to take your word for it?" I repeat the words he spoke to me earlier.

"One day, you will understand your value. Until that day, you will simply have to believe what I'm telling you is true." He says, leaning his head back on the tub's rim before closing his eyes. Thinking back to what he said before about how no one comes around him for fear of risking their own life. If I am the only one exempt from his judgment, then perhaps I can do something nice for him. Maybe it can be my last lesson.

I shift to gather the shampoo bottle and a container to collect water. If Death feels me moving, he doesn't give anything away. Sliding between his legs, cautious of where

I'm positioned, stopping just short of his man bits, I scoop up some water and pour it over his hair, careful not to get it into his eyes.

"Avalon, what are you doing?" He asks, lifting his head to look at me.

"Shush, just be quiet and enjoy," I tell him, bringing my hand filled with shampoo to his head so I can gently massage it into a lather. I'm painfully aware my breast, as well as my nipples, are no longer hidden below the sudsy water. And Death seems to realize this too, as his eyes move down to look at them. Admire them? I'm not really sure, but he seems content to stare.

I continue rubbing my fingertips against his scalp, applying various amounts of pressure as I go. His eyes move back up to mine, and his gaze is unnerving. I almost wish he'd look at my boobs again. When I shift to the back of his head, I have to slide closer, bringing my erect nipples inches from his chest and my mouth dangerously near his.

He hasn't so much as moved a muscle since he looked up at me, making me wonder if Thanatos finds any pleasure in what I'm doing or if he is only being a gentleman by not telling me to stop. Any fears or doubts I have drifted away when his eyes slip closed, and he bites down on his lip. Rinsing the shampoo from his hair, I realize I neglected to grab the conditioner. Not that his silky hair needs it, but I'm not ready to end our time together.

The instant I turn to get the bottle, his hands are on my hips, and his blue eyes question why I am leaving.

"I'm not going anywhere; I just can't reach the conditioner," I say, pointing at the lone container sitting at the other end of the tub.

His gaze moves down to my mouth before settling back on my eyes. With his hand still gripping my hips to hold me in place, he abruptly sits up. Once again, his face is precariously close to mine. Instinctually, my eyes slide down to those soft lips, and my desire to feel them against me has me leaning closer. Loosening his grip on my hips, he slides one hand around to my lower back as he reaches for the bottle behind me. Without saying a word, he hands it to me before leaning back against the tub again. He seems completely unfazed by what happened while I have to work to bring my breathing under control. Leaving me to wonder if a harbinger of death is this skilled in the art of seduction or if he is just this unaffected by mine.

Is that what the hell I'm doing here? Am I really trying to seduce a rider of the apocalypse? What's my end goal here? To fuck him in hopes of saving all humanity? But there is some deeper, darker part of me that knows the fate of humanity has no bearing on why I'm doing it. Realizing he is still watching me, I swallow before resuming what I started while I continually tell myself I'm doing it to prove to him there is more than just pain in our world.

Keep telling yourself that, Avalon. Maybe someday you might actually believe saving the world was the only reason you wanted to continue touching him.

When I meet his gaze, I find a subtle change in them. They are lighter than normal, not the crystal clear I've seen before, but definitely lighter.

Massaging the conditioner into his hair for the next couple of minutes, I try to keep my mind from overthinking this. His only response is to move his head with my actions to give me better access to what part I am working on. I also notice his hand has remained on my lower back. The force he applies there is light enough to allow me movement but firm enough not to permit me any further distance from him.

By the time I rinsed the last of it from his hair, the water had grown cool, yet I would stay here in freezing cold water for the rest of my days if it meant I could spend some more time with him. Picking up the sponge, I wait for him to tell me if he wants me to proceed or stop. When he dips his head, I pour soap over it to wash his body. I start with the arm he has draped on the tub. When I move to the one pressed against my lower back, he replaces it with his free hand. When this one is done, he does not place it on the tub as I suspected he would; instead, he returns it to my lower back, caging me between his arms.

As I continue washing him, his gaze follows the path I take with the sponge. When I move lower, a low groan escapes him when I brush against his hardened length. This is it. Either I have to stop now or step over the point of no return.

While I am busy debating everything and saying a silent prayer for it not to be just another dream, he makes the decision for me when he takes the sponge, so he can begin washing me.

Shifting, he uses the hand still sitting low on my back to pull me closer, forcing me to place my legs on either side of his torso. Which puts us in an extremely compromising position. How in the hell did this go from wanting to do something nice for him to me being held in his embrace? Worse, within his embrace, on the verge of moaning each time his hand glides over my skin. I wonder if he understands how turned-on I am. I wonder if he is.

The thought does not go unanswered for long when he readjusts to rinse the bubbles from my back. Yep, he's definitely still as turned on as I am if the stiff erection brushing against my lady parts is any indication.

He drizzles the water over my left shoulder, across my collarbone, and all the way over to my right side. His eyes follow the water as it cascades over my breast. The entire act is extremely erotic, but it's his eyes never leaving my body I find the most sensual.

He washes my right arm first, dropping the sponge long enough to massage my hand. As he finishes, he kisses each finger and palm before he moves to the left.

With my arms completed, he places the sponge against my chest, hesitating as his eyes come up to mine, almost asking my permission before proceeding. Just as he had done to me, I nod my agreement, an act which makes him smile. I can't say if he smiled because I gave him permission to proceed or because I mimicked his earlier response when I was the one asking for permission.

His gentle touch continues as he glides the sponge down over my sensitive nipple; on instinct, my head falls back as my breathing increases. Pulling me closer, Death guides my head back up so he can watch my response. When I open my eyes, I discover the crystal color has returned to his, and as handsome as I have always found him, he has never been more beautiful than he is right now. I want him, but I want him to want me as well.

Leaning forward, I brush my lips over his mouth. When he does not respond, I believe I have my answer. Figuring the desire is one-sided, I pull away until his arms tighten around me and his lips find mine. The kiss he initiates is everything I had hoped it would be. It's sexy, sensual, and passionate but mostly consuming. Here with this man, this moment is all-consuming. He is all-consuming.

Marcelle Valentine

Doing something I never thought possible, I break our kiss. I do it because the water has turned from cool to cold, and let's face it, there is nothing sexy about shivering while in the arms of a man like Thanatos. His questioning eyes quickly drop from mine. Does he think I didn't like it? I can assure him nothing could be further from the truth. I could tell him, but I would much rather show him.

Slowly standing, his eyes fly back up to watch as the last of the suds glide over my wet skin. I remain there, allowing him to look at me. To see me as I truly am, not as the pissed-off woman hell-bent on proving a point when he barged in on me, not the woman he saw when he mistakenly walked in on but as a woman who wants him to look, wants him to touch, taste, tease, fill as much as I want to do these things for him.

Reaching down, I take his hand in mine, encouraging him to follow me. He shifts, coming to full height, and as he did to me, it is my turn to watch as the water runs over the hard planes of his chest, abs, and glorious erection.

Dropping the sponge, he takes my other hand in his before stepping out of the tub. Unlike him, when I step out, I don't hesitate; instead, I keep his hand firmly encased in mine as I lead him to the bedroom.

Death pulls, whipping me back into his arms. Before I can ask what he's doing, he crushes his mouth to mine in a heated, needy kiss that makes my toes curl. Tongues chasing, hands roaming, once-in-a-lifetime kind of kiss. The one you can only experience when you have longed for it, imagined it, dreamed of what it would be like, wanted it so bad you ache just thinking of it, sort of kiss.

I need more than just a kiss as I glide my hand down, wrapping it around his thick, hard erection. The second my hand comes into contact with him, he hisses. When I glide it up to run my thumb over the head, gathering his glistening precum in the process, his hiss morphs into groans as his head falls away from me. I wonder if he has ever experienced this, or am I the first?

The thought of being the only woman to make him feel like this empowers me to take things further. To show him what he's been missing all this time.

Kissing my way down his chest, I sink to my knees in front of him. His questioning eyes watch what I intend to do. Sucking the thumb still glistening from his prerelease, the salty taste of him fills me with a wild desire to have more. His eyes follow every move I make. Keeping my gaze on him, wanting to see the emotion I can pull from him, I run my tongue up the length of his cock, licking up the liquid left by my thumb. He doesn't hiss, nor does he moan. He speaks in a language unknown to me. It's not Spanish, it's not French, it's not Italian, and I don't think it's Arabic; regardless, whatever it is, I like the sound of it when spoken from his luscious lips. It is beautiful, and I want to hear him say more.

I kiss the tip before sliding my mouth around him, taking him in as far as my throat permits.

"Jocu ru mlsufjlt, wyltus. Was afhi iae, aes ksuylas, dfazm ztyl mtu vaum la ru." Each word. Hell, each syllable Thanatos speaks makes my clit pulse with anticipation.

I pull back only long enough to tell him, "Say it again."

Before he can respond, I suck him back in and begin working to bring him to the edge. Do I want to make him come apart? Yes. Would I prefer to do it after I've sated the burning desire building within me? The same one I've had for him since my very first dream? I would. But will I fulfill whatever need he has of me right now? Ab-so-fucking-lutely. I only hope there will be a next time. Maybe even one where I speak in tongues.

"Iae ysu ltu raml nuyeloweh nuofj o tycu ucus hyov uium af."

Listening to his breathing and groans are my clues when I do something he likes and when I do something that makes him come unglued. On the edge of rapture, he is still talking to me in a language I now believe no human has ever heard. I increase my speed. The need to taste everything he wants to give is pushing me to a frantic pace. His hands knotting in my hair confirm how close he is.

"Ycyhaf ni jav ztyl ysu iae vaofj la ru." I reward him for doing as I ask by swirling my tongue around the tip of his erection down his shaft and back up, stopping only long enough to lick away the drop of precum.

"Fuck." His hissed response was the first thing he said I could understand.

"Ah-ah-ah, handsome, I understood that one."

"Avalon," I gently drag my teeth over him as I pull him back into my mouth, letting him know I do not approve of his disregarding my request.

"I nuj iae la tycu ruski af ru. Wekd. Wekd. Wekd."

"Good horseman." I moan, kissing away the pleasurable pain I just provided.

"Vaf'l mlat."

"Do you like what I'm doing to you?"

He nods, but this is not what I want. Clicking my tongue, I demand, "Tell me if you like what I'm doing to you?"

"Ium! Ium, O hodu ztyl iae ysu vaofj la ru. Thuymu vaf'l mlat."

"Mmmm, I'll take that as a yes then." His eyes seek mine; even if he wasn't nodding his head feverishly, I would find my answer written in his soulful eyes. I guess I know what it means now when his eyes change from blue to crystal. With his hands twisting viciously in my hair, his hips pivot as he thrusts deeper, desperate to satisfy the delicious ache I have skillfully built. Running my fingers up to his nipple, I apply pressure as I pick up my pace until he screams my name and spills his release. Remaining on my knees until I have taken it all, I pull back with a pop. As he pants madly above me.

"I suppose I can now ask you if a horseman enjoys the things Kenna did to Logan?"

He inhales deeply and pulls me to my feet, allowing him to kiss me frantically before pulling away, only long enough to confirm what is abundantly obvious.

"Very much so."

Chapter Twenty-Four: Control

*P*ICKING AVALON UP, I would like nothing more than to hear her scream my name as she made me growl hers. I have never known such rapture in all my long life. I should like to experience it again. The mere thought of her mouth on me, her tongue chasing my release, has me aroused again. And as much as I would like to watch her on her knees pleasuring me, I want this more.

Lying her on the bed, I run my fingers down her side and across her thighs, careful not to touch any part she is aching for me to explore. I want to enjoy her as she did me. Every moan, groan, and each whimper. She will beg me just as she made me beg her.

"Are you hard again already?" She asks, sounding somewhat astonished when my body responds to seeing her laid out before me.

Following her eyes down to my hard length, ready to have her again, the memory of her with her mouth wrapped around me is so vivid I have to stop myself from begging her to do it again. A spasm ripples through me, reminding me how it felt as I found my release.

Had I known how good sex with Avalon would feel, I would have taken her the first night she dreamt of me. My problem is I am unsure if I would have done anything else after that. As a matter of question, I should like to know how any male who has experienced such gratification manages to control their urges?

"Is this not normal?"

"Not for most men. No."

"I think you should know by now I am not like mortal men, Apple."

"You can say that again." With her eyes focused on the product her beautiful mouth caused, Avalon's mumbled response was not meant for me to hear, but I heard it nonetheless.

Moving my finger to the inside of her ankle, I trace the contours up her calf, along her knee to mid-thigh, where I stop. Her hips lift, hoping to encourage me to proceed but not yet. I can see the scars left by the man her mother sold her to. One day I hope she trusts me enough to tell me what he did. I may not be able to avenge her, but I have the power to help her move past it. But not until she is ready to do so. The instant my finger traces the first of her scars, she jerks, pulling away from my touch.

"Don't."

"No one can hurt you any longer, Avalon. I will not permit them to do so."

"It's a past I prefer to leave there," she advises as she sits up before pushing back against the headboard. She maneuvers, covering her naked frame from my wandering eyes.

"Okay, no questions about the scars. It was not my intention to hurt you." She relaxes, but I fear I may have ruined everything. Leaning on the bed, I kiss her arm and the tops of her knees, her shoulders, and by the time I kiss her neck, the desire I believed I had chased away leeches back into her eyes. As she bites down on her lip, I walk to the end of the bed; her eyes stay focused on my every move. Reaching up, taking an ankle in each hand, I slide her back down the bed until I can begin kissing the same path my hand followed before. Careful not to touch the scars, her breathing has returned to the needy breaths from before I screwed everything up.

Settling between her thighs, I take my time to memorize every shape and area she has to offer. Kissing the top of each thigh, I want nothing more than to bite into the tender flesh on the inside of her leg, pull it into my mouth, and hear her beg, but I believe she would enjoy it more if I move slightly higher. Taking one last look at her eyes, hooded by the desire for me to taste her, I give her what she wants as I run my tongue along the slick folds at her core.

"Oh, Jesus Christ," she moans, causing a new emotion to surface. Jealousy.

"Avalon."

"Yes," she pants.

"Please do not yell another man's name when you are with me."

"What?" The confusion written on her face forces me to explain myself.

"I am not Jesus. I am Thanatos, the pale rider and the bringer of Death—"

"You don't think I know who you are? I know exactly who is in bed with me. Trust me when I tell you I have no desire for anyone else to be here. Sometimes when mortals say this, it is not meant in the literal sense; it's more figurative. Said in the heat of the moment, but I promise I won't say it again."

Her hand comes to the side of my face. "I'm sorry, I didn't think."

Yanking to pull her off-center, she flops back on the bed, and before she can say anything else, I return to exploring her. She seems to like it best when I focus on the tight bundle of nerves towards the front of her wet folds, but she also moans loudly when my tongue slips inside her. Yet the action she becomes undone with, the one that makes her finally beg, is when I insert my fingers while sucking the bundle of nerves into my mouth. Remembering how pleasurable it was when she did it to me, I skim my hand up her bare frame until it strokes against her erect nipple. It is the final piece needed to send her into a frenzy. Her hand finds the back of my head as her hips lift to encourage me to continue my ministrations.

"Fuck, fuck, fuck. Don't stop." Yes, I remember this too. I also remember how close I was to releasing the waves of euphoria when I began begging like she is now. Increasing the movement of my hands, I switch from licking to sucking to biting.

"I'm gonna come, Holy fucking hell," her hand pulls me closer as she grinds against my mouth, chasing the inevitable outcome of my attention.

"Thanatos," she screams as she clenches around my fingers. The wetness explodes, coating my digits. Sliding them from within her, I continue licking and tasting until she collapses on the bed and her hand slides from the back of my head. After realizing how much pleasure I can give her, the erection I've had since climbing into the tub with her now aches to fill the space my fingers just occupied.

A thought occurs to me as I lick away the last of her desire; I could happily stay here in this house, in this bed, between these legs for all eternity, and it would still not be long enough.

Climbing up her body, I look down at the most perfect creation my father has ever made. She is my every desire realized.

"Are you ready for the next part?" she asks, stroking her fingers along my back.

"Dare I ask?" She nods before she reaches down to take my hard length and drags it against the warmth of her soaked core. Yes, I want this. I crave her more than I have ever desired anything in my long life. To slide inside her, thrusting again and again until she screams my name. The sweetest sound made all the sweeter when said by those lips. She slides her legs up mine until they rest behind me, locking them behind my back, and when she pulls them down towards her body while lifting her ass off the bed, I slide inside her.

Never have I been granted such utter pleasure as I experienced the second I was fully seated within her. Desperate to experience the intense sensation again, I withdraw, and when I thrust back down, it is every bit as pleasurable as it was the first time. Truthfully, it may be more since she is now kissing my neck in a way every muscle in my body has gone rigid.

Just like last time, I will happily do anything she demands of me as long as she continues moving like she is.

"I tycu fucus wuhl mekt thuymesu, ytthu." (I have never felt such pleasure, Apple.)

Her response is to shift her legs higher, but then she presses her ass back down, and the new position sucks me deeper within her.

"O kaehv hocu zoltof iae was ltu suml aw ri vyim yfv ol zaehv fal nu ufaejt. Ol zohh fucus nu ufaejt." (I could live within you for the rest of my days, and it would not be enough. It will never be enough.)

Her moans of pleasure are growing with each confession I make.

"O yhzyim dfuz iae zaehv nu ri efvaofj, ycyhaf. Y lselt o yr acusbaiuv la rydu y suyholi." (I always knew you would be my undoing, Avalon. A truth I am overjoyed to make a reality.)

I swallow her moan when I crush my mouth to hers. My tongue slides over her lips, begging her to grant me access. When she sucks it into her mouth, the climax I was holding off rips out of me, spilling everything I have inside her. Unwilling to stop until she finds her release, I reach between her legs to rub her.

"Fuck yes! That feels good, but I will explode if you keep rubbing my clit." Good, this is precisely what I want. Hoping to help her, I move my lips from hers down to the erect nipples I have wanted to lick since the first time I saw them. Running my tongue over the first one, she grinds against my hand and body harder, squeezing my erection in the process.

The growl she evokes from me has me moving my hips again. She forces me to roll so she can be on top, which I like as much as any of the other positions she has shown me. She can use my body to stimulate the nerves she likes me touching in this new position, allowing me to focus on the breasts, now teasing my lips.

Moving from one side to the other, I am unsure what she likes more, but I like it best when I hold her nipple firmly between my teeth as my tongue swipes away the pain I inflict. If done correctly, I have discovered pleasure and pain are one and the same, and Avalon seems to agree because the second I release one nipple, she pushes me to take the other.

Her movements are frenzied as her walls clench around me, sucking the last of my release from me, and like the previous time when she reaches the brink, she tells the world by screaming my name.

Our ragged breaths are the only sounds filling the otherwise silent room. With me still buried deep inside her, Avalon leans down to kiss me gently.

Avalon

That was hands down the best sex I have ever experienced, and even though I am completely sated, I hope he will be up for another round or two before we have to pack up and move on. Death, who I have surmised from our previous conversations, has never done this before, is a fast learner. Three sexual experiences down for him, with so many more to go. I am left with only one question.

"Will you tell me what you said?"

"No."

"Why?"

"You wished to hear me speak in my native tongue; in fact, you demanded it. So I did as you asked. I told you all my desires in my native language. However, this is where your request ended because you did not require me to translate after. If you wished to know what I said, you should have demanded it then."

"Seriously?"

"Yes. Besides, I did something I have not done before."

"What?" I ask while following his muscles down to the source of my extreme pleasure. The memory of controlling him even though I was the one on my knees has me licking my lips with the anticipation of when I will do this again. I enjoyed the control I had over him but loved the sound of my name on his lips when he found his release spilling every drop in my mouth. I am so lost in my thought of our first encounter I almost forgot I asked him a question.

"Spoke in my native tongue. It is a language not many mortals have ever been permitted to hear, but more importantly, I relinquished control. Something I have never done for anyone."

"Would you have told me what you said if I asked you then?"

"I would have done anything you asked of me. Then, Apple." His emphasis on the word then tells me it's not something he plans on granting me, at least not now.

"I'll keep that in mind for the future."

"You believe I will relinquish control again?"

Wrapping my hand around his hardening cock, I slowly begin stroking it until his eyes grow hungry; when a low growl fills the room, I grin. Satisfied I have proven my point, I release him. He watches as I suck the drops of precum I collected from my thumb. I triumphantly climb out of bed, sauntering towards the bathroom, as I declare, "Oh, I know you will."

*****

Over the next couple of days, we spent every second engaged in one sexual act or another. Thanatos seems to enjoy taking me from behind. He's bent me over the tub, the kitchen table, the couch, the wash basin in the basement, and the bathroom counter. Hell, he even took me against the glass patio set in the middle of a thunderstorm as I tried to gather the remains of our uneaten dinner. Completely naked except for the heels I wore for our romantic meal, he fucked me. Fingers digging painfully into my hips, my nipples stimulated from sliding over the glass top's wet surface. He took what he wanted from me, and I enjoyed every second of it.

Although I admit, our romantic dinner was uneaten because he told me feasting on me was infinitely more appealing than whatever we had managed to throw together from the food left in the house. And who am I to deny him what he wanted, so feast on me he did. Dress ripped in two, panties destroyed, he placed me on the table, scooted his chair close as if preparing for his evening meal, put my legs over his shoulders, and devoured me like a starving man. My clit still throbs every time I think about it.

He's learned I like my nipples stimulated when I come, and I've learned he likes when I drop to my knees and take what I want.

For the first time in my life, I found someone I felt comfortable enough to tell why I hated my parents and what happened when they sold me to Calvin. I told him about the scars and how Cal told me no one would ever want me now. He even carved his first initial on my stomach to prove he owned me. I told him about the shackles, the beatings, the sexual assaults. I admitted his beatings were so brutal because I refused to give in. Refused to say what he wanted me to say. Because I knew if I did, he would win, and if he won, it would mean he broke me. That thought alone was enough to deny him.

I confessed I only stayed to protect Janie, who died because of me anyway. I told him the darkest secret of all: when I drove the knife through his heart, I felt the most euphoric joy I had ever experienced. Well, until now, that is. And the simple fact is if I could find that much pleasure in taking someone else's life, it proves I am nothing like what he believes me to be.

Thanatos's response was to tell me it changed nothing. Truth be told, he finds me more worthy for having lived the life they forced on me and come out the strong woman I am today. Then he did something I didn't think possible. He took the power Cal held over me by kissing every scar he placed on my skin until they no longer belonged to Calvin. Until they were nothing more than a relic of a long-forgotten life. Even the ones I was most embarrassed by, the ones Calvin carved on my thighs.

Marcelle Valentine

In our mansion on the hill, we experience everything the world has left to offer. Until I woke this morning to find our bags packed and Thanatos waiting on the porch.

"Are we leaving?"

"It is long past time for us to be on our way."

Riding away from the house I claimed as ours, I can't help but feel everything has changed, and for the first time since I pulled him from that tub, I can't say if it's for the better.... Or the worse.

Chapter Twenty-Five: Time

Avalon Early Summer 2024

SEEING THE FIRST CREST of the Atlantic shimmering across the horizon below us, I want to beg him to turn around and take us back to the home we made together. But I know it would be pointless because he won't do it today, just as he wouldn't do it the last two.

Spring slipped away to Summer yesterday, and even the warmth from the sun feels incapable of thawing the freeze growing between us. Thanatos has been quiet since we left. Silent and distant would be better words to describe him. Even when we set up camp, he refuses to remain, telling me it would be best if he keeps watch in case anyone stumbles across our campsite, but I know it is so he doesn't have to be alone with me.

Marcelle Valentine

I guess the last hope I held we could get back to where we were four days ago disappeared when I begged him to join me in the tent, but rather than following, he let his wings carry him away from camp, away from me. I guess it was too much to hope my life had changed. Everything is different; hell, even Ghost seems sullen.

*****

"You brought me to the ocean?"

"It is where you wanted to come, yes?"

"I don't remember ever telling you that. In fact, I know I didn't."

"You may talk in your sleep."

"Shit, what the hell did I say?"

He smiles before taking my face in his hands. "Nothing that did not please me to hear."

Oh my God, what the hell did I say? Seeing my obvious discomfort, he breaks the silence with a confession I was unprepared for.

"I wanted to bring you here to experience one last thing with you."

"Last thing?"

"My father has summoned me home, Apple. I must return. I have fulfilled my assigned task."

"What? Now?"

"Yes. I have ignored his call far longer than I thought possible."

"When did they...."

"Two weeks ago."

"Why didn't you tell me?"

"I don't know. I suppose I did not know how to do it without hurting you."

"So you're leaving?"

"I can no longer defy his will."

"But what...." I want to ask him what about us since, barring the last couple of days when he has been somber, I have come to believe there could be an us. I care for him. Hell, I think I have fallen in love with him. How crazy is it to love one of the horsemen sent to judge us? But in the end, I chicken out, saying instead, "will happen to the people of this world."

Lifting my hands in his, he places a soft kiss against each one. "I will tell my father I found humanity beautiful and worthy of our forgiveness. I will advise there is no need to wake my brothers, and I will tell him it was a lesson taught by the best of them."

"I'm far from the best humanity has to offer."

"Not to me, Apple. To me, you are everything this world has to give."

"When will you go?"

"Soon." Closing my eyes, I finally understand why he has been so distant since we left the mansion. "I would like to give you something."

"A gift?" the sad little laugh I give him confirms I feel no happiness right now.

"Before I give it to you, would you like to know the fate of the coward who hurt you? The one named Calvin." I can sense he is desperate to give me the answer I never knew. Nodding my head, I will listen, but I cannot bring myself to look at him, keeping my gaze directed out over the rushing waves.

"He survived, but he was never the same. The man who made you beg for every scrap had to depend on others for his survival." A pained expression crosses my face, and as hard as I try to hide it from him, I know he saw it.

"So he is still alive."

"No. He died the day I met you, the day I destroyed the city I first saw you in. When you cross the city limits, I crumbled the place you called home, scattering his ashes to the four winds."

"He followed me?"

"He coveted you like he always had. So you see, Apple, you are not responsible for his death. I am."

My eyes slip closed as a lone tear trickles down my face. Weak. The mere mention of his name from Thanatos's lips and I am reduced to that defenseless, lost child he tried so damn hard to break. Death's finger wipes away the tear before it travels past my cheek, and his action is almost too much for me to bear. Too goddam humiliating for words.

"I also would like to give you something." he slips the compass I once gave him into my hand.

"I gave it to you."

"And now I am gifting it to you. To remind you anytime you feel lost or alone, you are not. I'm with you always." Running my fingers over it much as he did when I gave it to him, I can't bring myself to look at his gift. Feeling every bit as lost as he hopes this thing will prevent. When I gave it to him, I never thought I would have it back so soon.

"Do you regret it?"

"What?"

"Us."

"Yes." If a heart can break, hearing his confession shatters mine until he continues. "But not for the reason you think."

The sound of Ghost's soft whinny confirms our time is growing short. I realize I am not only losing Thanatos, but I am losing Ghost as well. Walking over to him, I run my hand down his forehead to his muzzle.

"You have to leave too, huh?"

Almost as if he understands me, he bobs his head.

"I'll miss you, Marshmallow." He snorts at the sudden name change. "Sorry, big guy, but I changed my mind. You're far too sweet to be a Ghost." He nuzzles his head against my face. I believe he understands at this moment while saying our last goodbye; I don't want to associate him with the man who haunted my dreams.

A lump forms in my throat as I whisper softly, "Take care of him for me, okay?"

He lifts his head so we look at one another, "and take care of yourself, sweet boy."

"I have to go, Avalon." Running my hand down his head once more, I turn to say the hardest goodbye I have ever had to say.

"Will I ever see you again?"

"Someday."

"When I die?" His gentle smile confirms my question is accurate. Closing my eyes, I can't bring myself to say the words. Telling him goodbye will all but assure Thanatos will leave me, and I don't want him to go. I want to beg him to stay with me, choose me, choose another path, another life. But I know I can't. To ask this of him would all but guarantee the other horsemen will come. And as much as I want to say screw everyone else, I know I can't be selfish. He has to return if humanity has any chance of surviving.

"Apple," hearing my nickname, the one I still have no idea why he calls me, makes my heart hurt, "I want you to know when I was first sent here, I only dreamt of returning to my previous life."

"And now?"

"I long for a life here with you," his words are whispered as his lips brush mine, followed by a kiss I know I will never experience again. A kiss that leaves me breathless and desperate to pull him back into my arms.

I can't watch him go when he pulls away. Keeping my head directed to the ocean, the one I was so desperate to see one more time. I realize he gave me my wish. A place I had always thought of with fond memories has shifted in minutes. Now I will remember it as the place where I lost what I valued the most. The saddest part is it will remain as such until my time here is done.

When I hear the creak of the saddle, I know he has mounted our horse to prepare for his departure. Forcing myself to look at the only man I have ever felt safe with; his gaze is focused on me. His eyes hungry for more, longing to stay with me.

"Return to Xander. He will assure you are kept safe." He pulls the reins to turn Ghost; with one last look over his shoulder, he says the one thing that finally breaks the gates, holding my tears at bay, "I will never forget you, Apple, and I will carry the memories of our time together for the rest of my days. Because of you, I learned what it means to be human."

And then he's gone. Taking my heart with his departure.

Sinking down to the sand, I whisper the one thing I was always too afraid to tell him, "I love you."

Chapter Twenty-Six: Life Moves On

That which is born of the flesh is flesh, and that which is born of the Spirit is spirit. John 3:6

Avalon Early Fall 2024

LIFE MOVES ON, THE world continues to turn; the sun rises as the moon sets, new life begins while others end, and I am still processing how to live in a world where he no longer exists.

The world learned of his departure as the months passed, and they rejoiced. I can't blame them, but I also do not have to pretend their revelry did not come at a steep price. One I paid for them to have their happiness.

Marcelle Valentine

The day he left me, I remained on the beach praying he would come back, but as the sun set behind me, I knew my prayers had gone unanswered, so I began the slow trek back to Suki and Xander. I do it because he asked me to; I do it because my heart aches in a way I never knew possible, and I want to be near someone who knows me.

By the time I returned to the place I had hoped to find her, the city was no more. It was nothing but a relic of what it once was. Buildings were destroyed or left in shambles. The burned-out shells left as an ominous reminder of what this place once represented and of the lives of the men and women who once thrived here.

I searched for any signs of whether my friend survived, but when I found the bracelet I gave her in another life, I sat down to wait for whatever death befell them to return for me. Without Suki to lean on, I could think of nothing I wanted more than to see him again. To have him hold me in his arms to tell me everything will be alright now.

The raven is back; his caws are the only sound remaining in this graveyard. Still, I wait. Wait and wonder when death, the state, not the man I love, will come for me.

To me, living or dying are two sides of the same coin. Just a flip in the air. Heads I go on, tails my friend, the raven has his meal.

I admit this is cowardly. I acknowledge it is not what he asked of me. But I can no longer force myself to care or pretend. No one, not my parents, not Calvin, not even Nevil with his band of thugs, could break me. It was finally allowing myself to love someone, to tell them every gory detail only to have him care for me regardless of my flaws; I lost. Because it was in loving him and losing him, our Creator did what none of the others could.... he broke me.

*****

You know the old adage, some shit about absence making the heart grow fonder. Well, I call bullshit. Because rest assured, I'm pissed, bitter, and ready to burn the world down around me; fondness is nowhere to be seen.

I want to know why he had to go back. I want to know why my friend, the one person I considered family, had to die. I want answers, so it is simple. I will not lie down and die until I fucking have them.

It's been seven days since I discovered the community I left my Suki in destroyed. Seven days of me waiting for something to guide me or take me. Until yesterday I could give a shit which it was.

A gang of assholes passed by last night. I managed to stay out of sight, but I had my blade poised and ready if any of them found my hiding spot. This is what made me realize I wanted answers more than I wanted to die. It would have been all too easy to storm out and force a fight I know I had no chance of winning, but it would have sent me to Thanatos.

The Raven's ever-watchful eyes seem to judge every choice I make.

"Yeah, I know you're sick of waiting for your meal," I wave him away as I wander down to the only freshwater around here. Unfortunately for the bird, I haven't given up quite yet, so he can continue waiting.

By the time I get back, the afternoon has slipped away to twilight, but my feathered friend remains. His incessant cawing is driving me crazy today. "Look, I'll make you a deal.

You can claim your prize if you bring Suki, Xander, and Thanatos back. If not, then piss off."

He squawks before flying away. Wondering what's gotten into him since he hasn't left my damn side for days, I watch as he glides along the currents. Huh, maybe he's given up on his free meal. He has just disappeared from sight when I feel the air shift around me, followed by the sweetest sound I have ever heard.

"Avalon." I know that voice, and the sound is one I never thought I would hear again.

"It's not him; you know it's not. When you turn around, the only thing you will find is empty space." When I turn, I swallow the fear of finding nothing, only to discover Thanatos standing there but not there. His silhouette flickers from the shifting light.

"Thanatos?"

"I see you at long last did something I asked of you."

"Fat load of good it did me." Stepping closer, I move my hand through the space his shape occupies. "Are you real?"

"I am real."

"But you're not really here."

"No, as much as I would like to be there with you, I cannot."

"Did your dad send you back?"

"No one sent me."

"Then I don't understand why did you come?"

"Your soul called out to me."

"My soul called you... And you came?"

"This surprises you?"

"No, I'm hoping you'll tell me how to do it again." His smile is everything I have been missing.

"You are not taking care of yourself as you should, Avalon."

Giving him an incredulous little laugh, I click my tongue before stating, "Don't have a lot to live for." Lifting my arms, I show him the state of the community I returned to.

"This is just a place, Avalon."

"Well, since every person I ever cared for was in this place or left me, this place is as good as any others." The pained expression he wears confirms he never wanted to leave me, and as much as I hate seeing this on his face, none of it does anything to ease the sting of losing him. Still, he doesn't deserve my shit. Not when he cared enough to come back. The simple truth is Death is big on the whole, obeying his creator thing, and I get the distinct feeling he didn't exactly get permission to come here.

"Why do you believe Suki perished here?" I lift my arm, pointing at the bracelet.

"I see." Figuring my point has been proven, I return it to my side and lift my gaze back to him. "She will thank you when you return it to her."

"What?"

"Neither Suki nor Xander was here when the community fell."

"Are you telling me Suki is...."

"Alive? Yes, she remains on your plane. She's searching for you, but I can tell you where she will go."

"Where?"

"When Xander and Suki learned of my departure, she told him they needed to go to the one place she thought you would return to."

"The cabin we were traveling to before we stopped in Cambridge." His smile confirms I'm correct.

"Before five foolish men brought the most precious cargo into my camp and presented me the greatest gift I would ever know."

"You're good." Okay, I admit the man knows how to give a compliment.

"I simply spoke the truth." He says with a wink.

"Do you still think about me?"

"You consume my every thought." I shouldn't be happy to hear he is suffering the same as I am, but I can't help it. I need to know if what we shared meant something to him too. "Thoughts of the most beautiful woman waiting in a tub filled with bubbles hiding her glorious body make it difficult to do much else."

Laughing, I return the smile he gives me. "It is a good one. I mean, it was the thing that started it all."

"No, it was merely the catalyst for what I had long desired."

"So I guess I'm heading back to Ohio."

"If you travel northeast from here, you will come across Suki and Xander within a community. They will stop for supplies but will choose to stay to help the residents. You should go there, Avalon, because nothing is left for you in Ohio."

"I guess the compass will finally have a use."

"A perfect gift to help you find your way."

"Maybe if I hadn't given it to you, you would have never left."

"I will always treasure the gift you gave me because it brought me to you."

"I miss you, Thanatos. I miss you so damn much. And Ghost, I miss him too. If I could have one wish, it would have been for more time."

"Close your eyes, Apple." Hearing my nickname, I bite my lip, hoping to halt the swell of emotion it brings. I can sense him moving closer. Doing as he asks, I close my eyes. The feel of his hand against my face is as real as the day he did it on the beach. But his lips against mine have me sucking in a sharp breath.

"I will not be permitted to return here, Apple. This was a one-time trip only because your body was failing."

Closing my eyes to the prospect of losing him again. I don't know which one was harder.

"Don't stay here. Live your life. Find happiness. Meet the man of your dreams, fall in love, have children, and know I will be there to welcome you when the time comes."

How do I tell him I had already met the man of my dreams and had fallen in love with him? Yet in the end, I don't say any of it because how would confessing this to him help ease the pain we are both experiencing? This is why I decided to travel Northeast, praying the weather doesn't turn foul before I can find her.

Chapter Twenty-Seven: Starting Over

Love is patient; love is kind. It does not envy, it does not boast, it is not proud. It does not dishonor others, it is not self-seeking, it is not easily angered, it keeps no record of wrongs. Love does not delight in evil but rejoices with the truth. It always protects, always trusts, always hopes, always perseveres. Love never fails. But where there are prophecies, they will cease; where there are tongues, they will be stilled; where there is knowledge, it will pass away. Corinthians 13:4-8

AND WHEN IT COMES TO MY HORSEMAN THANATOS, I WILL ALWAYS REMEMBER.

Avalon Early Winter 2024

*T*HE PEACE AROUND ME is shattered when Jared yells, "Avalon, I found it!"

"Hallelujah." I huff, tossing the stack of musty papers on my lap aside so I can wipe the dust from my hands and jeans.

I'm sure you are wondering who the hell Jared is. A week into my travels, I stumbled across a beaten shell of a man I took pity on. Fortunately for him, I didn't realize who he was right away; otherwise, he would have never lived to utter another word.

And what he told me sent my life careening on an alternative path....

*****

Nine Weeks Earlier

"Oh my God. I have never been so happy to find another soul." His brows pinch as a confused look covers his face. "You are real. Right? Please tell me you're real. I don't think I could survive if you are another hallucination."

"I'm real," I reply cautiously. Since Death was called home, I have encountered many people who were not what you would consider good sorts, and I would hate having to fight for my life when I am within a few weeks of finding Suki.

"That's good, really—really good. You cannot understand how agonizing it is not knowing...." he trails off, rubbing his head.

"What are you talking about? Not knowing what?"

"If the things you're seeing are real or not.... Wait. Oh damn, I see what you're trying to do there. No! You cannot make me talk about him," He says in a rush, backing away. I think he may actually be cowering. What the hell happened to this guy?

Lifting my hands to show I mean him no harm, I cautiously approach. I say cautiously because as much as I didn't want to traumatize the guy any further if this was a trap, I wanted to ensure I still had plenty of time to grab my dagger.

"It's okay. You don't have to say anything." His worried gaze flicks to the road behind me. He slowly straightens, obviously deciding I don't plan on hurting him.

"Where are you—where are you going?" he stutters as he continuously wrings his hands.

"I don't really know."

"Can I - Can I walk with you? Even if for just a little while?"

"I don't travel with other people." Especially people who may mistake me for an apparition and stab me while I'm sleeping.

"Please. Please, I-I won't talk. Please, just don't... don't leave me."

Now ordinarily, I would tell him to go pound sand, but something about him feels familiar, and this alone makes me disregard all the alarms telling me to walk away. "Only for a little while."

"Names Jared." He says as he stands abruptly.

"Amy," I may not have turned him away, but it doesn't mean I trust him, hence why I gave him a fictitious name.

"Nice to meet you, Amy." He extends his hand as he advances warily. Like a mouse terrified the cat will catch them, but desperate for the food left conveniently out for him to take, he approaches.

"Nice to meet you as well."

*****

Seven Weeks Ago

"Amy—"

"Avalon."

"I'm sorry?"

"My name.... As opposed to Amy." The confusion covering his face leads me to elaborate. "I guess I should have told you a while ago. Regardless, if you continue traveling with me, you would have found out soon enough."

"I suppose I understand why you wouldn't want to tell someone you just met who you really are, but Amy — I mean Avalon. Geez, it might take me a minute to get used to calling you this." I give him a sympathetic smile.

"I should probably.... You know what? It doesn't matter. Thanks for telling me."

*****

Four Weeks Ago

The sound of my fist smashing against his nose as he cries out breaks the tranquility of the night. "What did you just say, asshole?"

We had been traveling together for several weeks when he confessed to recognizing me. Jared told me he realized I was the female who traveled with the horseman, and he hadn't told me immediately because he feared I would leave him or kill him.

It turned out my new travel companion was the guy who stopped me from rushing out to save Thanatos that night in Charlotte all those months ago. The same asshole who hit me over the head before leaving me in a fucking basement while my horseman was being tortured.

"I suppose I deserve that."

Leaping at him, his desperate pleas as I held the blade to his throat loosened those lips enough for him to tell me he truly did what he did to save my life, thereby protecting my horseman's as well. After withdrawing the blade, I gave him five minutes to explain.

"I told you I grew up with the guy. His name is Robert, and he is the worst kind of sadistic prick left in this world."

"Was the worst kind," I correct.

"What do you mean, was?"

"Thanatos killed him."

"No. Robert is still alive. He captured me not long after you escaped, figuring I had something to do with it. He did.... horrible things to me. Things men never think will happen to them." He rubs the side of his head. His eyes dart from side to side. Figuring Jared may have suffered the same fate I had, my heart went out to the guy.

"But I escaped. I–I got away," he mumbled before finishing in a rush, "But he has others, and I promised them I would return after I found help."

"Others?"

"Men, women, children, anyone who opposed or spoke out about him. They all vanished, but I know where they are and what we must do to stop him."

"Children?"

"Yes, the newest is a child who was traveling with a couple. He took them too. I don't know what he did to the man but the woman.... He beat her and took her as a pet."

"A fucking pet?"

"I–I–I... I don't think he's human. The things Robert has done, Avalon. He can't be human and do the things he's done."

"He keeps people as pets?"

"Just the woman. She wouldn't stop fighting when he took the man away. Wouldn't stop crying when he removed the child from her too. So he seized the brokenhearted woman and put her in chains. Robert forces her to follow him around on her hands and knees. When she can't keep up, he beats her."

"Where the fuck does he have these people? Could you take me to them?"

"We can't—can't go there. He'll kill me. He'll kill you too. He knows you were with the horseman, knows you traveled with him, knows it was you who saved him. He hates you almost as much as the horseman for destroying his city."

"Well, I'm not going to leave them there. I have friends who'll help us. We have to get to Suki and—"

"What did you say?"

"I said we just have to get to Suki and Xander and then...." The color drained from his face as his eyes grew wide. "Jared?"

"Avalon, I don't know how to say this."

"Say what?" when he continues to stand there, shifting from one foot to the other, I snap, "What the fuck aren't you telling me?"

"Suki is the woman he has." My pounding heart is only overshadowed by his muffled response as the world spins around me.

*****

Present Day

Jumping to my feet, I see Jared waving something in the air. I watch as a rushing Jared trips over a box, the same box he's fallen over four other times.

"You're sure," I yell as I run back to where he is struggling to come to his feet.

"As sure as I can be. I only heard Robert talking about it, but it looks like what he described."

"And you think it'll work?"

"I don't know, Avalon," he says, shaking his head. His pained expression confirms he wants nothing more than to provide me with the answers I seek, but he can't. He only has slightly more knowledge of what we're doing than I do.

The instant he told me that Robert had Suki, I wanted to rush to her aid. Pull her ass out of the fire as she had done for me more times than I can count, but he refused to let me go.

Telling me that may have been Robert's intention all along, to lure me there so he could have his revenge for Thanatos. After a huge fight where I may have knocked him on his ass more than once, I finally agreed to hear him out.

At first, I thought Jared had lost his fucking mind when he told me we needed to find a spell. A fucking spell, *as in magic*. What century does this idiot think we are living in? It wasn't until he advised in a century that we saw the arrival of one of the fable horsemen of the Goddamn apocalypse. He had me dead to rights there.

So instead of rushing in with zero plan in place, I listened to Jared, which is how I ended up here digging through old relics in some forgotten museum barely across New York state lines.

"And you don't have any idea what it is?"

"No, other than it's something that could possibly help." He says, handing it to me.

"Why are you giving it to me?"

"Because one thing Robert made perfectly clear is it would only work if you loved the person you used it to save."

"And because you don't love Suki...."

"It has to be you," He tells me, leading me out of the basement. Once we arrive outside, I turn the paper over repeatedly. It is merely an old piece of parchment, but I guess if someone asked me to explain what ancient magical spells would be written on, this would definitely fit the bill.

"I don't know, Jared."

"It's the only way, Avalon." Swallowing hard before looking at me to continue.

"I managed to escape, but I heard bits and pieces of his plan before I did. He is hell-bent on doling out some revenge against someone. I believe that someone is you. I put most of it together when you told me your friend's name. And after everything that happened in Charlotte, it doesn't take a genius to piece together the rest."

"What if it doesn't work?"

"There's only one way to find out, Avalon. Besides, if it doesn't work, we go with plan B."

"Which is?"

"Storm the fucking gates and kill everyone we see."

"Now that's a plan I can get behind," I say, handing him the paper.

"Okay, we'll do it your way. I only hope he doesn't use your friend and the kids as a human shield. Maybe we should find a back entrance."

Sighing, I look down at the paper again. "What is this supposed to do?"

"Got no damn clue, but there's one way to find out." He pushes the paper back towards me.

"And you're sure it has to be me."

"Who the hell knows? Maybe it was always meant for you."

Without another thought, I snap the wax and open the parchment. I find only one word, "Pestilentia."

Confused, I look up at Jared, a small smile playing at the corners of his lips, "Loyal to the bitter end."

"Jared, what the hell is going on?"

"What was always supposed to happen. You merely delayed it when you went and fell in love with him."

Stepping away from him, I look down at the paper clenched in my hand. "What the fuck is this?"

"Rapture."

"Where's Suki? What the fuck have you done with her?" I ask, grabbing my dagger and pointing it at the man I know is not the poor defenseless man he pretended to be.

"I did not do anything with your Suki. She is safe at the camp Death told you to travel to. You really should learn how to listen."

"And Robert?"

"Dead. You didn't honestly believe your precious horseman would allow any of them to live."

"Who the fuck are you?" The smile he has been wearing turns wicked, and I know I just made a horrible mistake.

As the wind whips up around us and the sky turns gray, he throws his head back, grinning at the turn of events. Before I can say anything else, he transforms into the Raven.

His words whispered in the wind are more chilling than the cold air surrounding me. Swirling around me, mocking me. Screaming the confirmation of my mistake. And all but assuring I had played right into his fucking hands.

"And so it begins. Thank you, little lamb."

"What the hell did I just do?"

Marcelle Valentine

Coming Soon,

Pestilence's Judgment

Marcelle Valentine

Also by Marcelle Valentine

Scarred by Fate Series
Ritual Nightmare
Breaking Purgatory
Fate's Ritual
Opposing Tartarus
Sacrificial Endings

The Ash Rock Series
Shadow's Moon Season One
Shadow's Moon Season Two
Shadow's Moon Season Three
Coming soon Shadow's Moon Season Four

Arrival of the Four Horsemen Series
Death's Inquest
Pestilence's Judgment
Coming soon War's Verdict

Kindle Vella
Shadow's Moon Season One through Four
Seized by Sin
Coming soon Silverwood Throne

Marcelle Valentine

Acknowledgments

The premise for this series came to me while I was writing book two in the Scarred by Fate Series. That premise quickly became an obsession as I started writing conversations, jotting down ideas, and researching the biblical references regarding the four riders. Since I was aware there were already a few stellar Horsemen Series out there, I didn't want mine to be a carbon copy of theirs. Hence, I choose to have the series focus on one main character, Avalon. She is the catalyst that stopped and started humanity's end. So it's only fitting for her to meet the riders she released.

My deepest heartfelt thanks to every reader who took a chance on a relatively unknown author. I hope you get lost in their world as you read my books, even if only for a minute in time.

I could not have completed this series without the people who supported me, including my beta readers, my niece Ashley, my mom, and my daughter Melanie. Everything you each did to help me bring the series to life is something I could never say thank you enough. You each poured your time into this series to help me make it something worth reading.

I have several different projects currently in progress. Book two in the horsemen series is already underway. I also have a Vella I am writing about a serial killer, which is a step outside what I typically write, but I think you will enjoy it, especially if you read my Scarred Series.

Thank you to my husband and everyone else in my family who have been my biggest cheerleaders. I love each and every one of you.

And finally, to every author that has ever put pen to paper, fingers to keyboard, whose work only inspired me more to follow this dream, I hope I do not disappoint.

Thank you
Marcelle

Marcelle Valentine

Newsletter

Consider visiting my website and signing up for my newsletter to receive updates on this series and future projects.

https://www. MarcelleValentine. com

Please consider leaving a review on Amazon and Goodreads if you enjoyed the book. Any thoughts are appreciated and will only help me improve the story. Reviews also provide new readers with a way to find my books.

You can find this book on:

Amazon	Bibliotheca
Apple Book	Scribd
Barnes & Noble	Baker & Taylor
Kobo (including Kobo Plus)	Hoopla
Smashwords Store	Vivlio
Tolino	BorrowBox
OverDrive	Odilo
Google Play Books	

Follow me on social media.

Facebook

Goodreads

Instagram

TikTok

Marcelle Valentine

About the Author

Marcelle Valentine has long been an admirer of creating worlds in which people can get lost in. From the time when she was little, her active imagination took her on epic journeys to faraway places where troubles and friendships abound. Discovering Paranormal and Fantasy Romance books brought back memories of old friends and places, reigniting her passion for writing. She invites you to travel with her during these journeys and get lost in a world where you will find friends, enemies, and lovers all waiting to whisk you away. Marcelle is the author of the Scarred by Fate Series and the episodic series Shadow's Moon. She lives in Ohio with her husband. She has two children, three grandchildren, and one lovable, lazy Great Dane.

MarcelleValentine. com

Facebook

Goodreads

Instagram

TikTok